M000194678

NOVEMBER RAIN

ALSO BY MAUREEN JENNINGS

MURDOCH MYSTERY SERIES
Except the Dying (1997)
Under the Dragon's Tail (1998)
Poor Tom Is Cold (2001)
Let Loose the Dogs (2003)
Night's Child (2005)
Vices of My Blood (2006)
A Journeyman to Grief (2007)
Let Darkness Bury the Dead (2017)

CHRISTINE MORRIS SERIES
Does Your Mother Know? (2006)
The K Handshape (2008)

DETECTIVE INSPECTOR TOM TYLER SERIES
Season of Darkness (2011)
Beware This Boy (2012)
No Known Grave (2014)
Dead Ground in Between (2016)

NOVELLA
Shipwreck (2011)

SCREENPLAYS FOR MURDOCH MYSTERIES TV SERIES
"Staircase to Heaven" (co-writer) (2011)
"Victoria Cross" (co-writer) (2012)
"Murdochaphobia" (co-writer) (2013)
"Shipwreck" (adapted from the novella) (2014)
"House of Industry" (2015)
"The Missing" (2016)
"Game of Kings" (2018)
"One Minute to Murder" (2019)

33204701402413

NOVEMBER RAIN

A Paradise Café Mystery by

MAUREEN JENNINGS

Author of the Detective Murdoch Mysteries

WITHDRAWN

Cormorant Books

Copyright © 2020 The William H. Murdoch Corporation
This edition copyright © 2020 Cormorant Books Inc.
This is a first edition.

No part of this publication may be reproduced, stored in a retrieval system
or transmitted, in any form or by any means, without the prior written consent
of the publisher or a licence from The Canadian Copyright Licensing Agency
(Access Copyright). For an Access Copyright licence,
visit www.accesscopyright.ca or call toll free 1.800.893.5777.

The publisher gratefully acknowledges the support of the Canada Council
for the Arts and the Ontario Arts Council for its publishing program.
We acknowledge the financial support of the Government of Canada
through the Canada Book Fund (CBF) for our publishing activities, and the
Government of Ontario through Ontario Creates, an agency of the Ontario
Ministry of Culture, and the Ontario Book Publishing Tax Credit Program.

LIBRARY AND ARCHIVES CANADA CATALOGUING IN PUBLICATION

Title: November rain / by Maureen Jennings.
Names: Jennings, Maureen, author.
Description: Series statement: A Paradise Café mystery
Identifiers: Canadiana (print) 20200238647 | Canadiana (ebook) 20200238655 |
ISBN 9781770866041 (softcover) | ISBN 9781770866058 (HTML)
Classification: LCC PS8569.E562 N68 2020 | DDC C813/.54—dc23

Cover art: Nick Craine
Interior text design: Tannice Goddard, tannicegdesigns.ca
Printer: Friesens

Printed and bound in Canada.

CORMORANT BOOKS INC.
260 SPADINA AVENUE, SUITE 502, TORONTO, ON M5T 2E4
www.cormorantbooks.com

To my husband and great supporter,
Iden Ford

CHAPTER ONE

S ODDEN YELLOW LEAVES clotted the sidewalk; a thin mist
had crept up from the lake and was drifting hungrily
around the rain-blackened trees; damp, brown sparrows
lined up on the telephone wire, chirping irritably. All in
all, it was a miserable November morning already sliding
toward winter.

The fact that I was on my way to the city morgue to
investigate a tragic death didn't help my mood.

* * *

AS I USUALLY did, I walked to the office from home. It wasn't
far, twenty minutes at the most, but I had hardly reached
Yonge, the aortic street of the city, when a needle-sharp
rain began to fall, stinging my face. I chastised myself for
neglecting to bring my umbrella. I'd dressed properly for the
weather, but it seems as if nothing can protect you from this
kind of November chill that seeps through to the very bones.

I arrived at the Arcade. Our office was on the third floor,
but the elevator was engaged. Rather than wait an eternity

for it to clank its way down, I decided to use the stairs.

One of the electric lights had burned out and as I trudged up I had to virtually feel my way; my wellies squeaked on the uncarpeted steps. When I reached the hall, I was startled to see two women standing outside my door, still and black as crows. They were dressed in full mourning garb. Long black coats almost to their ankles, brimmed hats with dark veils that fell to the chin.

"Good morning," I said.

"We've come for a consultation," said the shorter one. "We've been here for at least ten minutes."

I didn't think that was a very polite way to greet a stranger, but there was something about her voice that demanded deference. Not to mention the seriousness of her mourning attire. I swallowed my defensive retort. As our sign stated plainly, the office didn't open until eight o'clock. It was ten to the hour.

"I'm so sorry. Please come in."

I eased past them, unlocked the door and snapped on the light. More than once, I'd moaned about how small our two rooms were. Not today. The smallness seemed cozy, the lack of windows shut out the bleak weather. My desk was neat and tidy, the typewriter centred and ready for action.

I removed my wet mackintosh and hat quickly and hung them on the coat tree.

"May I take your coats?"

The same woman spoke. "That won't be necessary, thank you."

Indeed, they were quite dry. No umbrellas to be seen.

"Please have a seat. I'll get another chair."

I pulled forward the single chair that was in front of my desk and quickly grabbed the only other one from Mr. Gilmore's adjoining office. The two women sat down. It felt a little cramped, but there wasn't anything I could do about that except return to my own desk. The woman who had spoken was obviously the senior one of the two. She moved carefully as if she had long worried about breaking something, although, closer, I could see she wasn't really that old. Younger than my Gramps for sure. This time it was the second woman who spoke. Her voice was soft and hesitant, and she gave the impression of somebody who doesn't want to be noticed if it can be avoided. "We are speaking to Miss Charlotte Frayne, I presume?"

"That is correct."

She bobbed her head. Underneath the veil, she seemed fair skinned, thin faced. What little showed of her hair was light brown.

"We are Mrs. Gerald Jessop and Mrs. Preston Jessop. We have come on the recommendation of Mrs. Walsingham, whom we understand was a client of yours."

"That is also correct."

It didn't surprise me that these two moved in the same circles as Mrs. Walsingham, one of Toronto's wealthier citizens. They had been spared the rain. They'd obviously been able to afford a taxicab to get here. That or they had their own car and chauffeur.

Mrs. Preston Jessop glanced around the office. I was glad Mr. Gilmore had hung up a portrait of the king's brother. He might not be as good-looking as his brother, but he had the advantage of being respectably married with two pretty young daughters and he conveyed dignity and propriety. The portrait was an affirmation of T. Gilmore and Associates' affiliations.

Her scrutiny seemed so intense and slow that for a moment I wondered if she could in fact see very well. I soon learned poor eyesight was not her problem. She was a woman in such a state of distress she was barely functioning. Virtually every move had to be slow and deliberate to keep at bay her complete collapse. Her daughter-in-law didn't speak, obviously used to the role of silent companion.

I waited.

Mrs. Preston Jessop eventually looked at me. "A few days ago, my son Gerald was found dead. The police have declared him to be a suicide. We do not believe that is the case."

Her eyes were obscured by her black veil, but I had the feeling they were normally keen and uncompromising. Her nose looked beaky, her mouth tight.

"Gerald would never have taken his own life. He was not that kind of person. The police say the case is closed. We would like you to do your own investigation. Find out the truth."

I hesitated for a moment not sure how to respond. She said, "I will pay whatever you ask. Double your usual fee if need be."

"That won't be necessary."

I don't like dealing with people who think that they can throw their money at you and you will say whatever they want you to say.

"We have a competent police department. I assume they investigated thoroughly. What if I come to the same conclusion?"

"That is highly unlikely. They are wrong."

The younger woman's eyes flickered over at her, but I couldn't tell if she agreed with her or not.

"Will you take the case or not, Miss, er ...?"

"Frayne." In spite of the woman's obvious state of upset, her tone was getting my back up. "I will need to have more details before I can say yes or no. I don't want to waste your money and my time if I think there is nothing to be gained from a further investigation."

I could almost feel Mr. Gilmore wincing. "They are clients after all, Miss Frayne. We can't afford to turn away business."

Mrs. Jessop nodded in the direction of her daughter-in-law. "Ellen, show her the coroner's report."

On cue, Ellen Jessop fished in her handbag. Like the women themselves, the purse, which was black velvet with jet beads, seemed frozen in a time when women were expected to display mourning very seriously indeed.

She took out an envelope and handed it to me.

They both watched as I opened it.

OFFICE OF THE CORONER OF THE CITY OF TORONTO.
REPORT ON THE DEATH OF GERALD SOMERSET
JESSOP AGE 43

I was called to view the body of Gerald Somerset Jessop at 7 a.m. on Friday October 30, 1936. He resided at 31 Pembroke Street with his mother and his wife. The body as presented to me was submerged in the water of his bathtub. It was in an advanced state of rigor mortis.

He was dressed in his nightclothes which consisted of a purple silk jacket top and trousers. His feet were bare. He had four medals around his neck (exhibit #1) and there were coins in all his pockets (exhibit #2). They are all British coins and of one-penny denomination. On a table beside the bathtub was an empty ceramic. On examination, it proved to have contained the residue of 80 proof rum. There was an ordinary household cup which contained rum residue in the amount of one ounce (exhibits #3 & #4).

Although I did not conduct an extensive search of the site, I did enter the adjoining bedroom. On the bedside table, I found a syringe and seven ampoules of morphine all empty (exhibit #5). Beside the bed was an empty bottle, labelled RUM. In addition, there was a folded note on the table (exhibit #6). It was addressed to the mother and wife of the deceased. It indicated he was quite despondent and intended to take his own life.

I estimate death to have occurred sometime between 11 p.m. and 1 a.m. the previous night. A more precise estimation is difficult as the body was immersed in water until it was discovered at 6 a.m. The body was transferred by ambulance to the morgue.

When rigor had receded, I conducted a post-mortem examination. This was at 9 a.m. on Friday, October 30. As follows.

The body is that of a male, six feet one inch tall, weighing 170 pounds. There was a considerable amount of alcohol in the blood stream and an additional amount of morphia in the stomach. The combination of these two substances in this amount would have engendered complete shut down of the central nervous system and subsequently brought about death. The surrounding tissue indicated the deceased had used this drug on a regular basis. Although the body was discovered immersed in water, there was no water in the lungs which indicates he was not breathing when he sank below the surface.

There is no evidence of a pre-existing disease except for liver damage which is described below. The face is quite severely mutilated. The nasal bones are absent as is most of the right lower mandible. There has been extensive reconstruction of both nose and jaw, including six upper teeth. There is considerable scarring on the right side of the face. Given the nature of the wounds I assume they were incurred in the war. Three of the fingers of the right hand have been amputated at the first joint. Again, no doubt from a wound suffered in war time.

The liver is enlarged and showing signs of early cirrhosis.

Given the circumstances of the body and the note, I conclude that Gerald Jessop met his death by his own hand, committed while the balance of his mind was disturbed.

Yours truly,

J.M. Rogers. MD. Dated this 30th day of October in the year of our Lord, 1936

The verdict seemed pretty unequivocal. I said as much. Mrs. Jessop answered.

"What is unequivocal is that my son died. But that is not sufficient. He had much to contend with in his life, but he was not suicidal."

Abruptly she turned to her daughter-in-law. "Isn't that so, Ellen?"

"Yes, Mamma. That is so."

I could hardly hear her.

"You say he had much to contend with. I assume you are referring to the fact that he was a former soldier and suffered significant wounds?"

Mrs. Preston Jessop's stiff body grew even straighter. She, too, was carrying a black handbag and she clutched it hard.

"He went to war on August 8, 1917 as a handsome young man of twenty-four. His future was before him and there is little doubt he would have had a happy and prosperous life. He was wounded at the battle of Valenciennes in 1918. He was an officer, a captain, and disregarding any risk to himself, he led his men into battle to capture an enemy machine gun that was decimating his platoon. The operation was successful, thereby saving many lives, but during the attack, Gerald was struck in the face by a piece of shrapnel. A second piece cut off three of his fingers."

The way she recounted this tale, she could have been reciting verbatim the report in the *London Gazette*.

"The tragedy, the dreadful tragedy, Miss Frayne is that, as you no doubt know, this battle was one of the last of the war. Armistice was declared a mere ten days later. By then of course, it was too late for my son."

Ellen said, "He was awarded the Military Cross."

"He should have received the Victoria Cross," said Mrs. Jessop. "He was very brave."

Unfortunately, bravery in battle was one thing, returning to a civilian life when completely disfigured required a different kind of courage.

"Ellen and Gerald were married in June 1917, two months before he went overseas," interjected Mrs. Jessop.

The bald statement was so loaded with possibilities that I was at a loss as to how to respond.

She saved me the trouble. "You asked why we are so convinced Gerald did not take his own life. Ellen has just informed me she is likely with child."

Even through the concealing veil I could tell the younger woman had blushed. If she could have dropped through the floor she would have.

She muttered, "Not quite confirmed as yet, Mamma."

As gently as I could, I asked, "Did your husband know this?"

"Of course, he did," answered the senior Mrs. Jessop.

I addressed Ellen. "How did he respond?"

The senior Mrs. Jessop wouldn't let her daughter-in-law get a word in edgewise.

"How would you expect? It has been a cause of great

disappointment to all of us that there has been no heir to carry on our name."

Okay. Got it.

"He would have been very happy," whispered Ellen.

"No reason to be despondent then?"

"None." This, again, was from Gerald Jessop's mother. She was a woman on a mission, which might be why she was blinding herself to the fact that her daughter-in-law, however submissive she might appear, was not telling the truth.

More to gain a little time than anything, I stood up.

"May I offer you a cup of coffee? It can be ready in a minute."

"Do you have tea?"

"I'm afraid not."

Neither Mr. Gilmore nor I drank tea and I'd forgotten to stock up on anything except coffee.

"Nothing then, thank you."

I sat down again.

"The coroner mentions a letter that your son left behind. Do you have it?"

She inhaled deeply. "It is currently in the possession of the police. They confiscated numerous items, including the supposed letter."

I didn't take her up on her use of the word "supposed."

"Did you read it?"

"I was not allowed to see it, but it was read aloud to us."

"And what was the content?" I kept my voice as gentle as

I could. I felt like a surgeon probing a very painful, infected wound.

She looked away. "Perhaps Ellen could answer better than I. I was too shocked to take in very much."

"Naturally."

The younger woman had shrunk more deeply into the chair.

"He said he was sorry to cause us distress ...," her voice, already soft, tailed off. Impatiently, her mother-in-law took up the tale.

"He said his life was unbearable and he could not continue. He asked that we get on with the kind of life we deserved. Whatever that is supposed to mean."

Ellen muttered something I didn't hear.

"I beg your pardon, Mrs. Jessop?"

She spoke up. "The last words were 'Forgive me.'"

Would they? Could they forgive? It was hard to tell at this point. Perhaps his wife, but his mother wasn't so soft.

"Who was the officer in charge of the case?"

I had dealt with the local police before. It was helpful to have connections with them.

"Who was it, Ellen?" Mrs. Jessop asked.

"His name was Murdoch. Detective Murdoch."

Good. I knew Jack well and trusted him totally. I was glad he was on the case. I also knew that meant he would have done a thorough investigation.

It was my turn to inhale. "Mrs. Jessop. I am truly sorry for your loss, but I really don't think there is much I can do.

The report is quite explicit. It is obvious Gerald intended to end his own life."

She interrupted me. "Every man has his darker moments, Miss Frayne. Given his war experience, my son was not immune to morbid thoughts. But that is not the same as actually committing such an act. It could have been an accident."

"True. But I'm afraid that might be something we will never know."

It did, however, look as if Gerald Jessop had made sure there would be no mistake. I hesitated. "I can understand how painful it must be to think someone you love has deliberately taken his own life. There may be some comfort in believing it was an accident; but, as presented, the facts do indicate Gerald committed suicide."

She started to cough. "I beg your pardon. My throat is dry."

I jumped up. "Let me get you some water."

She flapped her hand. Although the cough was subsiding, she still had difficulty speaking. "Thank you ... not necessary. Ellen will explain."

I sat down. I was starting to feel like a jack-in-the-box.

Mrs. Gerald Jessop took up the narrative. As soon as a word was out of her mouth, she ducked her head and swallowed it right back in. Her voice was so soft that at times I almost lost her. Her mother-in-law focussed on the floor as if she were listening to a pupil reciting a written text that she was ready to correct at any moment.

"When he returned from war, Gerald was in constant pain. His doctor prescribed morphia, but even that was not always sufficient. Gerald started to imbibe alcohol."

"He wasn't used to it," interrupted Mrs. Jessop, her dry throat now apparently eased. "We have always been a temperate family. My late husband enjoyed the occasional glass of port, but never to excess."

I didn't need to ask about her own habits. It was obvious what her position was. The nostrils were a dead giveaway.

"Was your son's use of alcohol problematic, Mrs. Jessop?"

She inhaled deeply again, nostrils pinching. It was her signal that she was navigating choppy waters.

"It became so. As I said, he could never quite escape the pain from his wounds." She halted. Another cough. She waved her hand again. This time, Ellen promptly took up the tale.

"He struggled with this dependency for some time. We tried sending him to special clinics, but the effects were temporary. However, last spring we were able to find a place in America where he could get help. He has been maintaining sobriety ever since. Eight months now."

"I'm afraid that is not what the coroner concluded. He said there was a considerable amount of alcohol in Gerald's system."

"That is what I don't understand," rasped Mrs. Jessop. "On the advice of the clinic, we allow no liquor whatsoever in the house."

"Then he must have been drinking somewhere else."

She shook her head. Her veil swung with the motion like black water. "He rarely left the house during the daytime. He was self-conscious about his appearance."

"It really wasn't that bad," interjected Ellen. "We'd become accustomed to it."

She said it so emphatically that I had the feeling it had become almost rote.

You may have got used to him, I thought, but that didn't mean he wasn't a fright to strangers.

"And there was no sign that he had been drinking when you had dinner together?"

"None at all. Absolutely not. I would have remarked on it at once if it were the case. The clinic advised us to confront him if he reneged on his commitment."

"When was the last time you saw him?"

"He came down for dinner at six o'clock."

"Did he seem in good spirits?"

The senior Mrs. Jessop didn't reply immediately. She turned her head away from me and shifted in her chair.

"This was a particularly difficult time of the year for him. Armistice Day always brings back memories of his service." She was gripped by the raspy cough.

This time I didn't ask. I jumped up, went into our pocket-handkerchief-sized kitchen and poured her a glass of water. I came back and handed it to her. She accepted meekly and took a sip.

"I had ordered the cook to make one of his favourite meals, braised beef, but he hardly touched it. He said he had a headache and he needed some fresh air. He went out." Another sip. "That was the last I saw him."

My heart ached for the woman whose only resort to reach her despairing and damaged son was to order their cook to make his favourite meal.

I turned to her daughter-in-law. "And you, Mrs. Jessop? When did you last see Mr. Jessop?"

"Earlier. I left before dinner to attend my Zonta Club meeting," said Ellen. "When I came home, shortly after ten, I could see a light in Gerald's room. He had not yet gone to bed."

"Did you speak to him?"

She dropped her head. "No, he didn't like to be disturbed when retired for the night."

I assumed they had separate rooms but before I could ask her, she volunteered the information.

"My room is across the hall from Gerald's. He was a restless sleeper and he never wanted to keep me awake as well."

Except on the occasion when he had come to her bed and impregnated her. If that was in fact the case.

"Can we just get back to the question of the alcohol for a moment? Could somebody in the household have brought your son alcohol?"

My question seemed to jolt Mrs. Jessop. "Absolutely not," she snapped. "We keep only a small number of servants and we have had them for many years. Not only are they utterly loyal, they know that any violation of our rules would result in immediate dismissal. Without a character."

I hadn't heard that term for a while, but even with today's high level of unemployment, a domestic servant might find it hard to get another position unless they had a good reference.

"And was he still on prescription morphia?"

"Yes."

I regarded the two women sitting in front of me. I felt terribly sorry for all of them.

Ellen was studying the pattern on my little wool rug as if she might copy it later.

The senior Mrs. Jessop placed the empty glass on the floor. "There is another possibility. Gerald might have been murdered."

CHAPTER TWO

O F COURSE, THAT possibility had occurred to me and it had
fluttered briefly around my brain like a lost moth. But it
seemed so unlikely it hadn't settled.

"Who might have done that, Mrs. Jessop?"

"I have no idea, but we can rule out nothing can we?"
She answered sharply, but it was impossible to determine if
she seriously believed her assertion or not.

What was clear was that she was not about to give in
easily. A hero has to die a hero. Nothing more, nothing less.
I knew the local police well enough to be sure they would
not reopen a case unless they absolutely had to. I was
about to turn down the job as gently as I could when I was
saved by the bell. Literally. The telephone rang. I excused
myself and answered. It was Gramps. His voice was loud
as usual. He'd never got used to the idea that he could
speak normally. I wasn't in another country where volume
was necessary.

"Lottie. You forgot your umbrella."

"Sorry I'm busy at the moment. Can I call you back?"

"Ha. I know that tone of voice. You're dealing with a difficult client, aren't you?"

"That is correct."

"Ha. I could tell. Call me back when you're finished. Remember what I always tell you."

"And what is that?"

"When it rains, you'll get wet unless you have your umbrella." Gramps chuckled at his own joke. It was so absurd that under different circumstances, I would have laughed too.

"Thanks for the advice. I'll call you back."

"Oh, and Lottie ..."

"Yes?"

"Don't take on anything you don't feel good about."

We hung up, but the call had been a welcome interruption.

"My apologies," I said.

The senior Mrs. Jessop sniffed, removed a black-edged handkerchief from her purse and dabbed at her nose. I couldn't quite tell if she disapproved of the interruption or if she was reacting to the smell of cooking onions which was beginning to drift through the room. My neighbour, Mr. Patchell, for economic reasons, was forced to live out of his office and he was starting to make his breakfast. As well as the onions, the sound of music was coming through. Sometimes he played his cello. Never mind angels playing harps, in my opinion, a human playing the cello was as close to heavenly music as you can get while you're still alive. Mr. Patchell had been a professional cellist in his native Poland, but here he eked out a living repairing watches and jewellery.

I was closer to the connecting wall than the Jessops who, so far, didn't seem to have noticed the music. I have to admit that for a few moments, I was distracted from the situation I was dealing with. Perhaps because of the necessity of paying attention to his frying onions, he didn't play for very long.

Mrs. Jessop put away her handkerchief. Before we could continue, the music started up again.

Mrs. Jessop glanced at me with a slightly raised eyebrow. "What is that?"

"My neighbour is playing his gramophone."

This morning, Mr. Patchell had chosen to play "Stormy Weather." It was a melancholy song at the best of times, and Ethel Waters's velvet voice seemed to wrap around the three of us like a soft shroud.

I was just about to apologize for the intrusion when Mrs. Jessop abruptly stretched out her hands in front of her. She stared at her own gloved fingers.

"Gerald loved music. He was an accomplished piano player."

She lowered her hands back to her lap.

Accomplished pianist indeed. Probably bloody brilliant. *Three fingers of the right hand are stumps.*

Ethel whispered through the walls, words to the effect that she could not go on because all she had in life was gone.

Mrs. Jessop appeared to listen for a moment, then she leaned forward in the chair.

"Miss Frayne. I appreciate what you are saying, and I realize this job might put you in an awkward position. However, I promise you I will respect whatever conclusion you come to."

She said this, having removed the bone-hard shield of wealth and privilege. I liked her far more.

"May I make this suggestion," she continued. "The police have released Gerald's body. The funeral home will pick him up from the morgue." Underneath the veil, she wiped her eyes. "We hope to have a funeral as soon as possible, but that might not be the case. We are Anglicans and according to the doctrine of the church, as a suicide, Gerald will not be given the funeral rites nor will he be buried in the church graveyard where both his father and grandfather lie."

That put another wrinkle on the senior Mrs. Jessop's need to prove her son did not die by his own hand.

"The detective has said he will return us Gerald's effects. He is due to come at three o'clock today. Perhaps you could meet with him? You also have our permission to speak to our servants. If after that, you still feel there is no point in pursuing the matter, I will let it drop. We will have to make other arrangements for the burial."

"Fair enough." I pulled over my notebook. I addressed Ellen. "I'd like to take down some details. Would you mind giving me your account of what happened, Mrs. Jessop?"

I would have liked to question Ellen more, but this

wasn't the right time. She must be close to forty but, even now, I could see she had been a pretty young woman of what? Twenty-one or less when she had married the handsome Gerald? After only two months of marriage, she had then had to live with the result of his injuries for eighteen years. It must have been tough being the wife of a severely disfigured man who wouldn't go out in daytime and who became dependent on alcohol and morphine.

My questions didn't take long. The senior Mrs. Jessop confirmed the events as Ellen had described them.

I finished and put down my pen. To my surprise, Mrs. Jessop actually mustered up a smile of sorts behind her veil. I seemed to have won her over, I'm not quite sure why.

Unexpectedly, she said, "It's likely going to rain all day. Rather than getting soaked again, I'll send the car to pick you up. Can you be ready at two o'clock?"

I could.

With various bobbing of heads and adjusting of veils, they left. In spite of everything, the senior Mrs. Jessop seemed a little happier. I seriously doubted I could lift her burden totally, but I guessed she was a woman who could deal with certainty better than the opposite.

In their absence, I could hear Mr. Patchell's record continue; Ethel was singing about there being gloom and misery everywhere when it rains and the weather is stormy.

There was the sound of a scratch as Mr. Patchell moved the needle arm. Then silence.

* * *

I ROLLED A fresh sheet of paper into the typewriter and typed my report. I had taken down Ellen's account verbatim. She was less difficult to follow when she got into describing the true drama of what had happened. She had a rather poetic way of speaking which is rather unusual. I added a few ellipses to illustrate the ebb and flow of her narrative.

CONFIDENTIAL. Monday, November 2, 1936. FILE OF MRS. PRESTON JESSOP. 31 PEMBROKE STREET, TORONTO. TEL. MAIN 683.

ACCOUNT OF MRS. GERALD JESSOP.

(widow of deceased)

I was awakened shortly before six o'clock on Friday morning (October 30) by the sound of Duffy (the dog) barking. Usually when she is so persistent, she needs to go out. Sometimes Gerald is so deeply asleep he doesn't hear her. I got up and went to Gerald's room to see what was happening. Duffy was scratching at the door, Gerald was nowhere in sight. I could see his bed was unmade. I went to the bathroom and knocked. There was no answer so I went in. Gerald was lying in the bathtub. He had sunk down in the water. It was obvious even to my eyes that he was dead. His skin was grey and he was completely still in a way that only death can confer. His hair was floating on the water around his head. Duffy was trying to get out, so I picked her up and ran out to fetch Sam (his valet). He was not in his room. Mamma (Mrs. Preston Jessop) also sleeps on this floor, but it was my instinct to fetch Sam first. He had much experience in

*the war. He must have heard the dog and my footsteps because
he came running up the stairs. He had been making his breakfast
in the kitchen. I had difficulty in speaking and could only point
at Gerald's room. Sam could see immediately that something was
terribly wrong, so he gestured to me to stay where I was and ran
into the room. I did in fact stay in the hall. He emerged a few
minutes later. "I want you to fetch Wilson at once (the chauffeur).
Tell him there seems to have been a dreadful accident. He should
telephone the police station immediately and then come up
here." I asked him what I should do about Duffy. He said to
take her downstairs and put her in the kitchen where she has a
pen. "Should I rouse Mrs. Jessop?" I then asked. We both knew
Gerald was dead and we needed police and medical assistance,
but we also had her welfare in mind. "Let's wait until the
ambulance arrives. I don't want her to see him the way he is."*

*That seemed like a sensible proposal so I hurried as fast as
I could to get Wilson.*

*(At this point in the narrative, she lost her composure. It
took several minutes before she was ready to continue.)*

*The police ambulance arrived quickly. The coroner, a
Dr. Rogers, was with them and a detective. I did not want to
get in the way so I stayed in Mamma's room. She had been
awakened by all the commotion, but Sam insisted she not go
into the bathroom. It was very difficult to persuade her, but I
knew that was the right decision. Finally, Detective Murdoch
came to speak to her. He was very kind. He said that Dr. Rogers
had confirmed that Gerald was indeed dead. He said, given the
circumstances, there would have to be an investigation. Mamma*

requested that she be allowed to see Gerald's body. Detective
Murdoch conferred with the coroner and they gave permission.
I asked if I could accompany her and they agreed I could. I
therefore went with her into the bedroom. They had moved
Gerald's body to the bed and covered him with a sheet up to
his neck.

(More upset.)

"What happened?" Mamma asked. The detective said they
couldn't make a final appraisal until there was an autopsy, but
it did look as if Gerald had committed suicide. "Did he leave a
note?" Detective Murdoch said there was a note on the bedside
table, but he couldn't let her touch it at the moment. However,
if she wished, he would read it to her. She said she did so wish.
She said then as she has repeated since that she could not believe
Gerald had killed himself. The detective said they would do a
thorough investigation. He expressed his deepest regrets and
asked if he could have her doctor sent for. She said that for the
moment she would prefer to be with her maid and myself. We
returned to her room while they removed Gerald's body. The
entire household was awake by now and Mrs. Jones was able
to comfort Mamma as best she could. She has been in our employ
for twenty years. We have all been coping until receiving the
report from Dr. Rogers which you have seen. I myself am ready
to accept these findings.

That was essentially it.

Given the facts as presented I could see no possibility,
other than suicide or misadventure, which we could prove.

As there was a clear suicide note, we had to accept intention and there was no way to know if Gerald had changed his mind at the last minute, but succumbed to the drink and the drug. At my request, Mrs. Jessop wrote a letter giving me authority to view the body and to speak to the police detective in charge of the case.

She agreed to our usual terms: two dollars an hour, not including travel time, and any additional expenses such as printed documents which are to be itemized.

I finished the report and filed one copy in the filing cabinet, the other in my desk drawer. Mr. Gilmore and I always shared reports on our cases.

I was hoping he'd call in today. He was on what he'd termed a leave of absence. "I will be incommunicado for a little while, I'm afraid, Miss Frayne, but I leave the running of the office in your quite capable hands." It was all a bit abstruse and he hadn't really explained, but given what he had gone through in July, I didn't begrudge him time off. Far from it.

Initially, I'd rather enjoyed the feeling of independence his absence had conferred, but it was going on for two weeks now and I was hoping he'd be back soon. When we weren't out on a case, we had fallen into a pleasant routine. He'd sit in his back room, sipping coffee and reading all the daily newspapers. This was an important part of our work. He claimed that no potential client would have faith in our abilities if we were ignorant of what was going on and who was doing what. "Private investigators act as physicians of the body politic. We know what is healthy and what is diseased." Mr. Gilmore liked these pithy little sayings. As he was reading, he often called out bits of news. I missed that, too. As well as forgetting my umbrella, I'd neglected to pick up the usual newspapers. I was curious to know what was happening in the so-called Toronto Stork Derby. Not to mention the latest escapades of our king. These superficialities were temporary distractions from the increasingly dire news filtering through from Europe. Armistice Day was coming up soon, when we'd stand together, quietly and respectfully, many of us weeping, and we'd remember the dead and the maimed, like Gerald Jessop. No wonder he'd found this time of year difficult.

It was after ten o'clock now. Oops. I almost forgot I'd told Gramps I'd call him back. I was just reaching for the telephone when there was the sound of the daily post being dropped through our letter box. I must admit that ever since our nasty episode in the summer, the sound of the envelopes sliding through the slot made me a tad apprehensive.

I went to retrieve them. Only three envelopes today, one looking like a cheque. Great. To my surprise, the second envelope was addressed to me. The return address was Mr. Gilmore's. I opened it. Short and to the point, it was written in typical tidy Thaddeus Gilmore style and it was utterly peculiar.

My dear Miss Frayne, I wonder if you could locate accommodation for me. It will be for a small family, a man and a woman and two children, a girl aged thirteen and a boy aged twelve. The best place would be close to the area of my residence on Phoebe Street. I am not at liberty to disclose the names of this family, but you can sign a lease in my name. If you need to, use one of the company cheques for the deposit. A modest two-bedroom apartment or the equivalent would be the best and should be available at once.

Yours truly,
T. Gilmore

I was used to my boss's reticence, but this was obscure to say the least. Who was this family? I assumed they weren't in the city to do their own search. I also had to assume the letter was connected with his mysterious absence. I turned the envelope and paid attention to the franking. It had been posted in Munich.

Staring at it, sniffing it, holding it up to the light, yielded no further clues so I put it in the desk drawer. I trusted Mr. Gilmore. I knew there would be a good reason for this strange mission.

Oops again. Gramps! I got put through.

He answered after two rings, his voice as usual too loud. I reminded him constantly that he should answer with the number, but he never remembered.

"Hello. Who's calling?"

"It's me."

"What kind of me?"

This was a hoary joke, but he loved it. I went along.

"How many 'me's do you know?"

"Dozens."

"Well this me is your granddaughter, Charlotte."

"Lottie! What took you so long?"

His voice was genuinely anxious.

"Sorry, Gramps, I had to write up a report while it was fresh in my mind."

"The difficult client?"

"That's right."

"You can tell me about it later."

"Okay. Aren't you going to meet me for lunch at the Paradise?"

"I don't think so, pet. It's raining cats and dogs. I've got a nice fire going and my programme is coming on soon."

"Okay. How's your boil?"

"Sore."

"Don't pick at it."

"I'm not. "

"I know you, Gramps. You're probably picking at it. The doctor said you've got to let it burst on its own."

"Stop fussing."

The odour of Mr. Patchell's onions was stronger than ever. My eyes were starting to sting.

"What are you going to have for your lunch?"

"I'll cook up some bacon and eggs most likely."

"Sounds good. Don't forget to turn the stove off when you're done."

"Lottie! Cut it out."

"You forgot last week."

"For a minute. I forgot for a minute."

"That's all it takes."

"Will you stop fussing. I've not lost my marbles yet."

Gramps is all the family I have. To tell the truth, since Gran died so suddenly, two years ago, I always have the nagging fear he might leave me as well. I do fuss over him, I admit it.

We hung up.

I was just putting on my still damp coat when the telephone rang again. Thinking it was Gramps with a follow-up comment, which was typical of him, I forgot myself for a moment.

"What now?"

The man's voice on the other end of the line was gravelly.

"Who is this?"

Certainly not Gramps calling.

"So sorry. You have reached the office of T. Gilmore and Associates. Charlotte Frayne speaking."

"Is Gilmore there?"

"I'm afraid Mr. Gilmore is not in the office at the moment, can I be of assistance?"

"When do you expect him back?"

"Not immediately. Is there anything I can help you with?"

There was a brief silence. "You're a woman, I presume."

I bit back a sarcastic retort referencing eunuchs. "You are correct in that assumption, sir. I am Mr. Gilmore's associate, Charlotte Frayne."

I waited while he contemplated the magnitude of my response.

"That might be even better," the man continued. Same harsh voice. This time, I also detected a hint of an accent. European, I thought.

"You are a trained investigator I presume?"

"Correct again, sir."

"Good. I have a job for you."

"All right. And what is that job, may I ask?"

"I own a manufacturing company. We make high-class women's clothes."

He stopped and cleared his throat. "I'll get straight to the point."

"Please do. I far prefer directness."

Stop, it, Charlotte, we need the work.

He didn't seem put off by my snippy response. Maybe he didn't notice.

"One of my workers is trying to cause trouble."

"I see." Of course, I didn't see. "Causing trouble" covered a wide range of possibilities. "Can you elaborate, sir?"

"I suspect I'm harbouring a commie agitator," he continued. "Might be more than one. I think they're trying to organize a union. Get the women to come out on strike. I can't afford that. There's enough competition in this trade without stoppages allowing the others to slip in."

I made an agreeing type of noise.

"What?"

"Nothing, sir. Please continue."

"I need somebody to come in and expose the troublemakers."

"And you thought a private investigator might the person to do that?"

I could almost see him snarl. "That's your line of work isn't it?"

"On occasion."

This wasn't the first time I been asked to do undercover work, but intervening in labour and management affairs wasn't particularly something I wanted to take on.

The man virtually barked at me. "So do you want the job or not? There are other companies I can approach."

"I'd like a few more particulars first. For one thing you haven't given me your name."

"Didn't I?"

He sounded genuinely surprised as if everybody must know who he was.

"I'm Saul Rosenthal. You can ask your boss if you want a reference. We know each other."

A pleasant manner was definitely not in this man's repertoire. But as Mr. Gilmore said, "If we only took on jobs for people we liked, we'd go broke fast."

"I'll hire you for a week," Rosenthal continued. "Regular rates. You can come on board as one of the workers. All you have to do is keep your eyes and ears open then report back to me about what's going on."

"What if there is nothing to report?"

"What do you mean?"

"What if there are no agitators stirring up trouble?"

Another pause and for the first time, a trace of humour in the voice.

"Then that would be a relief and I can sleep soundly. So yes or no? If there is a rotten apple, better to toss it out sooner rather than later before it affects the entire barrel. You'd have to start at once," said the gravel voice. "I can't afford to wait."

At this point I expected that the Jessop job wouldn't last long. Better to be overbooked than under. It had been a lean month.

"All right. I accept."

"You'll need to get yourself hired as one of the employees. Can you come by today?"

"What time?"

"Noon? There's a lunch break then."

"Okay."

"Come to the shop. Speak to the supervisor. Convince him to hire you. Can you handle that?"

"I'll have to, won't I?"

"We don't ask for a lot. As long as you move and breathe, we'll hire you."

And fire you if you cause trouble, I thought to myself.

"How many employees do you have, sir?"

"Nineteen. Are you on or not?"

"I'll accept the assignment."

"Okay. What is your fee? Gilmore always goes on about reasonable rates."

"We charge two dollars an hour."

"What! I could probably do a better job myself."

Naturally I was about to tell him to go ahead and do just that, but I refrained.

He snapped at me. "I'll pay you a dollar fifty. No extras."

"Make that a dollar seventy-five and I'll accept."

I wasn't sure if Mr. Gilmore would be wringing his hands or rejoicing. It had been a lean month for the agency.

I heard Mr. Rosenthal scowl.

"All right. The address is one-sixty-seven Spadina Avenue. East side. Just above Queen Street. Got that?"

"Got it. And the name of your company?"

"Superior Ladies' Clothes."

Appropriate name.

"Report to the supervisor. His name is Klein."

"What shall I tell him?"

"Nothing specific. This must be strictly between you and me. We're looking to hire new workers. You'll have to convince him you'll suit."

"And if I don't?"

Rosenthal almost chuckled. "No job. But if you can sell yourself to him, the other workers will probably accept you too."

I didn't particularly like the word "probably," but he was being realistic.

"Will you be there yourself?"

"I'm always on the premises. But don't indicate you know me."

"I wasn't planning on doing that, Mr. Rosenthal. It would open me up for speculation don't you think?"

He only grunted. "I'll pay you on receipt of your report. One week from today. If you feel you need more time, we can discuss it as we go."

He hung up. He may have said goodbye, but if he did I didn't hear it.

I must say I was quailing somewhat. What had I got myself into? I knew nothing about making clothes, superior quality or otherwise. I wasn't sure how I was going to get around that one. And Mr. Rosenthal hadn't given me any suggestions. "Convince him." Great. Very helpful. What bothered me more was the ethics of operating as a spy. You have to gain people's trust and then possibly betray them. I wished Mr. Gilmore was here to talk about this. I wondered how he knew Rosenthal.

I returned to my desk. Neither assignment had brought delight to my heart, but they still needed a proper contract. Maybe I should stick to retrieving lost pets. There was usually happiness at the end. Usually, but not always. Sometimes the pet was dead.

Time to go to the morgue.

CHAPTER THREE

THE MORGUE WAS solid red brick; square shaped and two stories high. Like so many buildings in the city, however functional, it still had made an attempt at dress-up. The high arched windows on the ground floor were framed by inlays of contrasting light-coloured brick. The entrance was a grand oak door, wide and high. A discreet brass plaque declared this was indeed the CITY MORGUE.

Unfortunately, somewhat detracting from this dignity, there was a large mattress factory directly beside it. No aspirations of beauty here. A four-storey-high block of grey brick, with small windows. Some wag had taken advantage of the location and there was a sign in front. *Marshall's. Need a good sleep? Come to Lombard Street. We guarantee quiet neighbours.*

I approached the massive door of the morgue. There was a note taped to the bell. OUT OF ORDER. KNOCK HARD. Ever obedient, I did just that. There was no response from inside, so I thumped again. Nothing happened and I was just about to knock again when the door was flung open.

"What are you trying to do, raise the dead?"

"Joe! That is a terrible joke."

The speaker was my friend, Joe Craig. He was an attendant at the morgue and he was the one I had arranged to meet. He stepped back and surveyed me.

"My god. Where did you get that outfit? Going out in the life boat again are we?"

I was wearing my Gran's old mackintosh, which hung to the top of my wellies. My hat could be described as a sou'wester and would have suited a fisherman. Although the rain had dropped back to drizzle, it was still inhospitable. I glistened.

I followed him into the foyer. "First of all, it's not polite to make personal remarks to a woman, unless they are complimentary. Secondly, I believe being practical is more important than fashion. In case you hadn't noticed, it's raining."

Joe grinned at me. "I'd give you a hug if you weren't so wet. How've you been anyway? Still going with that fellow?"

"If you mean Hilliard, yes."

"Let me know if it crashes. Just whistle and I'll come running."

"I suppose I should say thank you to that."

I started to take off my raincoat and hat.

"Here, give me those." He reached out and took them from me. Then he halted and scrutinized me.

"You know what, Lottie? Being in love suits you. You're glowing."

"Oh Joe, cut it out. That's just the rain."

He grimaced. "Shucks. I should have figured that out."

There was an expression on his face that made me feel bad. Joe and I had enjoyed a little dalliance previously. We had fun together and I liked him a lot. He'd made it clear he wanted more from the relationship and I might have been persuaded if I hadn't met Hilliard Taylor. Joe turned around and started to head through the foyer.

The bodies were kept in refrigerators in the basement which had white walls, stone tiles, and high windows. There was no doubt about its function.

"No room at the inn," said Joe as we entered. "We've had four equivocal deaths in the past week, two of them nippers. All of them died from carbon monoxide poisoning. When will people learn to be more careful? Two faulty stoves, one blocked fireplace."

Joe went over to the covered gurney that was in the middle of the floor. "Here's your man." Joe's voice dropped, "He got a bit puffy from being immersed in water, but before that he was no beauty, poor sod."

He pulled down the sheet, exposing Gerald Jessop's face.

I could tell he'd been warning me, but even so I was unprepared for the first sight of this once handsome ex-soldier. The senior Mrs. Jessop had said Gerald had received extensive plastic surgery on his mutilated face. With the pallor of death, the effect now was of a clay model that had been roughly thrown together by an amateur sculptor. Lopsided, uneven eyes, a crooked nose, no lips to speak of, and a twisted misshapen jaw. "You get used to it," Ellen Jessop had blurted. I'm sure that was true, but nothing could hide the fact that Gerald had the face of a monster. Poor sod indeed.

"Can I see his hands?"

Joe pulled down the covering sheet.

The left hand was smooth with long slender artist's fingers. An attractive hand that you'd notice in normal circumstances. The right was ugly. Scar tissue had fused three of the fingers together and the tips were all amputated just above the first joint. It was a claw not a hand.

I nodded at Joe to replace the sheet. "The coroner returned a verdict of suicide. Would you agree?"

Joe didn't hesitate. "Given the state of the chappie's insides, I'd say this was somebody who wasn't too happy in the world. He was obviously a regular morphine user and his liver was already a mess. Can't say I blame him. You saw him. How would you like to look at that in the mirror every morning?"

"You get used to it," I said echoing Ellen's words.

"Maybe. But even if you did, given those kind of injuries, I'd say he'd be hard pressed to shake off the pain in his face. The nerves would have been damaged."

"Okay. Did you find anything else that might indicate it wasn't suicide?"

"Like what?"

"Like homicide."

Joe stared at me. "Come on, Lottie. I know you've taken

on this job and you're doing it, but there is zero evidence that this was other than the chap offing himself. Not the slightest sign of defensive wounds, no bruises anywhere. If you can show me how somebody did him in, and more important who and why, I'll resign and get work as a dance instructor."

I had to laugh at that. I knew how efficient Joe was at his job, but dancing was definitely not his forte. We'd tried a couple of times.

Nevertheless, I could feel a certain stubborn streak in me, beginning to take a grip. I wasn't ready to call it quits on this case just yet.

"One more question. Given the prior injuries, do you think he was capable of fathering a child?"

Joe shrugged. "He's intact if that's what you mean. There's no genital scarring, so he didn't have the French curse. Other than that, it's impossible to tell. Why'd you ask?"

"Just following up all loose ends. Are all of his effects with the police?"

"Everything. Did you know he won the Military Cross?"

"Yes, his mother told me."

"Hefty price to pay."

I knew what he meant.

CHAPTER FOUR

P ROMISING JOE I'D at least come by for a coffee soon, I left and headed for the Paradise Café. A brief explanation. In July, my path had crossed with that of the Paradise Café. Literally and figuratively. One of the owners hired me to investigate what looked like embezzlement going on. Four men, all former prisoners of war, had come together and started a café. They had suffered terribly during their stint in the camp and they wanted to create a place where they would serve tasty, nourishing food at reasonable prices to people who were imprisoned in a different way. Poverty and no opportunities were their barbed wire.

Case solved; heart lost.

Whenever I approached the café, especially on such a chilly November day, I was cheered by the sight of it. The fresh yellow trim brought to mind summer buttercups. The word *inviting* certainly came to mind.

This stretch of Queen Street was a bit on the shabby side so for the café's sake I had been glad when the adjacent space, which had been vacant for a long time, was finally rented. I suppose it was like getting a new tooth to replace the gap left by an old extraction. Better still, the new shop sold books and the new tenant had given the outside a refurbishing. The deep blue trim was more subdued than the café, as befitted a serious book shop, and it was all clean and neat. The lettering, also neat, across the front said WORKMANS; a printed sign in the window declared *All relevant books stocked.*

Initially, I'd wondered about the wisdom of anybody starting a new business in these times, but almost since opening day the store seemed to have a steady stream of customers. The owner's name in fact was Workman. Wallace Workman. He was young and a passionate unionist and socialist, although he kept that fairly quiet. Smart thing these days with Chief Constable Draper seeming to have an obsession with rooting out communists. Or socialists. He didn't make the distinction. They were all apparently a threat to stable government.

Wally ran his shop rather like a library and provided comfortable chairs for his customers where they could sit and browse through the books they may or may not eventually purchase.

Wilf Morrow, one of the partners at the Paradise, was very enthusiastic about the place; Hilliard less so.

Wally was just changing the window display as I walked by. We exchanged waves.

There was the usual lineup outside the café itself, waiting for the next sitting. Mostly men, a few women; they weren't talking much, huddling into their coats, collars turned up against the rain. Knowing Hilliard, I expected he'd open promptly and sure enough, I saw him flipping over the sign. OPEN. He flung open the door.

"Come on in, folks," he called. "We won't be long."

The line shuffled forward, nobody shoved. They knew better. Lining up was now a way of life for many people. Hilliard saw me and to my gratification, his face lit up. Mine probably did too.

"Charlotte! Come in. Quick."

He raised his arm so I could slip underneath. He was tall.

"It's okay, folks, she's part of the team."

I liked that he put it that way. Hilliard Taylor was one of the partners of the café and back in July he'd hired me to find out who was lifting some of their hard-earned money.

Hilliard squeezed my shoulder as I went past.

"I need to speak to you," he whispered.

In spite of the warm smile, I thought he looked worried and I wondered what was going on. The customers moved forward, well-behaved and quiet, but there was steady pressure to keep moving into the warmth of the café.

Down the centre of the room was a long table with a few smaller tables around the perimeter. It was a tight space, but that added to the cozy feeling. The partners had made sure the electric lighting was bright; the walls were painted yellow; there were even pristine white tablecloths. I am rather proud to say that at my suggestion, a few jam jars containing cuttings from a couple of hanging plants were sitting on the tables. They gave a nice touch of greenery on this grey day.

Many of the customers were regulars and knew each other, but the greetings were muted. Getting to their seats was the priority. Some had proper hats and overcoats against the weather; others were dressed in a strange combination of shawls, both men and women. Two or three had socks on their hands instead of gloves. I knew those were the ones who would be given credit, if they asked for it, until the day they got work.

I exchanged greetings with several of them.

Leaving Hilliard to supervise the sitting, I headed for the kitchen where I almost collided with Pearl, the waitress, who was just rushing out. She had to be one of the moodiest women I'd ever met, but she was loyal and industrious and I'd become used to her.

"I wish he wouldn't do this," she exclaimed at me. "Wilf hasn't come down yet. We're not ready."

Without waiting for a response, she bustled off to start taking orders.

I went into the kitchen. As usual, it was steamy and redolent with cooking food. Thank goodness onions weren't the dominant smell. It wasn't a large space, but it had been designed for functionality. The appliances were fairly new and still looked shiny and ready for action, the shelves were tidy.

Calvin Greene was at the stove ladling soup into the bowls on a tray ready to go out. He glanced over his shoulder and nodded at me. His dark skin glistened with sweat from the heat emanating from the oven.

"Good day, Miss Frayne."

He'd only been with the café for three weeks and still maintained a formal address with everybody.

"Hello, Calvin. What wonderful creation have you devised today?" I asked.

I was being slightly hypocritical. Cal had worked for many years on one of the lake trawlers and he believed in serious economy. This translated into his using portions of the animal meat that were, shall we say, less than familiar. So far none of the customers had complained, but I can't say giblet soup was a big favourite.

"Cock-a-leekie soup for starters." He dipped the ladle into the soup pot. "Do you want to try it?"

There was a plate on the counter, and I could see where he'd put the pale chicken carcass and two pieces of scrag of mutton to be served later.

"Here," he said and offered up the ladle. I had no choice but to have a taste. The soup had a rather unpleasant, greasy, grey-green colour. I took a cautious sip. It was definitely better than it looked, but I wouldn't have put it at the top of my can't-live-without-it list.

"What do you think?" Calvin asked.

I was given a reprieve by Pearl who came banging through the swing door.

"We're ready to serve up, Cal."

She picked up the tray laden with steaming soup bowls.

She made it look easy. It was one of the skills that mitigated her less-engaging qualities.

Hilliard was close behind her.

"Stay here," he said to me. "I'll be right back." He was about to grab the two baskets of sliced bread from the table when at that moment there was a loud crash from the dining room and the sound of loud angry voices, women's voices.

"What the hell? What's going on?" Hilliard asked even as he started to head toward the door.

He stepped into the dining room. I followed him.

The cause of the crash appeared to be one of the chairs which had been knocked to the floor. The shouts were coming from one of the female customers. She was yelling at another woman, younger and attractive, who was standing nearby. I hadn't seen her before. The chair owner was actually shaking her fist.

"You're a troublemaker that's what you are, Miriam Cohen. You're lucky I don't go to the boss."

Her opponent snapped back, "Do what you like. It's a free country."

The face of the apparent initiator of this quarrel was distorted with rage. "You're a slut is what you are. I've seen you wiggling your arse at the boss's son. You're a laughing stock. He won't look at you twice. Not your kind."

I wasn't sure what kind that was. The other woman was neatly dressed; red raincoat and matching perky hat. She didn't look sluttish. Also, she wasn't backing down. Her voice too was raised.

"You're just jealous, Bertha. You'd turn off a blind man, you would."

Bertha grabbed one of the knives on the table and actually raised it. I'm not sure what she intended, but Hilliard got there in time and caught her arm.

"Hold on there. What's going on?"

The café had gone deadly quiet. Nobody was making a move to stop the fight. Pearl, too, seemed paralyzed. She was still holding her full tray. I stepped closer to the younger woman, prepared to intervene myself if things got worse. The café was no place for a brawl.

The Bertha person tried to shake off Hilliard who still had a firm grip on her arm.

"Let go of me."

Drops of spittle shot out as she spoke and hit him on the face.

"Put the knife down and I will."

She did so. Reluctantly. He released her arm, wiped off the spit from his chin and pushed the knife out of harm's way.

"This is no place to sort out your quarrels, ma'am. Why don't you sit down?"

A grizzled man who was seated beside her reached up and caught her arm.

"Come on Bertha. Do as the man says. You're disturbing everybody's lunch."

She snapped around and glared at him. "I don't give a damn. I don't have money to buy food because of that whore."

Even from where I was standing, I could smell the liquor on her breath. She'd spent her money elsewhere.

"She got me in trouble. I was docked a day's wages."

The young woman bristled. "I did not. You brought it on yourself. A little too fond of the booze, aren't we, Bertha. Look at you."

Hilliard spoke sharply. "Miss, I'm going to ask you to leave. I don't know what your quarrel is with this woman, but at the moment I don't care. You cannot bring it in here."

Miriam looked as if she was ready to take him on as well. "Why me? She's the one who should go. She started it. I just came in here for some lunch."

Hilliard's voice was calm. "Let's put it this way. One of you will leave this café right now. I'm not going to tolerate this kind of disturbance. Who's it going to be?"

"To hell with you," said the girl and she turned on her heel and strode out of the café. Whew. The sigh of relief that ran through the room was tangible.

Hilliard addressed them. "Sorry about this, folks. Continue with your lunch. Dessert's on the house."

That brought forth a subdued cheer and the customers broke into a buzz. Pearl started serving the soup.

"Come on, don't let it get cold. It's a nice cock-a-leekie."

Wilf Morrow, who was one of the partners, had come into the dining room to see what the row was all about. Calvin hovered behind him. Wilf went over to where Bertha had knocked over her chair and stood it upright.

"Everything all right, Hill?"

"We're fine, thanks. Maybe you could bring over a cup of tea for Bertha here."

The woman sat down. Whether it was the presence of the two men or the offer of tea I don't know, but even though steam was still coming out of her nostrils she was starting to calm down. Hilliard pulled one of the chairs closer and sat down beside her.

I snatched a look at the clock. It was a quarter to twelve. Much as I wanted to see the conclusion to this drama, I just had time to get over to Spadina Avenue. I gave him a little wave and mouthed, "I've got to go."

"I must talk to you," he called out. "Can you come back later?"

"Okay."

I felt a twinge of anxiety. He looked like he was under duress. I didn't have to be a super sleuth to deduce the cause. Hilliard was newly divorced and trying to balance his role as a father to two kids with that of owning the Paradise Café. That particular expression meant family trouble.

He turned back to the woman who was rather ostentatiously wiping her eyes with the end of her sleeve. A crocodile would have been proud of those tears.

"Okay. Tell me what that was all about."

Wilf approached with a cup of tea and I waved goodbye.

CHAPTER FIVE

QUEEN STREET WAS sprouting black umbrellas as pedestrians struggled to go about their business. It wasn't worth my while to get on the streetcar so I hunched as best as I could into my raincoat and tugged my sou'wester tighter on my head. A milk cart plodded past. The horse's head was almost dragging on the ground he seemed so weighed down by the weather. An old sack was his only protection against the rain. I wanted to run after them.

I could hear Gramps's voice. "There will always be cruelty, Lottie. What are you doing to do about it? Buy up all the horses in the city and turn them out to pasture? Might as well include the stray dogs, and don't forget the abandoned cats."

A motor car sped by, sending up a shower of water that I dodged by inches. Bloody motorists. They thought they owned the world.

Mr. Rosenthal had said his shop was just north of Queen Street on the east side of Spadina and it proved to be not too far from the café. I walked as briskly as the rain permitted and as I was turning onto Spadina, I collided with a woman, who had paused at the corner, presumably to think about life and the relationship between rain and destiny. At least that's what she might have been considering. She hardly seemed to notice that we had bumped into each other. She was standing stock still, staring down the road.

"Sorry," said I. Then I realized it was in fact the young woman who had been part of the heated exchange at the Paradise Café. She nodded at me in acknowledgment of my apology, but she didn't seem to recognize me as one of the, shall I call us, spectators. I would have let it go, strangers passing on a rainy street, but I saw that she was in fact crying. She'd faced her opponent with a fierce defiance, but she didn't look fierce at the moment. Before I could engage her, she set off down the street walking fast. As we were going in the same direction I followed. I was sorry she had been brought to tears. My sympathies had been with her. Bertha was not endearing.

Over the past few years, Spadina Avenue had become the primary location of the city garment industry. The buildings that faced each other across the wide thoroughfare were red brick, square and unprepossessing. Toronto being what it was, a city with a soul, not to mention artistic aspirations, around the upper level of each building were beautiful carved friezes, utterly unnecessary if you only wanted to be practical.

Miriam had headed south and not too far from the corner, she suddenly stopped again. This time I was ready, and we didn't collide, but I saw that we did in fact have the same destination. A sign above the door said, SUPERIOR LADIES' CLOTHES. There was a small display window with a view of a mannequin with amputated arms and head. The torso was clad in a brown suit, with matching hat, so dull and uninteresting, it could only have appealed to the most dull and uninteresting woman. If that was what Superior was producing, I wasn't surprised Mr. Rosenthal was worried about competition.

The young woman was shaking out her umbrella with a terrier-like ferocity. Suddenly she noticed I was standing nearby.

"I beg pardon," she said. It was my turn to nod an acknowledgement. She pushed open the entrance door. I followed behind her.

"Are you coming upstairs?" she asked in surprise.

"I'm here to see Mr. Klein. I was told to come to the second floor."

"Are you looking for a job?"

"I am. Do you work here?"

"I do." She frowned. "You look familiar. Have we met before?"

I didn't see any advantage to acknowledging my connection to the Paradise at this point. "I don't think so."

The door had opened onto a narrow flight of stairs, ill lit and uncarpeted. The wood was scuffed and worn as if many people had ground their despair and anger into the treads.

Miriam made her way up, me close behind. We reached

a small landing where there was another door to the right. More stairs continued on up.

"Are they a good company to work for?" I asked.

She gave me a little smile. "Let's put it this way. If somebody offers you a job cleaning spittoons, take it."

She pushed open the door and went in.

CHAPTER SIX

THREE TABLES RAN down the middle of the room and about a dozen women, all wearing white overall tops, were bent over sewing machines. A couple of them took a quick look over at us, but nobody stopped working. The air was filled with the sound of the treadles and the whirring of the machines. No chattering. No wireless squawking out music. A few high windows in one wall allowed in a little meagre light, but given the weather they weren't doing a very good job. Three hanging lamps on minimum wattage didn't offer much help. I had the impression not even the mid-summer sun could penetrate this dungeon. The place was long and narrow with low ceilings; bare, unpainted walls; and scuffed wooden flooring. It also smelled as if any fresh air that had ever been present was used up decades ago.

Miriam tapped me on the shoulder. "Come and hang up your coat."

She walked over to the nearby stand, already burdened with several coats, and started to remove her raincoat and hat. Her brown hair was short and curly.

There was a glass-fronted office at the end of the room. A man burst out of it into the work space. He was in full throttle and yelling as if we were at the far end of a parade ground.

"Miss Cohen, you are late. Unless you have an excellent excuse such as the sudden death of your mother and father, you will be fined. Again."

I stopped in mid-divestment of my mackintosh, but Miriam continued what she was doing. She slipped on her white top.

"Sorry Mr. Klein. Couldn't be helped."

She didn't say, "and stuff your fine up your jacksey," but she may as well have. Klein turned to me and glared. He was a short, chubby man and rather unfortunately had chosen to wear a blue overall that appeared to have belonged to someone much smaller. Or a younger self.

"Who are you when you're at home?" he said, his voice still at high volume.

Given the general aggression and rudeness of his manner, I felt like turning around and leaving, or alternatively, thumping the man. Neither option was open to me. Miriam came to my rescue.

"She wants a job."

"Does she? Hope she's not a friend of yours, 'cos if she is, she won't get one."

"Never met her before."

She turned around and walked over to one of the tables.

I realized that one of the workers was actually a young

boy who must have just left school. He had copper red hair and the abundant freckles that come with it.

His chair was beside Miriam's and as she sat down, she ruffled his hair. He gave her the adoring smile of a lad with a big crush on a pretty older woman.

Klein beckoned to me. "Come this way."

He turned around and headed for the office, stopping briefly to examine the work of one of the women at the end table. He threw it back at her and she cowered.

As I went past Miriam, I muttered, "Thanks," but she only gave me a brief nod. Perhaps she didn't want to spoil my chances.

The supervisor's office was glassed-in and elevated so it had a good view of the entire workspace. Klein went first, walked straight to his desk and sat down behind it. As there was no other chair in the room, I had to stand awkwardly in front of him, like a recalcitrant schoolgirl facing the principal. He didn't look at me, but opened a large black ledger and dipped a straight pen into an inkwell. I began to feel as if I had slipped back into a previous century. I sincerely hoped Klein would have some disturbing visitors in the night.

"Name?"

"Charlotte Frayne."

"Married?"

"No."

"Good. We don't hire married women."

"Why not?"

That at least made him look up.

"It's her husband's job to take care of her, not us."

"What if they need the income?"

"Not my problem, is it?"

I didn't see any point in getting into an argument I wouldn't win, so I muttered something indistinctive. He returned to his ledger.

"We're in need of a sewer. Can you sew?" he asked. His voice was still loud. Maybe he was deaf.

"Not really."

"Cut?"

"Not at all."

He stared up at me. "What the hell can you do?"

"There must be other work in a shop like this. I'll do whatever is needed. I need a job."

"You and half the country." He waved his hand at me. "Turn around."

"I beg your pardon."

"Turn around. Make a circle. I want to make sure you're not a cripple or retarded."

Feeling utterly ridiculous, I did as he said.

"Okay. You'll do. We need a bin pusher. Our regular girl left."

"May I ask what is a bin pusher?"

He began to speak slowly and deliberately as if I was dim witted. "The clothes have to be cut obviously. That's done on the third floor. Then the pieces are tied into bundles and they are put into a bin; this same bin has to be brought down to the sewers who are on this floor. When they have made the fabric into some semblance of a garment, those same clothes have to be taken down to the first floor where they are stored. As they are not going to get up and walk there, they are placed in a —"

I interrupted him. "Let me guess, a bin?"

To my surprise, he actually grinned. At least I think it was a grin that lifted his lip.

"That is correct. So do you want the job or not?"

"I'll take it."

"You'll receive twenty-five cents an hour. The shift is ten hours. Eight to six. Monday to Friday. Saturday eight to noon. Weekdays, you get half an hour for lunch. Ten-minute breaks. No more than two. We have a trial period of two weeks, but if your work is unsatisfactory you may be dismissed without notice."

He paused, looked up at me for a moment.

"Any questions?"

"I do as a matter of fact. As bin pusher how do I get the bin from one floor to the other?"

"There's a service elevator. Only big enough for the bin. You wheel it into the elevator, close the gate, push the button required, and go down the stairs to the assigned floor where you open the gate and wheel out the bin. When you have disposed of these goods as described, you have to pick up the bolts of cloth from where they are stored at the rear of the shop and take them back to the third floor where they will be cut. That's clear enough, I'd say."

"And how many times a day do I have to do that?"

"As many as it takes. In between times you will sweep the floors and dispose of any scraps. You will also help with the packaging of the final product on the first floor. If we're short-handed in the shop, you can assist with the display room. You're not bad looking and you speak well enough."

"And for doing this I get twenty-five cents an hour?"

I tried to keep my tone neutral, but I obviously didn't succeed. He scowled at me.

"Like I said, there's lots of women would jump at this job and take less. You're not skilled. Do you want it or not?"

"Yes."

"Be here tomorrow morning at eight. Any lateness will be deducted from your wages."

"Of course, only fair."

He laid the pen neatly on the ledger. "I don't know what job you had before this, Miss Frayne, and I don't care. I've dealt with all sorts in my time. What I do care about is running a tight ship. Employees are discouraged from wasting time; chatting to each other for instance. You know how you women are. The more we can produce, the better for all concerned. Loyalty is its own reward."

He gestured with his hand.

"You can find your own way out."

I did so, walking back to the exit. Again, nobody paid me any attention except Miriam.

"See you tomorrow?" she called out.

"You will."

She seemed glad of that.

At the door, I turned and looked back to the office. Mr. Klein was staring out. Watching me? Watching the workers? I wasn't sure. They appeared to be intent on their work. Mr. Rosenthal had hired me to investigate rebellious and riotous tendencies among his workers. So far, I thought he was delusional.

I hadn't even closed the door when a horrible shriek rang out. Then another.

I stepped back into the room.

CHAPTER SEVEN

THE YOUNG LAD seated next to Miriam was on his feet clutching his own hand which was dripping blood. Miriam, also standing, was attempting to staunch the flow with a piece of fabric which was rapidly turning red. The boy, the one who had obviously shrieked, was gasping, his face contorted in pain. The other women had stopped work and were frozen in place. Klein's door flew open and he rushed out, roaring.

"Move him away from the table. Don't get the blood on the fabrics."

The boy's face was white, and he looked as if he was going to pass out. Except for Miriam, nobody was making a move to help him. Throwing off my purported role, I hurried over, grabbed his chair and pulled it out.

"Sit down, there's a good chap. Now put your head between your knees. Can I have a look?" Reluctantly, the lad stretched out his hand. As far as I could tell he had pierced the nail on his middle finger with the machine needle, a piece of which had broken off and was protruding from the skin.

"Is there a first aid kit anywhere?" I asked Miriam.

"I think so ..."

"I'll get it," said a woman at the other table. She jumped up and scuttled to the door.

Miriam patted the boy's shoulder. "You'll be all right, Ben. Be a brave boy."

He was trying hard not to cry. Mr. Klein, who was standing close to us, stared down at him.

"What the hell were you thinking of, you stupid fellow?"

Ben didn't answer, only moaned.

"It was an accident," snapped Miriam.

I heard a couple of the women exchanging words, but I was not sure what language they were speaking.

Klein clapped his hands at them as if they were geese. "All right, ladies. Show's over. He'll survive. Get back to work if you please. We're behind as it is. Come on, no shilly-shallying."

Reluctantly the workers began to start up their machines.

The woman who'd gone for first aid returned holding a small tin box.

"There's some bandages in here."

The box didn't have much in it just a single roll of gauze, a couple of cotton pads and a bottle of iodine. I poured some of the liquid onto a pad.

"This is going to sting, Ben. You can yell if you like."

I dabbed the pad onto Ben's wound. He winced, but didn't cry out. Miriam pressed on his shoulder.

"We should get him to a doctor," I said.

"I'll take him," said Miriam.

"No, you won't," said Klein. "We'll fall behind."

The matter was settled by the young lad suddenly and violently vomiting onto the floor.

Klein jumped back in disgust while Miriam frantically looked around for something with which to help Ben. A woman seated across the table halted her machine, grabbed some cloth from the bundle beside her and tossed it over to Miriam. Another woman jumped up.

"I'll get him some water," she said.

By now, everybody had ceased working and was watching. Miriam held the cloth under the boy's chin, but he seemed to have expunged himself. More bile than anything else. He gagged a couple more times, at the same time tried to hold his injured finger in the air to protect it. Deep red blood continued to ooze from the wound and trickle down his hand.

Klein folded his arms, but made no further attempt to bully the women back to work. The woman who had gone for water returned holding a cup.

"Thanks, Rhoda." Miriam took it from her and gently raised the boy's head so he could take a sip. The sour smell of vomit permeated the air.

"Don't worry, Ben," said Miriam. "We'll get you looked after."

At that moment, to add to an already charged scene, the door opened and in came two men. Three of the women immediately leapt to their feet and bobbed their heads.

Another culture, another generation. This had to be the big boss. I was meeting Saul Rosenthal face-to-face.

"What's going on, Mr. Klein? Why has work stopped?"

"There's been a small accident, sir. This lad here ran a needle through his finger."

"How did that happen?" growled Rosenthal.

"He let himself get distracted," said Klein.

He glanced over at Miriam as if implying she was responsible for the distraction. She was having none of it.

"Ben wasn't distracted. The safety mechanism on the machine was broken. They need servicing on a regular basis if we are to have no accidents. Frankly most of them are antiquated and should be replaced."

"Indeed."

Rosenthal went quiet, but he might as well have been shouting. The tension in his body was palpable. No one else moved a muscle.

I was fed up with him. Both of them, to tell the truth. "That's something you people can argue about later. Right now, this boy should get to a hospital."

Rosenthal turned to look at me. If his voice was gravelly, he had a face to match. Some pox had ravaged his skin and it was pitted and rough. His eyes were grey as asphalt.

"And you are?"

Klein answered for me. "This is Charlotte Frayne, sir. Our new employee."

"Doing what?"

"I've been hired to be the bin pusher," I spoke for myself.

He grunted. Then he moved closer to the injured boy, making sure he didn't step in the yellow puddle of vomit.

"Let me see your finger."

Ben lifted his hand again and Rosenthal peered at it. "There's a piece of the needle still embedded. It will have to be removed."

Over his shoulder he beckoned to the young man who was hovering behind him. Not as hefty, more hair, darker and all together much better looking, he was nevertheless obviously the heir apparent.

"Joel. Take care of him, will you?'

Joel moved in closer which necessitated him squeezing past Miriam who didn't cede an inch. Their bodies brushed. He seemed highly awkward and I remembered the argument at the Paradise. "You think you can get the boss's son."

I'd say Miriam had already got him by the look of things. Joel put his hand out to the boy.

"Can you stand up? There's a good chap."

Ben gripped him and struggled to get to his feet, but he was so shaky it was clear he might pass out at any moment, never mind vomit again.

"Tell you what. Why don't I give you a piggy-back ride?" He turned around. "Up you get."

Ben managed to hold on and Joel hoisted him up on his back. Mr. Rosenthal nodded at Klein.

"Go on ahead and call for a taxicab."

"Yes, sir."

Klein hurried off and the women shifted so Joel and the boy could get by.

They left and the women began to return to their workplaces, speaking to each other in soft voices.

Rosenthal held up his hand to get their attention. "I'm sure this has been most distressing. Before you get back to work, why don't you all take a fifteen-minute break. Make some tea. On me."

The woman Miriam had called Rhoda spoke up. She was small, rather bent and scrawny, but with a pride of demeanour that was unmistakable.

"That's very kind of you, sir but I wonder if we mightn't make that thirty minutes? We'd be happy to use our regular break time. Right ladies?"

The muted reply could only be described as tepid.

Rosenthal pointed his finger at the woman. "Miss Baum? Have I got that right?"

"Quite right, sir. Rhoda Baum. I've been here for three years."

"Tell you what, Miss Baum, why don't we saw it off in the middle? Let's say a twenty-minute break. A good strong cuppa will revive us all."

The other workers stood up promptly and began to make their way to the door. I'm sure they didn't want to give him a chance to change his mind.

Miriam didn't move. "What about the things I said, sir? Are you going to address them?"

"Of course, Miss Cohen. But not at this moment. Perhaps

somebody would be so good as to clean up the floor and dispose of the soiled clothes."

The helpful one who'd gone for the first aid box said she would get a mop, and off she trotted.

Rosenthal turned. As he passed me, his eyes met mine ever so briefly. He was inscrutable. He'd certainly acted more decently than I would have expected from our earlier conversation. Concerned boss? Exploitive ogre? Hypocrite? As yet, I hadn't the faintest idea.

I, too, started to exit. Miriam called after me.

"Thanks for your help. See you tomorrow."

The rest of the women also called out to me. At least two of them spoke in the language I'd heard earlier. I think they were the ones who had stood up when Mr. Rosenthal had come in. I saw Klein was watching me. It wasn't hard to guess what he was thinking.

Whew.

CHAPTER EIGHT

THE SENIOR MRS. JESSOP had said she'd send the car for me at two p.m. I was going to be late.

It was still raining and seemed as if it would continue to do so for forty more days. At this point, however, I was actually glad to feel the cooling damp on my face. It had been quite a morning.

I half-ran, half-walked, back to the office and when I reached the Arcade, I could see a car was parked at the curb just outside. It had to be the Jessop vehicle, a shiny black Packard sedan, beside it a chauffeur holding a large umbrella, also black and shiny. He was tall, dressed in a grey uniform, smart peaked cap, very military in appearance. His heavy moustache was white.

I went up to him.

"Hello. Are you waiting for me?"

"You are Miss Frayne?"

"That's me. And you are?"

"Wilson, Miss. Mrs. Jessop sent me to fetch you."

I didn't think there would be two fancy cars with fancy chauffeurs idling in front of my building waiting to whisk me off somewhere, but confirmation of intent and identity is always reassuring. Holding his umbrella aloft, Wilson went to open the rear door.

"I'd rather sit in the front if you don't mind."

Proletariat and all that, but also, I wanted the chance to talk to him. I beamed at him.

He looked rather startled as if I had made a racy proposition, but he nodded and opened the other door. I slipped in.

The car was warm and smelled of leather with a thick overlay of tobacco. I wondered who was the smoker.

Wilson turned the ignition key, shifted the car into gear, and the Packard roared to life. As we drove away, it settled into a soft growl like the tamed lion it was.

I waited until we were underway, then I opened the conversation.

"I assume Mrs. Jessop has told you why I am coming to the house?"

"Yes, she has, Miss."

"Her son's death must have been a dreadful shock for all of you."

"Yes, it was, Miss."

He was concentrating on driving. The windshield wipers squeaked and didn't do a very good job. Visibility wasn't great. He had to lean forward every few minutes and wipe away the condensation from the inside. I thought he was wary.

"I know you've already spoken to the police, but I wondered if you could just go over things again. I'd like to hear your version of what happened."

He didn't answer immediately, once again rubbing moisture away from the windows.

"What do you mean by 'version' Miss? I was called to the main house in the morning because Mr. Gerald's valet had found him dead. I was asked to call the police, which I did."

"Were you yourself surprised that he had taken his own life?'

"Surprised, Miss? I was shocked."

"Of course. But did you expect this to happen? I understand Mr. Gerald had a lot to contend with."

"He certainly did."

"He must have got very down sometimes."

"That is true."

More wiping.

"Had he made any previous attempts?"

"Not that I know of."

Wilson was doling out bits of information like a pauper paying taxes.

"How long have you known him?"

"I joined the household about twenty-five years ago. Mr. Gerald was then a young man of seventeen."

"I understand your wife is also employed by the Jessops."

"That's right. She does the cooking."

He was being impeccably polite. Frankly, I didn't know

how to penetrate his reserve. "Talk to my servants," Mrs. Jessop had said, but if Wilson was going to be typical of the servants, I had no way of knowing what she expected they'd tell me.

"There's always a way in. Even the most closed subject will open up if you hit the proper note." Mr. Gilmore was fond of sayings like this and mostly he was right. In this case, however, the drawbridge was fully drawn. I fished around for the password.

"You said Gerald Jessop got down in the dumps sometimes, but it's one thing to be blue, it's another to actually kill yourself isn't it?"

He glanced over at me. I continued.

"I mean to say a dreary day like this is enough to depress anybody. The rain seems like it's never going to stop. There's no sun for days. I myself have a hard time in November."

"Do you, Miss?"

Was there a softening? Hard to tell.

"Was Mr. Jessop in better spirits in the nicer weather would you say?"

"Sometimes. To tell the truth, I didn't have a lot to do with him, especially in the past few years. He kept himself quite sequestered in his rooms. He turned the extra bedroom into his library and he spent a lot of time there."

"That sounds very lonely."

Wilson shrugged. "I suppose it was from our point of view, but it was what he wanted. He didn't like to go out in public because of his appearance."

I thought I detected a note of disapproval in his voice.

"He must have been quite a sight given what happened to him. But that happened to an awful lot of soldiers didn't it?"

I could see Wilson's lips tighten. His voice was sharp. "I've seen worse. Much worse."

He looked too old to have been in the war, so I wondered what he was referring to so vehemently, but he was definitely warming up.

"It's hard to believe that there might be another war brewing, but all the indications are that there will be."

He frowned. "If there is, I hope we learned our lesson."

"Which is?"

"You can have all the artillery and firepower in the world. What wins wars is character. Never mind guns. You need brave men."

Before I could continue with this now fruitful line of talk, he turned the car onto Pembroke Street. The Jessop house was close by. He entered the adjacent lane and pulled up in front of the garage.

"If you'll just wait here while I get the umbrella, Miss, I'll take you around to the house."

"One more question, Mr. Wilson. According to the coroner's report, Mr. Jessop was wearing his medals when he died. Including the Military Cross. Were you aware of that?"

"The detective mentioned it."

"It seems to me a dreadful pity that a man who had shown such bravery would end his life in this way."

He looked at me for a moment, but I'd be darned if I could tell from his expression what he was thinking. Then he said, "He's not the first and most likely won't be the last."

End of conversation.

CHAPTER NINE

WILSON ESCORTED ME to the front entrance of the house. The door was opened immediately by a uniformed maid. Her dress was a sober dark blue, but the white, lacy apron and cap appeared more decorative than functional. She had a black arm band on her sleeve. She looked to be of middle age, middle height, middle weight.

"This is Miss Frayne," said Wilson.

"Please do come in, Miss. The mistress is in the drawing room."

There was a trace of a Welsh accent in her voice.

"I'll drive you back when you're ready to leave, Miss," said Wilson.

Before I could accept or refuse, he left. I surrendered my mackintosh and sou'wester to the maid and followed her.

The foyer was a mix of old-fashioned ornate and more contemporary simple. A thick plain carpet, burgundy flocked wallpaper (too much), light oak trimmings (always in style), a crystal chandelier (awe inspiring). The staircase curved up from the foyer itself (the best feature). The maid paused in front of a door to the right, tapped, and went in.

Probably in summer, the room was bright and pleasant as there were deep windows to one side, but today it was both cold and dim. There was a low fire in the grate and only two lamps were on. The green velvet curtains were drawn. The outer world reflecting the inner. The two Jessop women were seated by the fireplace. I had the feeling they hadn't been doing anything but sitting in silence.

As I entered, a small brown and white terrier leaped up and rushed at me barking ferociously. Like most small dogs, it thought it was a mastiff. And I suppose I was some kind of rodent. It certainly gave the impression it was about to take a nip to find out.

"It's okay, Duffy," I said in my most canine friendly voice. The dog was not convinced.

Ellen Jessop also jumped up.

"Stop that. Bad dog."

Duffy ignored her. She hadn't yet made her position clear.

The senior Mrs. Jessop's voice rang out.

"Cut it out."

Duffy stopped barking immediately, took a twitchy sniff at the air in front of me and with a little grumble, went back to the chair and collapsed. Mrs. Jessop patted its head.

"Silly girl."

The dog ignored her.

"I'm sorry Miss Frayne," said Ellen. "She's very protective. Gerald rescued her from the streets about a year ago.

She still seems to act based on the survival instinct." She gestured to the armchair by the fireplace. "Please have a seat."

I did so. The senior Mrs. Jessop was in the other wing-back. She leaned forward a little so she could see me.

"We have forewarned the servants that you will be speaking to them. You can use this room if you wish."

I did not wish. This room was so drenched with grief, so cold and dark, I thought any frank discussion between me and the faithful servants would be stilted at best, or worse.

But it might be better if I talked to them in a more familiar place. Perhaps the kitchen?"

She gave me a frosty look. "We are not totally in the Victorian age, Miss Frayne. For some time my servants have had their own quarters including a parlour. Would that be more suitable?"

"Sounds as if that would be ideal."

"I should tell you that we have heard from the detective and he will be here at three o'clock."

She pulled herself to her feet causing Duffy to leap up at the ready.

Rationally, I knew Mrs. Jessop could not have lost weight in the last few hours, that the illusion was because she wasn't wearing her outdoor clothes, but she looked as if she were shrivelling away by the minute.

"I am going to my room. Ellen will help you with the servants. I shall come down at three." She walked slowly to the door with the little dog trotting after her, nary a backward glance at me although I knew better than to move without her permission. Ellen left with them.

"I'll just be a moment," she said.

I took the opportunity to look around the room. Two wing-back brocade armchairs, a matching three-piece chesterfield, good carpet, nice lamps. Nothing unusual in the furnishing. They weren't any different from any modestly well-to-do household. What was unusual was that there was no mirror over the marble fireplace. Nothing that would reflect images. I guessed the curtains would be drawn before dark and that this would be true of any room in the house. No wonder the servants had their own quarters.

There was a single framed photograph draped in black silk on the mantelpiece. It was Gerald Jessop, in a captain's uniform as he must have looked when he joined the army. The senior Mrs. Jessop had said he was twenty-four. He could have been younger. Slim, blonde, well-defined features; he was smiling into the camera, the sun shining on his fair hair. A golden boy indeed.

CHAPTER TEN

ELLEN SOON RETURNED.

"Please come with me, Miss Frayne."

This was the first time I had been in the presence of Ellen Jessop alone and she was a little more self-assured, but not much. She had a way of ducking her head when she spoke as if she regretted what she'd said as soon as the words left her mouth and she sought to swallow them before they caused offence.

She led the way down the hall and opened a door to the left.

"This is the servants' parlour." She immediately switched on one of the lamps.

"Mrs. Greta Wilson, our cook, will come in first as she has a little time before dinner preparations."

Ellen slipped away.

The parlour was warmer and lighter; tidy enough, but certainly looked lived in, which was more than I could say for the drawing room. There was even a mirror over the mantelpiece and some paintings on the walls. All land-scapes. Here, too, there was a fire burning.

A gust of wind flung a smattering of rain against the window and I went over to have a look out in case the world was about to end abruptly.

I could see into the back garden which was surrounded by a high brick wall. At one end drooped a couple of denuded trees; some spindly shrubs edged the flower beds. In the greyness, there was one splash of colour. Near the far wall there was a wrought iron bench. It had been painted a bright, vivid blue.

The sight made my throat tighten. Right after the war, the city council had some of the park benches painted blue. The mutilated and the disfigured veterans were expected to sit there so passersby could be warned of what they might see as they walked by or tried to take a seat. I was only thirteen at the time, but I still remembered them.

I wondered who had placed this particular bench in this back garden.

* * *

THERE WAS A tap on the door and Ellen Jessop poked her head in.

"Mrs. Wilson can speak with you now, Miss Frayne. Shall I bring her in?"

"Yes, please."

I moved over to the table.

Ellen vanished and the cook entered. She stood on the

threshold waiting for instructions, but her demeanour was not submissive so much as wary. This woman had a mind of her own. Her grey hair was slightly frizzy, but pulled back in a neat old-fashioned bun. She, too, was in a plain, dark blue dress with white collar and cuffs. Like the maid, she was wearing a black arm band.

"Hello, Mrs. Wilson. Please have a seat."

I pulled out a chair at the table and sat down across from her.

Close up, she seemed younger than my first impression. Her skin was smooth and fair, her lips plump. As my Gramps would say, she must have been a smasher in her younger days. I thought Rudy Wilson was handsome too. A well-matched couple, physically at least. Maybe she was able to soften him up when he wasn't on duty.

I took my notebook and pen from my handbag and placed them on the table.

"I hope you don't mind if I take notes?"

"You have to, don't you?"

A bit of an ambiguous answer but I plunged ahead. She was actually hard to read. It was clear she had gone through quite a lot of weeping herself. Her eyes were swollen and red-rimmed.

"I believe you have been informed as to why I am here."

I wanted to know exactly what she'd been told.

She nodded. "Mrs. Jessop said you would be asking questions about Mr. Gerald's death."

"That is correct. I realize the police have already spoken

to everybody in the household, but Mrs. Jessop wants to make absolutely sure they have reached the correct conclusion."

She nodded again. "You mean about him killing himself?"

"Precisely."

At least she wasn't going to shy away from the facts.

"What is your opinion, Mrs. Wilson?"

Her gaze shifted immediately.

"Whether it was an accident or not, I hope he's finally at peace now."

Her eyes filled with tears and she quickly fished out a handkerchief and wiped them.

"I understand he had suffered severe wounds during the war that left him quite disfigured."

This time, she focussed on some spot over my head. "He got a medal for what he did, but it didn't give him back his fingers or his face did it?"

"Would you say he had adjusted to these injuries or did he get down?"

"Course he got down. I've been with this family for more than twenty years. I knew Mr. Gerald when he was one of the handsomest young men you'd ever seen. He wasn't vain about his looks, mind you. Never that. But the girls made eyes at him wherever he went. He could have had any woman he wanted."

"He married Ellen just before he went off to war, didn't he?"

"That's right. They were only married two months then

she didn't see him for more than a year, and when he came back ... well ..." She paused. "I do give her credit, though. She's stuck by him. It wasn't just that he'd been disfigured, he was changed."

I wasn't sure if she was going to continue. I prompted her. "Changed in what way?"

"He used to be such a jolly fellow. Always good humoured and pleasant. He liked dinner parties, going to vaudeville. But when he came back, he didn't want to go out anywhere. He was ashamed of how he looked. As if it was his fault, for goodness sake. I used to say to him time and time again, 'Mr. Gerald, you got those wounds honourably. You've no need to hide yourself away.'"

She dabbed at her eyes.

"I understand he took to drinking more than was good for him?"

She grimaced at me. "Not surprising was it?"

"Not at all. Unfortunately, many of our returning soldiers ended up with the same problem."

"Mrs. Jessop doted on him. Her only child. She sent him to fancy clinics more than once and he'd come back all chipper and optimistic, and we'd think, Thank the Lord he's all right now. He'll be all right ... but it didn't last. And when he did go back to the bottle, it was worse than ever."

She stopped and stared at me. "Sorry Miss, here am I talking on. Rudy always says I can babble like a stream let out of the dam once you get me started."

"Don't apologize, please. This is all very helpful. I can see how much you cared for him."

Suddenly wary again, she shot me a glance.

"All of us did."

"One last question. Did he seem particularly upset recently?"

"Wasn't any different really from any other year. Come late October, November, he'd get very blue. He found all the remembrances and ceremonies difficult."

"Did he attend any of them?"

"No."

"Nobody saw anything to worry about in terms of his mood?"

"We was always concerned, but we'd learned it would pass."

She looked out of the window. "He'd go and sit on that darn bench for hours. We weren't allowed to talk to him. 'Just leave him,' said Mrs. Jessop. 'Let him have his privacy.' I wanted him to at least have his tea or a cover or an umbrella but, no, we weren't allowed."

"No one?"

"Nobody but Sam Weaver, his valet. They'd sit together by the hour."

Once again, there was a hint of some deeper feeling. Jealousy perhaps? Did Greta want to be the special one?

"Was there such a vigil this year?"

"Oh yes. Every year since he got home."

"How long did it last?"

"Two, sometimes three, days. Early on it was longer."

"Did he and Sam sit outside at any time before he died?"

"They did. That very morning, they were there."

There was a soft tap on the door and Ellen came in. Tentative as usual.

"I wondered how long you would be, Miss Frayne. Mrs. Jessop wants her maid to do some errands for her, but she would like you to speak to her before she leaves."

Mrs. Wilson got to her feet. "I don't know as there's much more I can say, is there Miss?"

"Not at this time. Thank you. You have been most helpful."

"I'll get on with dinner preparations then."

She left.

"I'll bring Mrs. Jones, shall I?" said Ellen.

"Please do. Will Mr. Weaver be available after that?"

"I believe so. And the police detective will be here at three."

She backed off to the door. Closing it firmly seemed too definite a commitment, so it was slightly ajar when she left.

CHAPTER ELEVEN

THE MAID MUST have already been waiting in the hall, because she came in right away. I got her settled at the table.

"My name is Dorothy, but everybody calls me Dolly." She was indeed originally from Wales, "Cardiff to be exact. A lovely city to be sure." She'd come to Toronto as a young bride full of hope and optimism about a new and different world. Both she and her husband were taken into service by the Jessops.

"Nineteen-thirteen that was. I was a young lassie of twenty-two. Aled, my husband, was twenty-three."

Suddenly she stood up. "I'm just going to liven up that fire. It's cold in here."

It was the servants' parlour as Mrs. Jessop had said.

She went to the fireplace and banged on the coals with the poker. It did liven them up. She returned to the chair.

"Where was I?"

"You were telling me about the time you arrived in Canada. You were a bride you said."

"I was that and I'm a widow now. When war broke out Aled was proper keen to fight for the Empire. I couldn't stop him. He was wounded early on. Bullet through the leg. I thought he'd paid his dues, but not him. Back he went and wouldn't you know he got himself killed for his troubles didn't he? Battle of Vimy Ridge. Nineteen-seventeen. April. Spring had just come to Toronto. Never forget it."

She said all this in a matter-of-fact fashion. It had happened many years ago. It was hard to tell what her feelings were now.

"Mrs. Jessop was very good to me. And wouldn't you know, not much more than a year later, her own husband died. Not the war. Caught that wretched Spanish flu. Terrible that was. So many people died. You could be fine in the morning and dead by night-time. Mr. Gerald, poor laddie, didn't even see him. He was overseas in the army."

"How did he take his father's death?"

She gave me an odd look. "Like any young man would. Bravely. He could've got an honourable discharge, but Mrs. Jessop wouldn't hear of it. She will never gainsay her son and he wanted to stay and serve his country. And look what happened." She wiped at her eyes. I couldn't tell if she was still affected or if it had become a gesture of rote.

"It must have been completely shocking when he returned with such terrible injuries."

"It most certainly was. I've not seen such a change in a man. Not just that he was such a good-looking fellow before, but he was also what you might call very good-natured.

Always had a nice word for us. 'You're looking sprightly this morning, Dolly.'" She chuckled. "Truth is I didn't rightly know what sprightly meant at first. So I says to him, 'And so do you, Mr. Gerald. Most sprightly.' That made him laugh out loud. Sometimes on Sunday nights we'd all have a little sing song. He played the piano as good as can be. So jolly it was."

She fell silent and, as Mrs. Wilson had done, her gaze drifted to the window where outside, the blue bench dominated the dreary garden.

I prompted her. "And after he came back from the Front there was none of that jollity?"

"None."

"Was there any improvement over the years?"

"Not to speak of. I mean he tried, I know he did, but ..." She stroked the black band as if it was creating physical pain on her arm. "To tell you the truth Miss, he might as well of died out there on the battlefield. It might have been better for all concerned if he had."

But he hadn't died. He'd gone on struggling with his mutilated life for the next eighteen years.

Dolly was looking so upset I wanted to offer some comfort. It was obvious Gerald had had a deep impact on this household. Before I could say anything, I saw over her shoulder that a man had come into the backyard. He was short and stocky, huddled into an old army greatcoat. He was bareheaded. He walked over to the bench, sat down, fished out a package of cigarettes and started to light up.

I nodded in his direction.

"That must be Sam Weaver, Mr. Jessop's valet?"

Dolly turned to look and an expression of worry clouded her face.

"So it is. I thought he'd gone out."

"You know what, Mrs. Jones, I think we're done here for the time being. I should go and talk to Mr. Weaver right now."

Her eyes widened in alarm. "You sure? It's pretty miserable out there."

Given what she'd already told me about Gerald and Weaver spending hours on that damn bench I thought I might glean something by joining him.

"I'll risk it. Will you show me the way?"

"Golly. Why don't I fetch him in and you can stay here in the warm?"

She was looking at me anxiously. Was this bench the sanctuary? Not to be touched?

I stood up. "Don't worry, Mrs. Jones." I tried a little joke. "If Mr. Weaver can tolerate the weather, I'm sure I can. We women are made of tough stuff are we not? Never mind sugar and spice."

I didn't leave her much choice, although she seemed ready to protest. She was a nice woman and I felt badly I was obviously causing her such anxiety. I guessed the rules about not disturbing the master were strict. Too bad for all concerned.

CHAPTER TWELVE

Mrs. JONES LED me through the kitchen to the back door that opened to the garden.

"I can call him, Miss, if you'd rather."

Weaver either had not noticed us come to the door or refused to pay attention. I couldn't tell.

"Don't worry. I'm sure you've got things to take care of."

I didn't particularly want her to remain at the door watching us, although the bench was well out of earshot. Reluctantly she stepped back inside and I started to make my way toward it. The rain was a cold slap. The yellow leaves strewn across the lawn were splotched with dark circles like some arboreal warning of the Black Death. I was almost at the bench before Weaver turned around. He didn't seem startled. He didn't get up, just drew more deeply on his cigarette.

"You have to be the private detective Mrs. Jessop has hired."

His voice was totally neutral, neither friendly nor hostile.

I extended my hand. "I'm Charlotte Frayne. You must be

Sam Weaver. You were Mr. Jessop's valet."

Rather slowly, he accepted my handshake. His hand was icy cold. No gloves, no scarf or hat. The rain had reddened his face, which had an oddly squashed look to it as if he had spent time as a pugilist. He must have been in his forties, but he looked much older. *Ravaged* was the word that came to mind.

"I've already said everything I know to the police."

"I'm sure you have and I wouldn't be asking again, except that Mrs. Preston Jessop has hired me to go over the facts. I believe she has informed you of that."

He blew out smoke. "She won't accept it, will she? He killed himself, like the doctor said, when the balance of his mind was disturbed."

"You accept that verdict, do you?"

That got a bit of a reaction out of him. "What else could it be? He'd had it. Couldn't stand it anymore. He finally did the deed."

"You mean he'd tried to kill himself on other occasions?"

"No. I didn't mean that. I meant it was something he'd thought about over the years."

"He shared his thoughts with you, did he?"

"That's right."

"That must have been hard for you. Was there no professional help available?"

I hadn't meant to offend him, I was sincere. But take offence he did. He scowled at me ferociously, intensifying the impression of a man used to violent exchanges.

"He went to several clinics, but they was useless. Just wanted their money. None of them white coats were soldiers. None of them had been out there like I had. He got comfort talking to me. I was there. I knew what it was like. I don't know what you mean, 'hard on me.' It wasn't hard to listen."

"I'm sorry. You're referring to your experiences during the war? You were Mr. Jessop's batman were you not?"

"I was. We was lads together, a few years apart only, but he was as good a master as you could ever hope for. Then and since."

His lips were trembling and he struggled to contain his tears. I wanted to touch his hand, but I suspected such comfort would not be welcome.

He got another cigarette from the package. Then in the middle of lighting it he remembered his manners.

"Would you like one?" He shook up a cigarette.

"No, thanks."

"I'm not used to women puffing else I would have asked you right away."

"Of course. Thanks. I haven't taken up the habit."

"Good for you. Tell the truth I don't like to see women smoking. Bad enough us men do."

"Did Mr. Jessop smoke?"

"No. It was too painful. He'd lost pieces off his mouth you see. Anything too hot or too cold hurt him."

He had regained his composure and was focussing on taking in smoke to the bottom of his lungs.

"You mentioned clinics just now. I understand Mr. Jessop was a heavy drinker."

Weaver reacted. "Course he was. You'd be too if you suffered like he did."

"The morphia didn't help?"

"It sent him to sleep. He didn't like that. His brain was too clever."

"Hadn't he just come back from a stint in a clinic?"

"Yep."

"But he went back to drinking almost right away?"

Again, I'd inadvertently hit a trip wire and he glared at me.

"No. Not right away. He was sober as a judge for the last eight months. He was doing really well until—" he stopped abruptly.

"Until the night he died? I've read the coroner's report. There was a lot of alcohol in his system."

He nodded.

"Do you know where he obtained the liquor?"

"The policeman asked the same question and I gave him the same answer I'm giving you. I don't know."

"Nobody brought it in for him?"

"No. I sure didn't, if that's what you think. Nor any of the others. We all wanted him to stay sober. All of us. Besides I'd of seen it."

"So you all had to be temperate whether you wanted to or not?"

He shrugged. "We're none of us prisoners, you know.

This is an old-fashioned household it's true, but we do get days off. If anybody wants to go to the pub and have a bit of a tipple they can. Just not allowed on the premises."

He didn't have to tell me he was one of the servants who tippled on occasion. The message was clear.

I pressed on. "Many people drink heavily, but they don't die from it. In this case Gerald Jessop took a heavy dose of morphia as well as a large amount of rum and got into a bathtub full of water. He seemed pretty determined to kill himself. I'm assuming in these previous attempts as you call them, he didn't go that far."

I was being a bit brutal, I know, but frankly I didn't know how else to reach this man.

He slid a little further on the bench.

"No, he never went that far. Just took too much morphine."

"Why do you think he did this time? Went too far, I mean."

He shrugged. "Like I said, it was one thing too many."

"What was that one thing?"

He went very still. "I don't know. I couldn't read his mind, could I?"

"There was no specific thing that happened? No arguments with anybody for instance? No bad news?"

He snorted. "Ha. We get that every day, don't we? Mister Hitler is having fun over in Europe. Somebody's going to have to stop him soon or we'll all be at war again."

"Given what Mr. Jessop went through in the previous

war, I can understand that might have depressed him."

"Depresses all of us that were over there. Bloody waste wasn't it?"

He seemed as impervious to the weather as a tree, but I was starting to freeze. I was about to suggest we go inside when he began to stub out his cigarette. Old army style, he had a little tin box where he stashed the butt.

"You're perishing," he said. "Let's go in. We can talk some more in there if you want to."

At that moment the back door opened and barking at top volume, ears flapping, Duffy raced over at us. I could see that Mrs. Jones was standing on the threshold. I kept still, but Weaver reached down and snatched the dog up in his arms.

"Stop it you silly mutt. Nothing's happening." He gave her muzzle a little shake. "Quiet."

She managed a muffled woof and he let her go. "You'll never learn will you, silly goose. We're all friends out here."

"She must be upset by what's happened."

"Nah. Dogs don't care. Here today, gone tomorrow. Long as you feed them, they'll love you. Right Duffy?"

He put his face close to the dog's and she licked him. In spite of his words, his voice was tender and to my eyes the little scoundrel loved him.

I heard Mrs. Jones call to us.

"You two are going to catch your death. I've made a pot of tea. Come and get it."

We both stood up and Weaver placed the dog on the

ground. She gave me a "I'm not giving up yet" sort of bark, but trotted after Weaver as we all headed for the door.

"The policeman is here," the maid said to me. "He's with Mrs. Jessop in the drawing room. I'll bring you some tea, shall I?"

She was either a mind reader or my face was too revealing because she smiled at me.

"Would you prefer coffee?"

"That would be nice, thank you."

Sam Weaver was one step ahead of us and without any farewell, he and Duffy disappeared into the servants' parlour. Dolly backed into the hall and I followed her. From the direction of the kitchen, I could hear a woman crying.

CHAPTER THIRTEEN

JACK MURDOCH AND the senior Mrs. Jessop were seated across from each other in the fireside wing-back chairs. There was a large cardboard box on the coffee table in front of them. They'd been talking, but the conversation stopped when I entered. Jack politely got to his feet. Mrs. Jessop actually looked slightly less constrained than she'd been at our last meeting; I put that down to Jack's indubitable charm. He was a tall, good-looking man with thick dark hair and lean features; more importantly, he conveyed sincere interest and concern.

"Ah, Miss Frayne, I understand I have no need to introduce you to Detective Murdoch. He says you are already acquainted."

I couldn't tell by her tone of voice whether she considered this a good thing or not.

Jack and I greeted each other. I assumed Mrs. Jessop had told him about hiring me to probe further into Gerald's death. I was glad about that. Keep everything above board.

"Detective Murdoch has also declared his willingness

to discuss his conclusions with you," she continued. "I am content with that, although I do trust it will not influence your own investigation in any way."

I caught a flicker of amusement cross Jack's face. We'd had enough interaction over the summer that he knew me well enough by now. I took pride in being independent. Open-minded, but not easily swayed.

Mrs. Jessop got to her feet. She was stiff and slow. Jack stepped forward to offer a helping hand, which she accepted.

"I have decided to let you examine the contents of the box first, Miss Frayne. I am not yet ready to do so myself."

"Of course."

Ellen had been waiting quietly at the door and now she came forward to take over from Jack.

"I will be in my room," said Mrs. Jessop. "You can have me called when you wish."

Taking Ellen's arm, she left.

When the door closed behind them, Jack came over, his hand outstretched.

"Charlotte, great to see you. I was taken aback when Mrs. Jessop said she'd hired a private investigator and she told me who it was."

"She said why I presume?"

"She can't accept that her son committed suicide. She's hoping you will find some evidence this was not the case."

"And?"

"I'll go over everything with you, but it's pretty ironclad."

He indicated the box. "I collected what purports to be

a suicide note which was on his bedside table, together with a syringe and some empty ampoules of morphia. In addition, there was a ceramic jug, also empty, which we ascertained had contained rum."

"I read the coroner's report. He declares the cause of death was nervous prostration caused by the excessive amount of morphia and alcohol in his system. He thought that Gerald was likely in a semi-conscious state when he got himself to the bathtub. He may have stayed afloat for a while. Drowning was not the cause of his death."

Jack nodded. "Even if he accidently fell into the water, he had obviously intended at some point to drown himself. You don't get yourself pie-eyed then walk around the bathroom wearing your medals and weighed down with coins in your pockets. There were twenty British pennies which are ridiculously heavy. The bathtub was deep and filled to the top." He fell silent for a moment. "I suppose our only question is whether death was by his own hand. And there are absolutely no signs that either the morphia or alcohol were forced on him. I suppose persons unknown could have guided him to the bathtub and helped him in, but even with him semi-conscious that would be difficult and if he was already unconscious, it would have been almost impossible for just one person."

Jack removed the lid of the box and took out an envelope which he handed to me. The writing was messy; Gerald's hand had been shaky.

To Mother and Ellen.

"I've compared the handwriting with other letters," said Jack. "There's no doubt, Gerald wrote it himself."

I took the letter out of the envelope. The writing here was also uneven with large splotches of ink throughout.

> *For my dear women. I am deeply sorry for the pain I know my death will cause, but I hope you will forgive me. Quite simply, I cannot continue with my life. There is no hope that my state will change. The thought of dragging on like this from year to year is unbearable. I want you to know I love you both more than I can say. Please do not hold me to the earth by your grief. I want you to have the kind of life you deserve.*
>
> *Forgive me.*
>
> > *Gerald.*
> >
> > *It was so sad I could hardly stand it.*

I returned the letter to the envelope.

"I'd say that was conclusive."

"The intent is there of course, but, as I say, we had to make sure he was unassisted. We had the fingerprints on the syringe and ampoules checked and on the jug. They are definitely his. Quite distinctive. A thumb and little finger only."

"No others? No valet's? No maid's?"

"Nope."

"I assume he was able to inject the morphia himself?"

"Apparently so. He had become adept. Both the valet and his wife testified to that."

Again, Jack reached into the box.

"The liquor was in this."

He lifted out a ceramic jug. "This is the kind of jug they used in the war to issue rum to the soldiers."

There were black letters stencilled on the side. S.R.D.

"What do those stand for?"

Jack grimaced. "S.R.D. stands for SPECIAL RATIONS DEPARTMENT. Or as the lads often said, SELDOM REACHES DESTINATION."

There was no cork in the jug and I took a sniff.

"Wow. That's strong stuff."

"It was. Eighty proof. Lots of soldiers came to rely on it. Who can blame them? It was hard to endure those conditions unless you had a fire in your belly."

I knew that Jack had been a soldier in the war. He had been honourably discharged when he was seriously wounded, but, every so often, it became obvious he was still carrying internal scars.

"Where would Gerald have got one of these jugs, not to mention the rum?"

"He probably brought the jug back with him," said Jack with a shrug. "The rum he'd likely get anywhere in the city. There was an empty bottle by his bed."

"Mrs. Jessop says no alcohol was allowed in the house."

He nodded. "I doubt it would have been difficult for him to smuggle it in."

"By the same token for anybody else, I assume."

"Such as one of the servants, you mean?"

"Possibly."

Jack frowned. "The night of his death all of them swore they were tucked up in bed by ten o'clock. The last they saw Gerald was at dinner. He went to his room about eight o'clock. When they next laid eyes on him, he was dead."

"Any way to verify that?"

"Not really. The only two people who shared a room are the Wilsons and they vouch for each other. We have only Mrs. Jones' word for herself. Same with Weaver. The Jessops say they were in bed."

"I guess Gerald's stay in the clinic didn't stick."

"I guess not," he said with a grimace. "Speaking of which, his old uniform was at the ready. His revolver was in the holster still in the belt. It was not loaded. We found a box of bullets in his desk. Obviously, he chose not to go that way."

"Slightly less upsetting to those who were to find him."

"Maybe something like that."

"You said his uniform was ready for him?"

"Yep. Everything. Boots polished. As were the buttons and belt buckle. Apparently, when the whim took him, he wore his uniform, and his valet kept it in tip top condition."

"That's curious. The maid told me he didn't go to ceremonies."

"The valet said the same thing to me, but every Armistice Day Gerald insisted on donning his uniform."

"For eighteen years?"

"Yep. Eighteen years. On that particular day, he'd sit in the garden." Jack sighed.

"You saw the blue bench I take it?"

"I did. I don't know about you, Charlotte, but I found the whole thing very sad. I remember those bloody benches."

"Me, too."

Jack shook his head. "I was such a mess when I came back from the Front. I liked to walk along the boardwalk. Lake Ontario is big enough to act and feel like a sea at times and I found it comforting to be close to some powerful force of nature. One day I took a rest on one of the benches. People walked along the boardwalk trying to pretend they couldn't see me. I might have been a monster seated there. This was right after the war ended. A man came and sat beside me. I guess he thought I was one of them. He flew into a rage when he saw I was intact, at least visibly so."

I gaped at him. "Why did that make him angry?"

"I suppose he thought I was cheating. Getting undeserved attention. He had been injured himself. He was almost unrecognizable as a human being. He'd lost his nose completely. He had no jaw."

"Not unlike Gerald Jessop, I gather."

Jack got up and walked over to the mantelpiece. He picked up the photograph of Gerald.

"He certainly was a handsome fellow."

He replaced the photograph, walked over to one of the lamps and switched it on.

"This darkness is getting me down."

I waited for him to return to the chair.

"All right. Now, I'm just thinking like a private investigator. If this was homicide, who would benefit? Have you seen his will? Is there any kind of life insurance?"

"I checked that. There was a copy of the will in his desk. He made it years ago; his lawyer confirmed there was no change. Unless he had another lawyer, and a new will shows up, we have to accept his estate was to be disposed of exactly as he requested when he was discharged from the service."

"What's the gist?" I asked.

"He had quite a large estate. Mr. Jessop senior was a wealthy man and Gerald inherited most of his money. He left decent bequests to the servants."

I thought about the grieving, loyal widow. "What about his wife?"

"He left everything to her, except for the bequests. In the event she predeceased him the estate would revert to his mother on his death and further to any issue he might have."

"So far there haven't been any children. So were there any insurance policies?"

"Right. You asked me that. In fact, he made out a policy a year ago. One year plus two days."

"So it just cleared the year-long hold back if the insured commits suicide?"

"Exactly."

"And the beneficiary?"

"Ready for this? It is his valet, Sam Weaver."

Frankly, I was taken aback. "Not his family?"

"In addition to his estate, his wife received some money as death benefits, about three thousand dollars. She will also continue to receive his military pension unless she remarries. She will be quite well off."

"She doesn't need the insurance money?"

Jack shrugged. "It would seem not."

"Is there anything else in the box I should look at?"

"Not much to speak of. I went through his desk, but it was surprisingly bare. No journal or diaries. No bills or receipts."

"I assume his mother took care of all of the expenses."

"I don't know about you, Charlotte, but I tend to hang on to letters and cards that people have sent me."

"I do too. I've got several from years back. I like to keep them. Makes me feel I matter to people."

"The only letters Gerald kept were those letters from his mother and his wife which they sent to him when he was at the Front. There was nothing from beyond that, although he was recovering in England. I'm sure people were writing to him, but he either left them there or destroyed them. To all intents and purposes, his life ended in 1918." He handed me another brown envelope. "This was the only other thing he retained."

Inside was photograph, a group picture of young soldiers standing against an artillery gun which they must have captured; fresh-faced and optimistic, they were beaming into their destiny. Each was waving his tin hat in the air. To one side, also smiling, was Gerald Jessop looking very smart and every inch an officer.

At the bottom of the picture was a notation in ink.

Afternoon of October 31, 1918 before Valenciennes.

Some of the faces were circled in black and initials written beside them.

"They're all privates," said Jack. "Fifth Infantry. The same regiment as Jessop so I assume they were under his command." He sighed. "We were all so damned young."

I peered at the photograph.

Underneath the date was a list of names. Six of them, corresponding with the circled faces.

K.-R. Haight; W.-T. Masefield; K.-P. Woods; K.-F. Cooke; W.-Y. Dawes; K. (Died from wounds.)-P. Allen.

Of the original eleven, four had died, two were wounded, who knows how badly. Only five had escaped unscathed. And as Jack had remarked, they were all so damned young.

"I think that's it, Charlotte," said Jack. "As I say, his desk was pretty empty and there was nothing else that I could see in his room that might be relevant. The coroner's office will return the clothes and effects found with the body. His medals which were on his chest."

"Thanks, Jack. I've agreed to investigate, and I will. So far, I've spoken to the servants, but there is absolutely no sign that anybody did anything nefarious. Nobody has anything significant to gain from his death and their grief seems genuine. They were all devoted to him."

"Too bad it wasn't sufficient to keep him away from suicide."

All I could do was agree.

"Do you think I could have a look at his room?"

"I don't see why not. We've closed the case."

Fortuitously at that moment, Ellen, after the softest of taps, re-entered the room.

She agreed to my request and, after saying goodbye to Jack, I went with her upstairs.

CHAPTER FOURTEEN

THE UPSTAIRS HALL was wide, quietly decorated with dark wallpaper and dark oak trim. Gerald's room was at the front of the house. Ellen opened the door, snapped on the overhead light, and we entered. Like the drawing room, it was chilly and the curtains were drawn. I wondered if they would ever be opened again.

Suddenly, Ellen gave a little gasp. "If you don't mind, Miss Frayne, I think I'll wait for you outside."

She didn't need to explain. I'd never met Gerald Jessop, but his presence was almost palpable.

It was not a large room, but in dead centre, dominating everything, was a table on which was spread a map. I walked over to have a look. It was labelled as the Village of Valenciennes. Dotted lines criss-crossed from end to end and a red circle was drawn just outside what must be the village itself. I assumed that was where Gerald had been wounded but, as I looked closer, I could see the circle was actually around a drawing of a machine gun. In front of it were four crosses and initials. I didn't need to check the list I'd made. I knew these referred to the men who had been in that battle; the young men in the photograph.

In the corner of the table was a sheaf of loose papers. Quickly I riffled through them. All seemed to be notations. The kind of thing the army commanders would have made to direct the battles. I glanced around the room. Pinned on the walls were similar large maps all labelled with the names of battles that had now been blasted into Canadian history. Ypres. The Somme. Cambrai. Canal du Nord. All were marked extensively. It might have been in a military headquarters.

Gerald's bed was beside the table, jammed against the wall with hardly enough space to get into it. It was tightly made and looked more like an army camp bed than the kind you'd find in a gentleman's home. It was hard to imagine it as a conjugal bed. Perhaps Gerald and Ellen had enjoyed intimacy in her room.

Somewhat disconcertingly, there was a faceless manne-quin at the foot of the bed, dressed in full army uniform. Jacket brushed, boots gleaming, and leather belt polished. All ready for Gerald to step out and bravely lead his hand-ful of men to their death.

I went over to the desk, an old-fashioned rolltop. It wasn't locked and when I pushed up the lid, it revealed nothing. As Jack had told me, all the contents had been removed, but what struck me was how clean everything was. Gerald might have been a recluse, but the servants made sure no dust gathered on his privacy.

The only other thing of interest was an upright piano on the other side of the room. Mrs. Jessop had mentioned Gerald had been a talented musician. Did Gerald play even with his crippled hand? There was one piece of music on the stand. I suppose I'd expected some Chopin or Schubert, but it wasn't. The single piece of music that Gerald had left behind him seemed to be original. It was a poem which he had transcribed to music.

DREAMS GONE.

I had dreams once,
Love, family, a future.
All gone.
Broken like the bodies
Strewn on this grey wasteland.
No growing old for them:
No shared memories with friends
At gatherings
Where others look at us askance.
'Those men laugh.
Have they no reverence
For the fallen?'
They see not the truth.
We must cradle each other
And press to our hearts
Our dead brothers
Who had dreams once.

I wished I knew how to read music so I could at least play the song, but I didn't.

Again, there was what was now becoming an all too familiar tap on the door. I went to open it. Ellen was there.

"Have you finished, Miss Frayne? Mrs. Jessop would like to speak with you before you leave."

"Almost. I was just going to take a look at the bathroom."

She actually flinched. "Of course. I'll wait in the hall."

The bathroom was ensuite.

I went in. Like the bedroom, it was pristine. The tub was deep and large. Claw footed. Obviously, the water that had embraced Gerald in his death had been drained; the jug that had been on the small table beside the tub was in police possession, but everything else looked undisturbed. A nearby shelf held several thick, white towels, all folded and at the ready. There was a flushing toilet and a sink with fancy gold-plated taps. In an alcove near the window sat a leather tilting chair, barber style, and in front of it were a comb and hairbrush, silver backed; a shaving brush in a silver bowl; a soap dish and a straight razor with leather strop. I didn't need to test the razor to know it was razor sharp. All this bespoke luxury and comfort. The only thing to set it apart from the bathroom of any other well-to-do gentleman was that there was no mirror. Nowhere for Gerald to admire Sam's handiwork. Nowhere for him to smooth his own hair into place. I was also struck again that Gerald could have chosen other means to kill himself that were much messier. Razor. Pistol. I could only assume that he chose his method out of consideration to those who had the misfortune to discover him.

I went to join Ellen.

CHAPTER FIFTEEN

W E WENT INTO the drawing room, which was if anything colder and dimmer than before.

Mrs. Jessop was already seated in the wing-back by the feeble fire. Quietly, Ellen slipped into the other.

From the beginning, when I began to work for him, Mr. Gilmore had warned me, "Clients will put great pressure on you, whether they realize it or not, to have you tell them what they want to hear and not what they don't. Whether that's about the lost pet, which is most likely dead, the husband or wife who is most likely unfaithful. You must resist that pressure to create any fairy tale they might long for. Our job is to tell the truth however unpalatable." He'd given me that little sly grin of his. "Even if they are paying the bill."

Mrs. Jessop did not seem to be any exception.

"Well, Miss Frayne. Do you have anything to tell me?"

"Not so far, Mrs. Jessop."

She sighed and slumped a little. "Very well. We will

continue with our arrangement. When you are certain you
have concluded your investigation to the utmost, we will
consider the case closed as the police say."

There was a this-is-the-end-of-the-interview tone to her
voice, but I remained where I was.

"I believe Detective Murdoch asked you if you were
aware of any precipitating reason why Gerald might have
committed suicide when he did."

"That is correct, and I said I was not so aware. Other
than the newspapers being full of the upcoming Armistice
Day ceremonies. He was always in low spirits at this time
of year."

"But he had endured such a time for many years. Eighteen to be exact. Why this year? What pushed him over
the brink?"

"I have already said I don't know."

She had become stiffer, but she didn't get up. She was
still desperate for an answer.

"I understand your son lived a fairly reclusive life. A
predictable routine in fact. Could you describe that routine
to me?'

Mrs. Jessop nodded at her daughter-in-law.

"Ellen, you might know that better than I."

"He went out once a week, occasionally twice. Other
than that, he remained mostly in his room, working over
his battle maps." She glanced over at the older woman.
"He planned the battles as he thought they might have
gone, not as they did. He had become disillusioned with

the generals for the most part. Except General Alderson, whom he admired."

"When he did leave the house, did he go by himself?"

"Yes. He preferred it that way."

"But on those evenings when Mr. Jessop did go out, did he ever say what he did?"

"If the weather was clement, he'd walk about the city. If it wasn't, he'd go to some place where he felt comfortable." She stopped.

"A club?"

"No. He dropped his clubs some time ago."

"He never said where these comfortable places were?"

"They changed. He didn't like to go to the same location all the time. He didn't want people to become too familiar."

"Would you say this was a restaurant? A tavern?"

I felt I had to give them both a bit of a jolt if we were going to get anywhere.

Mrs. Jessop answered. "I believe he did frequent taverns previously, but since this last stay at a clinic he avoided them. On occasion, if he wanted to have dinner, he went to a restaurant."

"Do you recall the name of any of these establishments?"

She shook her head.

"I do," Ellen whispered. "At least I think I might."

"Yes?" I resisted the temptation to shout at her to speak up.

"When he came back from one such establishment, about three weeks ago, he seemed happy. He said he had enjoyed himself because 'they understood.' I knew he was referring to his war experiences. I got the impression where he had gone was a gathering place for former soldiers." She halted as if she'd said too much.

I nodded encouragingly. "It might be useful for me to go there just to see if anything in particular did happen. Can you remember anything at all that might identify it?"

"It has something to do with Heaven." She tapped on her head. "I remember now. It was called Paradise. The Paradise Café. It was on Queen Street somewhere."

CHAPTER SIXTEEN

WHEN I GOT outside, daylight was slipping away and it was almost dark. The rain-wet wind was blowing hard. The streetcars were packed as they trundled by, light spilling from the inside, passengers silhouetted. I had declined the offer of Wilson's services, saying that I had some work to complete. Truth was, I wanted to get over to the Paradise and I didn't want to reveal my connection to the place. Not necessary at this point.

I walked fast. Not just because of the weather. I hoped to see Hilliard before the first sitting took up his attention.

The café was not due to open for another half an hour, but as usual there was a line already forming outside. The usual group of men huddled into their shabby overcoats, a handful of quiet women with umbrellas, even two young children pressed for meagre shelter against their mother.

As a regular, I now had key privileges; I walked to the side door and let myself in.

I was just about to enter the kitchen when I heard a loud

thump and an exclamation of "Oh, no" expressed with definite alarm. I pushed open the door and went in. At this point, I started to feel as if I were some dreadful harbinger of destruction. First the factory, now this. The thump was the result of a large pan of oven-hot rice pudding falling on the floor. The "Oh, no" had come from Pearl who was standing near the oven, her hands clutched to her mouth. A choked-back moan of pain was coming from Calvin. Unlike young Ben, he was not screaming, but it was obvious he was hurting just as much. He was hopping around trying to hold back his yelps and shaking his hands as if he could cast off the pain of the burns.

Before I could even ask what had happened, Pearl saw me. Her face was ashen.

"I was only trying to help."

"With what?"

"He was slow. We've got a queue already. I went to take the pan out of the oven and it slipped. He tried to catch it and the rice spilled on him."

Calvin had hopped over to the sink. He managed to turn on the tap and run the water over his hands.

I hurried over to him.

The skin was bright red and already starting to blister.

"You've got to have that looked at."

"I'll be all right," he said over his shoulder. "I learned this from the trawler. You've got to cool down a burn right away."

Pearl, still shaken, crept closer.

"Where are the others?" I asked her.

"Wilf's downstairs. Hilliard's left already for Sudbury."

I knew that meant a new dealing with trouble and strife.

"Go and fetch Wilf."

She scuttled off fast.

"What's ready?" I asked Calvin.

"Everything, thank goodness. We were just about to serve it up."

He was looking woozy although the water trick seemed to be helping with the pain.

"Do you want to sit down?"

"A few more minutes."

Pearl had moved fast, and Wilf came rushing through the door.

"What the hell happened?"

Calvin grimaced. "A little accident. A pan of rice pudding landed on my hands. Bit of a waste I'm sad to say."

Wilf peered over Cal's shoulder. "My god. You'd better go and get that looked at."

"I already explained to Miss Frayne that I'll be all right. All I need now is the honey pot. It's over there on the shelf. Would you mind getting it for me?"

Wilf obeyed at once. Pearl started to clean up the rice pudding. I took Calvin by the elbow.

"Come and sit down."

He did, holding his burned hands in the air. Wilf brought over the pot of honey.

"Miss Frayne, if you'd be so kind," said Calvin. "Just

take that spoon and daub as much honey as you can over my hands."

"Another tip from the ship?"

"Exactly."

I started to plaster on the honey as gently as I could. He didn't flinch but remained with his hands on the table.

"What shall we do about the sitting?" Pearl asked.

Wilf dithered for a moment.

"Everything's ready," said Calvin. "Soup just needs to be doled out into the bowls. We're having cold mutton pie and a salad choice. All ready. The pie has to be sliced and put on a plate. They get two pickles each. The rice pudding has had it but there are chocolate cookies in the jar. I made them for tomorrow, but we'll use them now for dessert."

I jumped in. "I can cut up the pie."

Wilf gave me a rare, grateful smile.

"Okay. If you and Pearl handle all that, I'll go and let in the hordes." He put his hand on Calvin's shoulder. "You'll be all right, chum?"

"Yep. It's not the first scalding I've ever had."

"Do you want a tot?"

Cal grinned at him. "Won't say no."

Wilf hurried over the corner cupboard and returned with a bottle. I could see it was rum. He splashed a measure into a glass and handed it to Calvin who tried to take hold of it, but couldn't. Wilf held it to his mouth.

"Here. Big gulp's better."

Calvin did as he was told while Wilf watched him. He

had an expression of tenderness on his face that, like his gratitude toward me, seemed rare.

We heard a loud knocking from outside the other door. The customers were getting restless.

Wilf stood up. "I'll go keep them under control. Do you want another tot?"

Calvin shook his head. "Not just now. That put a fire in my belly to match my hands."

"Pearl? Charlotte? Five minutes?"

We both nodded agreement and he left. Calvin put his hand on the table and closed his eyes. His honey-sweet hands remained thrust in front of him.

CHAPTER SEVENTEEN

THE THIRD AND final sitting ended promptly. The response to the cock-a-leekie soup was mixed and I wouldn't say the mutton pie was a huge hit, but the cookies were. By closing time, they'd all been devoured.

When the last customer eased out, we all returned to the kitchen and virtually collapsed.

Wilf made some tea, which he laced liberally with rum. No wonder it was considered to be Britain's secret weapon in the last war. It certainly was a pick-me-up.

I was exhausted. It had been a full and busy day. After the accident, it was obvious that Calvin couldn't continue working. Pearl had dug out some aspirin powders, dumped them into a glass of water and, in spite of his protests, made him swallow every drop. Wilf had wanted him to go upstairs to rest, but he'd refused, saying he had to supervise the proceedings and it would take his mind away from his burns. There had been no arguing with that and he remained at the kitchen table until all customers had left.

By then he was looking better. His trawler remedies seemed to have helped.

Gramps was also with us.

During a short, very short, lull in between servings, I'd run to the telephone and begged him to come over to the café to help out. He agreed, as he wasn't exactly giving up an evening full of lively entertainment. He'd actually helped at the café twice before over the summer when Mrs. Reilly, Pearl's mother, who was the other waitress, fell ill. Although he was a bit slow in the hustle department, Gramps was friendly and capable. Most important as far as I was concerned, he really liked it and ever since I'd been keeping my eye out for something he might like to do on a part-time basis. Unfortunately, there was not much available and Gramps refused to take the bread out of some poor fellow's mouth by taking a job he didn't really need. We could live well enough on his pension and my earnings.

"Do you think the soup needed a bit more salt?" asked Calvin.

Not every bowl had come back licked clean.

"Maybe just a little," said Pearl with what was, for her, unusual tact. "Now that chicken soup you made last week was a big hit."

As far as I was concerned, that particular soup could have done with a little more, well chicken, but I wasn't going to point that out right now.

Suddenly Wilf slapped down his cup.

122 • MAUREEN JENNINGS

"Damn, I almost forgot. Hill left you a letter, Charlotte. He said he'd telephone as soon as he could, but he at least wanted you to know what was up."

That was a relief. There had been no time to enquire any further into Hilliard's sudden departure.

Wilf went over to the cupboard. An envelope was propped against the biscuit jar and he brought it over to me. The letter was scrawled. Haste for sure.

My dear Lottie. You haven't come back yet and I have to catch the four o'clock train. I'll ring you as soon as I can, but in the meantime here's what's happening. I received a telegram this morning. Frankie has come down with tonsillitis and he's got to have his tonsils out right away. Pauline says she's working and can't take time off. She says he's pretty miserable and she wants me to come up to Sudbury and be with him for the operation.

Frankie was Hilliard's eleven-year-old, Pauline his ex-wife. They were amicable enough now, but getting to that place had been rocky. He had been a prisoner of war and when he returned, like a lot of veterans, he'd found it hard to settle down, as he put it. Finally, fed-up, his wife had left him for a saner, calmer man and she and Hilliard were now officially divorced. He was still grappling with the balancing act of taking care of the son and daughter he'd fathered, and trying to build a new life here. Sometimes it worked, sometimes it didn't. From the beginning of our relationship,

I'd determined not to be the one factor to tip the see-saw. Other than his children, the café was his focus in life.

Back to the letter.

I don't know how long I'll be gone. At least a week, if not more. I can't leave until I know Frankie is in the clear. I miss you already. Keep an eye on things for me. Wilf has another bee in his bonnet about the Cave. Watch him. Big hug and kiss from me.

Hilliard

While I read the letter, the others had waited patiently pretending they weren't curious.

"I guess you know the gist?" I addressed Wilf.

"Yep. His kid's sick and he needs to be with him."

I was a bit put off by Wilf's tone. He made it sound trivial, which it wasn't.

"I had to have my tonsils out when I'd just turned eighteen," said Calvin. "I'd only been in the army three months when I came down with tonsillitis."

"No!" exclaimed Pearl. "That can make you sterile."

"You're thinking of the mumps, Pearl dear," said Wilf.

She shrugged. "It's still bad."

Calvin continued. "There was talk they'd discharge me, but along came a kind English doctor who declares, 'Don't worry, young fellow, I'll fix you up in a jiffy. I'll take out those old useless tonsils. Snip, snip. Nothing to it. Few days and you'll be right as rain.'"

He was doing such a good imitation of a posh English accent, we all started to laugh. Calvin went on.

"'And tell you what,' says the good doctor, 'after the surgery, I'll make sure you get ice cream.'" Calvin himself was smiling. "I'd heard about ice cream, but never tasted it. So sure enough, out came my tonsils, snip, snip. It hurt a lot. A lot. Oh boy was my throat ever sore. But after, just as he promised, the doctor came in followed by a nurse carrying a little dish of ice cream. He gives me a pat on the cheek. Only one scoop, but my oh my," Calvin leaned back for a moment and stared upwards. "It was heavenly."

Wilf grinned at him. "When we were all POWs we talked a lot about food that we loved. We tried to share this just before Lights Out and we had a little ritual at the end when we'd go, 'One, two, three' and we'd all say together, 'To taste that again would be Paradise.' It became a sort of bedtime story."

His voice was jolly, but I well knew by now that the POW years had been horrendous. But that was where the concept of the Paradise Café had been born.

I saw that Gramps was valiantly trying not to yawn. Time to go.

"Before we get out of here, Wilf, I wanted to ask you something. I'm trying to nail down some details concerning a new case I've taken on. A man. Apparently, he was in the café a few times recently."

"Here? In the Paradise?"

"You might have noticed him. He was injured in the war and was quite disfigured."

Wilf scowled. "Don't tell me his wife wants to divorce him?"

"No, nothing like that."

"Good. I'd hate to think of another bloke who's been ditched because of what's he's gone through."

His tone was bitter. It was a hot point for many of the ex-soldiers.

"Pearl? Did you see this fellow?"

She screwed up her face with the effort of thinking.

"Don't know about disfigured, but there's a man come in two or three times recently. He's always got a scarf wrapped around his face. So's some of the others if it's cold. I didn't pay much attention till he went to pay and I saw he'd lost some of his fingers. His gloves didn't fit properly." She demonstrated how the three middle fingers were flopping.

"Did he say anything to you?"

Pearl yawned, but not as politely as Gramps. She had a large mouth.

"Come on. It gets busy in here. You can't expect me to remember that."

"Think back, Pearl, there's a girl. He came in more than once perhaps as recently as Thursday. Other than being wrapped up, was there anything that stood out about him?"

"Like what?"

I held on to my patience. Like maybe he was sobbing and crying.

"Well, did he seem upset in any way?"

"Not that I noticed. I gave him his bill and he paid right off, no scratching around for a bit of change that might have fallen into his pocket from God like some of them do. They know the lunch plate costs twenty-five cents, but some of them act as if this is news to them."

Before she could continue her disgruntled harangue, Wilf interrupted her.

"I remember that bloke now that you mention him, Charlotte. He was here on Thursday. Met up with an old pal."

"An old pal?"

Suddenly, Pearl's memory woke up. "I remember now. The first man was already sitting here. He was one of those who came up short with his change. Expected us to subsidise him." She must have caught Wilf's expression. "Don't worry, I let it go. I told him to pay next time."

I knew one of the reasons the Paradise wasn't rolling in money was because all four of the partners allowed the down-and-out customers to carry an account, some of which were never paid up.

"How did you know these two men were old pals?" I asked Wilf.

Pearl answered for him. "They were shaking hands and thumping each other on the back. The wrapped-up man in particular seemed glad to see the other fellow."

"I agree with Pearl's assessment," added Wilf.

"Did they leave together?"

"Yes, I know that because the first fellow still hadn't paid. I haven't seen him since."

"Did you hear anything they said?"

"No," Wilf answered. "I was over in the corner trying to get my king out of a cunning check that Jacobs had dropped on me."

The on-going chess match was highly competitive, and I could believe that Wilf would have not paid any attention to much else.

"What's he done, Miss Frayne?" Calvin asked. "You said it was a case."

Wilf glared at me. "God, Charlotte you're not working for Draper are you?"

Gramps jumped in immediately. "Course not. Who do you think she is? She wouldn't have anything to do with Draper."

They were referring to our esteemed chief of police who was notoriously obsessed with the danger of communists to the community. It didn't matter to him that the Communist Party was now completely legal. He had believed in the "red scare" and still did. Wilf Morrow was an ardent communist. He had also never quite forgiven me for initially coming to work at the Paradise under false pretences.

"No, Wilf I am not now, nor ever would I work for Draper."

"Why are you interested in this bloke then?"

I could see no reason not to tell them.

"I'm afraid he appears to have killed himself."

The others stared at me in shock.

"How?" asked Wilf.

"Alcohol and morphine. His mother wants to make sure that this was the correct verdict."

Pearl nodded. "Insurance probably. She won't get it if he's a suicide."

I didn't want to get into an argument about it. "Back to what you said for a minute. I'd like to talk to the man who was supposedly an old friend. Is he a regular?"

Pearl answered. "Don't know about a regular, but he has been here before." Suddenly she snapped her fingers. "Wait a minute. Like I said I gave him some credit and he had to sign the book. I'll get it." She jumped up and rushed off to the dining room. I must say Pearl was nothing if not enthusiastic if it was something out of the ordinary. That girl didn't get enough challenges in her life as far as I was concerned.

While she was gone, I took a look at Gramps. Both he and Calvin were looking a bit wiped out.

"Listen you two. It's time to wrap up for the day."

"She's right," said Wilf. "Calvin, no ifs or buts, you're going to spend the night here. We'll get you another couple of aspirins. You can sleep in Hilliard's room. As for you, Mr. Frayne, I can't thank you enough for helping out. If you can come back tomorrow, I'd really appreciate it. I'll be in your debt forever."

"Be glad to," said Gramps. He meant it and I felt a twinge of guilt. His life was lonely, and I wasn't doing enough to help him in that department.

Pearl returned, banging through the swing door. She was holding the ledger where they kept track of the customer accounts. She opened a page.

"Here it is. I know the others. They're regulars. Never have enough money. We carry them." She pointed at the page. "Thursday, October 29. He owes ten cents. He had an extra cup of coffee with his meal. All he could come up with was five cents. See I got him to initial the book."

She glanced at me. "I know it's not a lot of money, but it all adds up. If we didn't keep track, we'd go out of business in a flash."

I looked. The writing was spidery and hard to make out.

"I can't read it, Pearl, help me out here."

"Happy to. After a while you get good at deciphering their handwriting." She peered at the book. "T. N."

Wilf looked over her shoulder. "It's not N. It's M. T.M. I remember him. When the other fellow saw him, he called out."

"That's right," said Pearl not to be outdone. "He's got the same name as that poet."

"What poet is that, Pearl?"

"Fairfield or Masedon. We had to learn his poems in school."

Wilf rolled his eyes at me, but I held back from joining him laughing at Pearl.

"Can you quote one of them now?" I asked her.

"Let me see. Yes, here we go. 'I must go down to the sea again, to the lonely sea and sky and all I want is a something ship and a something something star to steal her by.'"

Wilf and I practically spoke together. "Masefield."

"John Masefield," finished Wilf. "Was that it, Pearl?"

"Masefield is right, but not John. I'd have remembered that. It was another name. Like Tom."

"Okay. Let's go with that. Tom Masefield. Did you notice anything out of the ordinary about him, Pearl? Anything at all?"

"Can't say I did unless you include him not having a pong like some of them do. That might be considered out of the ordinary."

"What did he look like?"

"I don't know. Thin face. Wore round spectacles, you know the kind." She made circles with her fingers and held them up in front of her eyes. "About the same height as Mr. Hilliard. His hand shook, I can tell you that, and I heard him cough a couple of times. Deep down."

She coughed herself to illustrate. "I will say this for him, he had nice manners which not all of them do. That enough?"

She looked at me rather like a pupil wanting the teacher's approval.

"Excellent. Thanks Pearl."

She cast a glance of competitive triumph at Wilf.

"Has he been back since?" I asked.

"Not that I've seen. I'd get him to pay up if he does come back."

She slapped herself on the head. "Oh, I almost forgot. He asked if he could have a job at the café. We didn't need anybody then. If he'd asked now, I could have used him with some of the chores."

I stood up. "Come on Gramps. Time to hit the trail."

"Will you take a few pamphlets?" said Wilf. "We've decided to go with the play. It's opening on Saturday. We need to get the word out."

He thrust some pamphlets into my hand. *EIGHT MEN SPEAK. This play was banned only three years ago, but we're bringing it back. Of vital importance in Canadian history, it must be seen by all thoughtful people.*

"Does Hill know you're opening with it?"

Wilf shrugged. "We all have equal shares. This will bring us a lot of attention."

The partners had recently finished building a special entertainment room in the basement of the café, but I knew Hilliard and Wilf had disagreed as to what to start with. Hill wanted something light-hearted and uplifting. Some vaudeville acts perhaps; Wilf wanted to remount this controversial play which was strictly propaganda for the Communist Party.

Wilf gave me a sneaky grin. "Your granddad liked the idea. I've given him a small speaking role. Right Gramps?"

"What!"

Gramps was standing beside me. "I'm playing one of

the crowd. Don't worry. It's legal now. I won't get arrested."

"If you do, I'm not coming to bail you out."

I put the pamphlets in my pocket. "Let's get going."

It's not that I was against the Communist Party as such, far from it, but at this moment in time, it was all so chaotic. The party seemed to be more interested in being against employers than in trying to bring about co-operation and better conditions. Mistrust abounded and the CCP was always on the fringes of the law.

We all said our goodbyes and Gramps and I walked through the darkened dining room and stepped out into the street. A gust of wind threw the rain in my face so hard it hurt.

We halted briefly to get our bearings in front of Workman's shop. The lights were still on and I could see a young man and a woman were inside. They were standing close together, facing each other. Everything suggested an intense conversation was taking place. She brushed a strand of hair tenderly from his face. The young man was Wallace Workman himself. The young woman no other than Miriam Cohen. Given this interaction, I could understand why Joel Rosenthal wasn't in the running for her affections.

"Come on, there's a tram coming," said Gramps and he took my arm.

At that moment, we almost collided with a man who was hurrying toward us. He had a cap pulled down tight on his head, his head bent into the upturned collar of his overcoat.

"Beg pardon," he muttered as he stepped around us. He pushed up the spectacles on his nose. Touched the brim of his cap. No gloves, just mittens.

Gramps pulled me in a bit tighter to hustle me onward. Over my shoulder, I saw the man had stopped at the shop door. He rang the bell and immediately Wallace rushed to open it. I heard him say, "Come in, come in," with great enthusiasm. Miriam too came to greet the newcomer, smiling.

Whomever he was, the visitor, derelict or not, was getting a warm welcome.

I saw Miriam take him by the arm and head for the back room and Wallace came to the window and pulled down the blind. Shop closed.

"For Heaven's sake stop dawdling, Lottie," said Gramps and I had no choice but to move on.

CHAPTER EIGHTEEN

THE STREETCAR WAS almost empty, not too many people were out and about. We sat down on the bench, and as Gramps turned his head, I saw him wince.

"Is your boil hurting?" I asked.

"Yep. But you know what? Calvin said he's got a good remedy for boils. He's going to make it for me tomorrow. He said he used it a lot on the crew when he was sailing on the high seas."

"What is it?"

"He steams up some onions, ties them in a soft cloth, and puts it on the boil."

"Onions! Heaven forbid."

"He swears it's easy and there are lots of onions in the pantry. As well he says my blood needs purifying so he's going to make a drink from burdock which I will drink three times a day."

The ticket collector came to collect our fares, swaying against the movement of the streetcar as he punched our tickets.

"Miserable night, eh? We'll get you home as soon as possible."

It was a friendly greeting and, given the tough day, I was grateful.

Gramps continued. "He's a good man, that Calvin. He was telling me some stories about when he was in the war. Fascinating. In the beginning, they wouldn't let the coloured men fight. Thought they'd get emotional and run away. Just like women."

"What! I didn't hear you say that, Gramps."

He grinned. "Thought that'd get a rise out of you. But it's true. That's what they said back then. They also gave them all the joe-jobs. Digging latrines. Building the barracks. Short-sighted, if you ask me. I tell you, if I was in one of those trenches, I'd be happy to have a man like Calvin next to me."

"I'm with you on that one, Gramps."

"He knows a lot too from being on the trawler. He wasn't just the cook, he was the chief medic, especially on a long voyage."

"Okay. I'm going to put a hot cloth on the boil, but without the onions, make you a hot toddy and aspirin and we're both going to turn in early."

"Sounds good."

We clanked along Queen Street for few minutes. Then Gramps leaned in closer and whispered at me.

"I've always had a secret desire to be on the stage, Lottie. I'm right chuffed that Wilf asked me to take part."

"That's great Gramps. Don't get carried away. It's a competitive field."

He laughed. "You never know. I'm not too old to become famous."

I gave his arm a little punch. "You're certainly handsome enough."

CHAPTER NINETEEN

THE NEXT MORNING, I woke up too early, pushed from sleep by unpleasant dreams. At one point, I was trying to telephone Hilliard, but I kept getting the wrong connection. Then I couldn't find Gramps who didn't seem to be in the house. Let me say that dreams of this kind were quite familiar to me. I didn't need Dr. Freud to analyze me. I like my loved ones to be accessible at all times.

It wasn't yet light, but I got up anyway. I was wondering how Hilliard was faring with the tonsil situation and I anticipated the sound of the telephone. Nothing happened. No sound from Gramps either.

I got dressed in some of my plainest clothes. Tweed skirt, white blouse and navy cardigan, sensible shoes. Except for the shoes, this was my office garb. I actually like fashionable clothes, but I don't get to wear them that much. Most of my work calls for me to be inconspicuous.

I made myself a strong cup of coffee and drank it with a slice of bread before I slipped out into the grey, predawn light. Technically sunrise had occurred half an hour earlier, but you wouldn't know it. There was no mistaking it — rain was waiting in the wings. The damp air was undeniable.

I walked as quickly as I could, not wanting to be late for my first day at the Superior Ladies' Clothes shop. I arrived at ten minutes to eight. There was already a cluster of women and men standing outside, among them Miriam Cohen, her cherry red hat and raincoat vivid among the ubiquitous dark-coloured rain gear. All of them appeared to be focussed on one of the men who was banging on the door.

As I approached, I heard him shout.

"We know you're in there. Klein. Let us in. It's cold out here."

Young Ben was also present, his injured finger wrapped in a big bandage. He greeted me shyly, but with genuine pleasure.

"What's happening?" I asked no one in particular.

"The door's locked," one of the women answered. I recognized her as Rhoda Baum, the woman who got Ben a glass of water yesterday.

Next to her was angry Bertha. To my mind, she still looked angry, perhaps that was her permanent expression. I didn't particularly want her to recognize me from the café, so I tugged my scarf up around my face. One of the others glanced at me over her shoulder. She was the first aid woman. She was wrapped in a brown shawl like a parcel.

"Who usually lets you in?"

"Mr. Klein. You'd think he was guarding a castle. He's here first thing every morning and he hustles us all out every night at closing time."

Bertha gave a derisive snort. "The reason he shoves us out of the door at six is because they don't want us to claim overtime. As if we can."

Miss Baum chimed in. "And he's never late, I can tell you that. Never."

The shawl woman seized back the narrative. "He's always standing there counting us as we come in. God help the woman who's late. They get docked."

The man who'd been knocking on the door scowled. He was somewhat older than the others, with a lined, weather-beaten face. Life had taken its toll. He had the butt of a cigarette at the corner of his mouth, clearly reluctant to part company.

He saw me and gave me a bit of smile. "You're the new girl, aren't you? I heard about what you did for young Ben here. Good for you."

Another man now focussed on me. "Listen, you can bandage my fingers any day."

Miriam gave him a slap on the arm. "Cut it out, Arthur. She hasn't even started yet. Give her a chance."

The little group seemed to be getting more interested in me by the minute. I decided to deflect the attention.

"Somebody's inside. The lights are on."

I indicated the upstairs window where a feeble light struggled against the gloom.

"You're right. Damn it. He's in his office."

"Probably counting the gold," said Arthur. "Knock again, Fred."

He did so, but there was still no response.

"What shall we do, Mr. Lishman?" asked a woman, one of the two I referred to in my mind as the bobbers. She had an accent that sounded east European to me.

"If we can't get in, we can't work, can we?" he replied. He threw his arms up in the air. "Maybe old Rosie has decided to give us a holiday. He just forgot to tell us."

Miss Baum actually yelped in alarm.

"I can't afford to take the day off. I'm behind with the rent already."

"And Christmas is a-coming."

"What?"

Lishman started to sing. "Christmas is a-coming and the goose is getting fat. Please put a penny in the old man's hat. If you haven't got a penny, a halfpenny will do. If you haven't got a halfpenny, you're a skinny old Jew."

That was one version. Some of the others laughed, some didn't, but at that moment, a motor car turned the corner and headed down toward us.

"It's Mr. Rosenthal," called Ben.

"Fred. Hope he didn't hear you," said Arthur.

Lishman spat out the butt of his cigarette.

"Don't care if he did. If the shoe fits, wear it."

The car was a long, silver-grey McLaughlin-Buick, sleek as a shark.

It drew up to the curb and stopped. Joel Rosenthal was driving, chauffeur style, and his father was seated in the back. Rosenthal senior looked alarmed at the sight of the group of workers. I suppose he thought they could have been on strike.

He rolled down the window. "What's going on here?" He was The Boss in voice and attitude. The two bobbers curtsied again.

Fred Lishman approached the car. "We seem to be locked out."

"That's ridiculous. Where's Klein?"

"Don't know, sir. We've been here a good ten minutes, banging on the door, but he's not showed up."

Miriam approached the car. "We're losing work time. We wouldn't want to miss making the quota. We all know how important it is." Her voice was polite, but I could see the underlying sarcasm stung Rosenthal. He was no fool. He tapped his son on the shoulder.

Joel jumped out of the car and hurried around to help his father. I hadn't really noticed yesterday, but now I saw that Rosenthal senior was stiff around the hips and he leaned on his son's arm as he unfolded himself from the car. He went directly to the door and rattled the handle himself, but it remained adamant. He turned and faced his workers who were watching him quietly and curiously. The little drama was certainly brightening up a dull morning, especially as they were not the ones responsible for the inconvenience.

"We'll be inside in a jiffy, folks."

This was the good boss side of the man. He nodded over to his son.

"Joel. Get me the key box." He rubbed his hands together, although his doe skin gloves looked warm enough. "Darn chilly this morning," he said to nobody in particular. The two bobbers smiled and nodded in agreement.

Joel took a metal box from the car and brought it to his father. Rosenthal senior unbuttoned his overcoat, a soft cashmere, I might add, and unclipped a small key that was attached to his watch chain. He opened the box, took out another key, relocked the box and handed it back to his son. His movements were slow and studied and I felt an unexpected twinge of admiration for him. If he ever ended up on the gallows — and who knows, he might — this is how he'd face his end. Don't give the peons the satisfaction of looking troubled.

He fitted the key into the lock and the door opened easily. Rosenthal glanced over his shoulder and his eyes met mine.

"Miss Frayne, you seem to possess a clear head. Come with me while we see what, if anything, has happened. Everybody else, I'd like you to stay here. Joel, perhaps you would be in charge. We will be right back."

"Are you sure we can't come in?" asked Miriam. "It's bloody cold out here."

Rosenthal turned fully. The benign façade slipped and his expression could have stopped the waves.

"As I said, we will be right back. These circumstances seem very unusual to me and I'd like to find out why they have occurred." He dragged the smile back. "I promise that as soon as you can come inside, we will delay work starting until you have all warmed up with a hot cup of tea."

Unless she had bodily run over him, there was nothing Miriam could do. She stepped back. With Mr. Rosenthal leading the way, I followed him upstairs.

"I don't like the look of this at all, Miss Frayne," he said. "Those Commies have done something, I'm sure."

We entered the second floor sewing room.

It was immediately obvious why Klein had not unlocked the door.

He was lying spread-eagled across one of the tables, a pair of scissors protruding from his chest.

He had been dead for some time.

CHAPTER TWENTY

MR. ROSENTHAL MISSED his step and staggered foward. "My God."

"Please stay here." I went over to the body, being careful to make a wide circle so as to introduce as little confusion of footprints as possible. There was no doubt Klein was dead. His skin was the colour of ashes in a cold fireplace; his eyes and mouth were frozen open in rigor mortis. As is usually the case, his bowels had evacuated on death and I could smell him from where I stood.

The front of his overalls were soaked with blood.

I addressed Mr. Rosenthal.

"I'm going to check the office. Please don't move until I give the signal."

He didn't protest and remained frozen on the spot.

I could see into Klein's office. Unless somebody was underneath the desk, the place seemed empty, but I had to make sure.

"If anything happens, Mr. Rosenthal, you must go for help immediately. There's a telephone in the office and

I'm going to ring the police. When I know it's safe, I want you to go downstairs. Have everybody go into the lunch room. Nobody must leave until the police arrive."

"What shall I tell them?" His voice was a whisper.

"Say there has been an accident and the police are on their way."

"Shall I say anything about Klein?"

"Better not at this point. Stick to the absolute minimum information."

"Right. An accident. Police coming."

"Exactly. I'll stay here until they arrive."

His colour was returning. As I'd thought earlier, Mr. Rosenthal was of tough stock.

"Do you want me to come back up here?"

"No. Stay with the others."

"Very well." He choked a little. "I can hardly believe what I'm seeing Miss Frayne. Who would have done this?"

"The police will investigate."

I wasn't carrying any kind of weapon, defensive or offensive. All I had was my handbag which I grasped ready to strike out if necessary. Not that it could have been very effective, but it was better than nothing. Then, walking carefully, I walked into the office.

Nobody was hiding underneath the desk. I exhaled and relaxed my grip on my handbag. I took out my handkerchief, wrapped it around my hand, lifted the receiver and telephoned the police. Connection made, I gave Mr. Rosenthal a wave and he turned away, heading downstairs.

I was standing behind the desk, which was wide, more a table than a desk. Klein must have been putting up the employees' wage packets when he was interrupted, because there was an open metal cash box to one side containing dollar bills and several rolls of coins. Next to it was a cardboard box in which were the packets, some already labelled and some not. A sheaf of papers, pinned together, the weekly time sheets lay on the chair. There was an adding machine. Given the presence of the money I expected robbery, but it was hard to tell. Nothing here or in the workshop seemed disturbed.

CHAPTER TWENTY-ONE

THE POLICE ARRIVED quickly, but when you're standing guard over a man who has been violently murdered, nothing could be fast enough. My brief exchange with Mr. Klein hadn't been warm and fluffy, but the murder of anyone in such a manner was shocking.

I heard the sound of the officers coming up the stairs and I hurried to greet them, trying not to flinch as I passed Klein's body.

Two men entered, followed by three uniformed officers. The first man was a big heavy-set fellow with a rough-skinned face. I recognized him. His name was Walter Arcady and we'd met before. I thought he consistently displayed the disposition of a disturbed wasp. When he saw me, he tipped his hat, "Miss Frayne. What are you doing here?" I couldn't tell if he was unpleasantly surprised or neutral or perhaps even happy, although that possibility was unlikely.

"I was with the shop owner, Mr. Rosenthal. We found the body."

Arcady walked over to the table where Klein was sprawled. The other detective followed. The officers waited at the door.

In the short time that had elapsed, Klein looked even more dead, his skin more bloodless.

"Do we know who he is?" asked Arcady.

"Oscar Klein. He was the supervisor."

"I gather this is a clothes manufacturer?"

"Yes, Superior Ladies' Clothes."

"Where are the employees?"

"I asked Mr. Rosenthal to keep them on the first floor."

"Did anybody come up here?"

"Only Mr. Rosenthal and me. When I arrived this morning, the front door to the building was locked and the entire staff were all waiting outside."

The other detective spoke for the first time.

"How did you get in?"

Arcady jerked his head. "Miss Frayne, this is Detective Parrish."

He smiled shyly at me. He was much younger than Arcady, barely regulation height, and he looked nervous. I hadn't met him before in any of my dealings with the police department. I assumed he was newly promoted.

"In answer to your question, Detective, Mr. Rosenthal himself arrived. He had a key, and he and I entered. When we came upstairs, we found Klein's body."

Arcady glanced over at me. "Am I to assume you have taken on another line of work in the clothing business, Miss Frayne?"

"Not quite. I am currently working for Mr. Rosenthal as a private investigator."

He grunted. "Perhaps you can fill me in on that a little later."

He stood for a few moments studying the scene. Then, cautiously, he tried to move Klein's foot, but it was completely rigid.

"Given the state of rigor, I'd say he's been dead for ten hours or more. Do you agree Miss Frayne?"

I was shocked at the question. He was consulting me. You could have knocked me down with a feather.

"I'd say so. At the very least."

"Do you know what time the shop closes?"

"The workday finishes at six."

"But Klein was still here?"

"Apparently it was his responsibility for closing up at the end of the day."

I indicated the office. "He was in the process of making up the wage packets."

"And you say the door was definitely locked when you arrived?"

Arcady had perfected a tone of voice that implied he didn't believe a word you said. I suppose it worked with those labouring under fear and a bad conscience, but I found it highly irritating.

"It was. Definitely."

"Is there any other way to get in?"

"Not that I'm aware of. There's no fire escape."

Arcady sighed. "So, are we are likely looking at some-body else having a key? Or did he pretend to be an early Father Christmas and come down the chimney?"

There was a small fireplace in the corner of the work-room, but it was boarded over. The shop used radiators these days.

He seemed rather proud of the joke and actually grim-aced at me which I now knew could be a smile.

I managed to bite back a sarcastic response.

Arcady continued. "He — or she, we mustn't rule out the fairer sex, Parrish. Women can commit violent crimes just as easily as men. Don't you agree, Miss Frayne?"

"That's an equality we don't particularly clamour for."

"What?"

I let it go. "At this point I suspect the attacker entered the normal way. Through the door. And that Mr. Klein probably knew him. Or her."

Arcady looked at me with deep skepticism.

"Hm. Why do you say that?"

I couldn't tell if Arcady genuinely hadn't figured it out or if he was just testing me.

I pushed on. "I do think that would explain why Mr. Klein was killed out in the workroom and not his office. His light is still on which suggests he was in there when the intruder entered. He left his office and went toward this person, male or female to be determined. The lights are also on in the workroom so he could have seen well enough who it was. He wasn't alarmed by his visitor and was facing him when he was stabbed at close quarters. There is no obvious sign of a struggle. He doesn't seem to have tried to run for instance."

I could see Detective Parrish was taking all this in. He said, "Perhaps he didn't have a chance. There may even have been more than one intruder."

Arcady wasn't praise heavy.

"There may have been a bloody army for all we know. And three dogs and a cat. Let's not jump to unwarranted conclusions. Nothing will destroy an investigation sooner."

Detective Parrish looked discomfited. Arcady, as intended, had made him feel foolish.

I pointed at the table. "I think a warranted conclusion is that the killer grabbed one of the pairs of scissors that are kept in that jar. There are two other identical pairs remaining."

"That tells me that he didn't bring his own weapon," said Detective Parrish trying valiantly to restore himself.

"Not necessarily," grunted Arcady.

He was right again, but common sense was on the side of his young colleague. If you are trying to burgle a place you likely either have a weapon ready to use or to threaten. If you don't and you're surprised in the act, you will probably grab what's handy. My acquaintance with Klein had been brief, but he didn't strike me as the kind of man who would back off from a trespasser. I'd guess some kind of confrontation had occurred.

"The coroner will be more exact I'm sure, but the angle of the blades suggests they were thrust downward ..."

I paused to see if he was following me. He gave another of those economical nods. I resumed.

"It would seem that Klein was pushed backward onto the table and the attacker grabbed the scissors while he stood over him."

Arcady waved his hand. "Klein could have been stabbed somewhere else and staggered to the table."

It was a test, it had to be.

"There is no blood trail. As you can see."

I thought for a moment that he actually smiled. "You appear to have already conducted an investigation, Miss Frayne."

"Just making observations, Detective."

We heard the sound of footsteps coming up the stairs and there was a sharp rap on the door. One of the officers ushered in a tiny, stooped man who was muffled up in heavy rain gear. He was carrying a black leather bag and he came toward us unwinding his scarf as he did so.

He addressed Arcady.

"I'm Doctor Lewis, the city coroner. You summoned me?"

He sounded like Puck talking to Oberon. This impression was reinforced by his diminutive size; a round, pink-cheeked face; and a shock of curly white hair. Given his occupation, I was impressed by the cheeriness of his demeanour.

He glanced over Arcady's shoulder. "Ah. I see."

He went over to the body and stood for a moment,

looking down. I realized he was not studying the corpse as such. He was praying. He finished and turned around to us.

"Do we know anything about the circumstances?"

"Not at the moment," answered Arcady. "His body was discovered about half an hour ago."

The doctor placed the back of his hand on Klein's pale cheek and then gently tried to move the jaw. It was rigid.

"He's been dead ten to twelve hours. Maybe more." He reached down for his black bag. "I'll ask you all to leave the room while I do my preliminary examination. When that's done, I will need to borrow a couple of your officers to help me convey the body to the morgue."

"Of course, doctor."

I hadn't heard Arcady speak quite so sweetly before, but Dr. Lewis brought out that quality of niceness. It's a wonder Klein himself didn't get up and thank him.

Arcady walked back to the constables at the door. One of them, who also looked like a new recruit, was fidgeting with his truncheon.

"Plotnik, go downstairs. Don't let anybody in or out. Especially out. Liotta. You and Kelly, I want you to start taking down the names of the employees. Tell them we'll have to talk to them. Try not to alarm them, but don't give them any information."

"Shall we say somebody has been killed?" the nervous officer asked.

Arcady pulled on his lip. "Better to use the usual waffle. Just say that there's been a serious incident and one of the detectives, that's me, will be coming down to address them very soon. Okay, lads. Off you go. And don't forget you are police officers. You might even become detectives one day. Keep your eyes and ears open. Note anything that might seem relevant."

"Yes, sir.

They clattered off.

"All right, Miss Frayne. You said Klein was in the middle of making up the employees' wages. Was any money stolen?"

"I didn't have the chance to check that yet."

He started for the office. "Let's have a look, shall we?"

The three of us trooped past the coroner who was doing unspeakable things to the corpse.

Arcady closed the door behind us. We could still see if we wanted to, but it gave a semblance of privacy. He walked around the desk and picked up one of the packets from the cardboard box. A name was written on the front. He read it out loud.

"Bertha Koenig. Fifteen dollars minus fifty cents. Slow work."

He riffled through the packets. "There are ten filled. He hadn't finished."

There was a white business envelope tucked to the back of the desk. It was labelled "Deductions" and Arcady looked inside it.

"Let's see. Two two-dollar bills and one one-dollar bill. Five dollars in total."

He gave me a wink. "Miss Frayne, will you take out your trusty notebook. Let's do a bit of accounting. Ready?"

He picked up the bank statement. "There was a recent withdrawal to the tune of three-hundred-and-eighty-two dollars. Now here's the weekly time sheet. Starting Saturday, October twenty-fourth to Saturday, October thirty-first. There is a column for deductions. Let's do the earnings first. I'll call out these numbers. Jot them down and we'll add them up. Klein had got as far as ten employees. Ready?"

"As ready as I was a moment ago."

"Here we go. Parrish, count the money in the packets as we go. One, F. Goldie. Wage seventeen dollars; fifty cents deducted for lateness."

Parrish confirmed the amount. "All correct."

"Second, Mary Koski. Seventeen dollars, minus one dollar and fifty cents. Also for lateness. What was wrong with these women?"

Neither Parrish nor I considered he wanted an answer.

Arcady continued with the list.

"Number ten, Rosario Pasquale, forty dollars. No deductions. That's as far as he got. What does that add up to?"

Before I could answer, Parrish called out. "Two hundred and forty dollars in earnings, less seven dollars in deductions. There should be one hundred and forty dollars in the cash box that was not yet apportioned."

Both Arcady and I stared at him in astonishment.

He turned a little pink. "Mental arithmetic is a strength of mine, sir."

Arcady couldn't quite concede. "Do you agree, Miss Frayne?'

It took me a little longer. To be sure, I used the adding machine. "Confirmed."

"Shall I count the cash, sir?" Parrish asked.

"Be my guest, I'm surprised you can't just stare at it and know the answer."

His tone was actually good natured. Parrish slammed through the cash with amazing speed.

"Were you a bank teller, or something?" I asked.

"I worked in my father's butcher shop when I was younger," said Parrish.

"So? What's the verdict?" Arcady asked.

"All correct, sir." He indicated the white envelope. "There appears to be some money in there. Can I take a look?"

Arcady waved his hand.

Again, Parrish flipped through the cash. "There's only five dollars in here. There should be seven. I'll double check the cash box."

Watching him was rather like watching a magician do sleight of hand.

"One hundred-and-forty-two. That is correct. That is what the remaining nine employees earned." He picked up the time sheet and scanned it. "According to this, there are a further six dollars to be taken out in deductions."

I added my bit. "Klein had put that money aside. I wonder if he really intended to deposit it? If he was skimming a bit off the top every week, it could eventually add up to a tidy sum. Mr. Rosenthal said he left all the practicalities of running the shop to Klein. Given this system, there's no way he'd know anything about it."

"Miss Frayne, I'm not sure if you have a suspicious mind or a good grasp of the criminal one."

"They go together. Don't you think, Detective?"

Parrish jumped in. "There's another thing to take into account. Total of deductions for all employees is thirteen dollars. Of which we have in hand eleven dollars. Two dollars are unaccounted for."

Arcady pursed his lips.

"Are you certain?

"It's not in the desk, so unless it's on Klein's person, yes, there should be another two dollars."

Arcady sighed. "Surely we're not looking at a man being killed for a mere two dollars?"

CHAPTER TWENTY-TWO

Dr. Lewis was closing up his bag and Arcady sent Parrish to fetch a couple of stalwarts while he went to talk to him. I stayed in the office until all was dealt with. I was almost sorry to see Dr. Lewis leave. He made violent death seem less disturbing.

Arcady returned. "Dr. Lewis has not found any money on the body, Miss Frayne, so it's still unaccounted for." He gave me what I presumed was meant to pass for a smile. "You have clerical skills do you not? Shorthand and typing and what not."

"I do."

He looked relieved. "Good. Fact is, the best place to interview these people is here on the premises. The stenographer at the station has come down with the flu so I can't get him. I wondered if you would consider acting in that position on a temporary basis? I will make sure you are reimbursed."

I gave him a nice smile. "As well as having clerical skills as you put it, I am a licensed private investigator. At the moment, I'm employed by Mr. Rosenthal. If I am present during the interviews, I'd like to be free to ask questions."

He frowned, but he was smart enough to understand what the leverage was.

"All right. I assume I can rely on you to be discreet?"

"I've interviewed a lot of people in the course of my work. I know how to do it."

He hesitated just long enough to get his point across.

"I promise I will not intrude," I said chirpily. I almost crossed my fingers behind my back. I hoped I wouldn't regret saying that.

"Very well. Let's go. The sooner we start, the better."

I have to admit I was pleased. I'd been wondering how I was going to insinuate myself into the investigation. Although Mr. Gilmore had warned me more than once that we mustn't get personally involved in our cases, in this instance it was hard not to.

Mr. Rosenthal was waiting for us in the entrance. He'd removed his outer clothes already and a rather pleasant rich man's smell, probably from a recent visit to a barber's shop, wafted in our direction.

He greeted us immediately.

"Ah, Detective. Everybody's down in the lunch room waiting, but I wanted to offer my office for your use as I assume you will need to speak to them individually."

"Thank you, sir. That would be most helpful. I'll also need the address of Mr. Klein and the name of his next of kin."

I must admit that, reluctant as I was to attribute any redeeming features to the detective, he was crisp and efficient when it came to conducting the investigation.

Mr. Rosenthal rubbed his forehead, a gesture I was beginning to recognize as habitual. It was as if he was waking up his brains, or calming down his thoughts.

"We must have that in a file somewhere. I believe he was a bachelor. He didn't live too far from here. I know that."

"Okay. I'd like that information as soon as possible. Oh, by the way. Miss Frayne has agreed to help us with the notes and so forth."

Mr. Rosenthal looked at me quizzically, but he didn't acknowledge our prior acquaintance.

"Come this way."

We followed him through the side door into a short hallway. Straight ahead I could see the storeroom.

A flight of stairs on the right led down to the basement.

The lunch room was low-ceilinged and dim. There were no windows, but electric lights on low wattage could be said to illuminate the room. A sink and two stalls for the toilets were at one end. A shelf on the far wall held a smattering of cups and saucers, a kettle, and a few tin containers. No effort had been made to make it in any way pleasant or conducive to a work break. I thought the little galley kitchen that Mr. Gilmore and I had in our office offered more amenities.

Most of the employees were seated around a centre table, talking among themselves. There wasn't room for everybody and some of the men were leaning against the wall. It seemed as if most of them had lit up cigarettes. So had a couple of the women. I wasn't surprised to see that one of the smokers was Miriam Cohen. The air was going to get choking fairly soon. They went silent as soon as we entered and there were several curious glances cast my way. I suppose nobody could figure out my position.

At Arcady's request, Mr. Rosenthal had agreed to address the workers first. He took up a position in front of the door, leaving Joel, me, Detective Parrish and the young constable to squeeze in around to him. "Ladies and gentlemen, friends and colleagues. I'm afraid I have some very bad news. Mr. Oscar Klein has been found dead." He clasped his hands together in prayer-like fashion and, like a good actor, he gave them time to react. I saw Miriam pulled young Ben closer to her. Several of the women turned to each other exchanging shocked whispers.

Fred Lishman was the first to speak up. His voice was loud and hard.

"Are you going to let us in on what happened to the bloke or do we have to read it in the papers?"

He was seated beside Rhoda Baum and she reached over to him and touched his arm in a placating manner as if she were soothing an angry dog. He ignored her. Arcady answered him.

"My name is Detective Arcady and I am in charge of this investigation. I realize this has come as a great shock, but we are treating this as an equivocal death."

"By that do you mean the fellow was offed?"

Arcady was not the man to tangle with. Faced with hostility, he became even more formidable.

"By 'equivocal', I mean just that. We do not yet know with absolute certainty what was the cause of Mr. Klein's death, but we are proceeding as if it was a homicide."

Gasps and more exchanges. I watched them all closely, but as far as I could tell, this was indeed a surprise to all of them. Except for Miriam Cohen, who was not registering any emotion. She looked frozen, clutching at Ben as if he was her protector and not the other way around.

"We will need to speak to each of you individually," continued Arcady. "To that purpose, Mr. Rosenthal has kindly offered us the use of his office. Detective Parrish here will stay with you and then you will each be brought up for questioning. If we are satisfied with the interview, you will be allowed to leave the premises. But not before."

I suppose it was a rough way to put it and Lishman took exception.

"You're treating us as if you've already decided we're criminals. Klein was a right pill, but that doesn't mean it was one of us that killed him."

"I thank you to watch your language," said Arcady. "There are women present. Any more talk like that and I'll lay a charge."

Again, it was Rhoda Baum who tried to mollify the man. She did the arm stroking thing again.

"Don't fret, Fred. It's just regular procedure."

She'd spoken softly, but Arcady heard her.

"Precisely, madam. A very serious crime has taken place on these premises and I intend to find the guilty party. Is that clear?"

Nobody answered. Frightened eyes gazed up at him.

Arcady pointed at the younger, ruddy-faced constable. "This is Constable Liotta. He will be in charge of escorting each of you upstairs. You will be asked to give a statement. Any questions?"

"How long is this going to take?" asked Lishman.

"It will take as long as is necessary," Arcady answered.

Again, it was Lishman who threw down the gauntlet. "It's going to be a long day. I assume we'll have time to eat."

"Work that out among yourselves."

I was at a total loss as to explain my presence to the others. Miriam, in particular, had given me glances that were puzzled and not a little hostile.

Fortunately, for once, Arcady showed some sensitivity.

"In case you're wondering, I've asked Miss Frayne to assist me. She has clerical skills as it turns out. She will take down your statements and then when that same statement is typed up, you will be given a copy to verify that is what you said and that nobody coerced you or changed your words. You will then sign said statement."

He waited for a moment. "We have not yet had the chance to contact Mr. Klein's next of kin. Does anybody have information about that? And, also, we need his address."

Rhoda put up her hand as if she were in school.

"Yes, ma'am."

"He was a confirmed bachelor. He was living on Sullivan Street. I don't know the number, but he boarded with Mrs. Mary Liddell."

She lowered her head, aware that the others were staring at her. "Mrs. Liddell and I go to the same church. When she found out where I was working, we'd chat sometimes."

She didn't need to elaborate. I thought Klein was lucky that his mourner after death was this kind woman.

"Thank you, ma'am. Much appreciated."

Arcady beckoned to Detective Parrish and took him aside. It was clear from Parrish's expression that he was being assigned the job of going to Klein's residence to deliver the news. Arcady directed Constable Plotnik to accompany him and they both left.

Arcady turned to Mr. Rosenthal. "Shall we?" He nodded to the remaining constable next to him. "Give me a few minutes, Liotta, then you can start bringing them up."

Mr. Rosenthal jumped in. "I realize how upsetting this is and of course there will be no work today. But as Mr. ...?"

"Lishman. Fred. I'm one of your cutters."

"Yes, yes, of course. As you said, it might turn out to be a long day. We might as well make the best of it. I'll have something brought in from the bakery. I don't know about you, but I'm quite famished." He beckoned to Joel. "Take their orders will you."

There's nothing like something tasty to lift the spirits and the mood in the room changed. I felt a flash of pity for the dead man. There wasn't much grief for him.

CHAPTER TWENTY-THREE

A RCADY, MR. ROSENTHAL, and I went back upstairs to his office.

This turned out to be tucked away at the end of the show room, where the finished clothes were stacked on high shelves and where a row of naked mannequins waited to be dressed. Unlike Klein's glass fort, the boss's office was enclosed and only the modest brass name plate on the door revealed what it was. Tucked next to it was a much smaller office. An equally modest plate named Joel Rosenthal as that resident.

Saul's smelled like cigars and was smaller than I expected, just room enough for a gleaming mahogany desk, devoid of any papers; an equally gleaming cabinet took up one wall. It suggested important files, but it could have been empty for all I knew. Beneath the window was a burgundy velvet chaise lounge. Here Mr. Rosenthal could relax, if need be, from the stresses of running a shop and putting down communist agitators. I wondered if the presence of the chaise had anything to do with the stiffness of the hips he'd demonstrated when he was getting out of the McLaughlin-Buick. There was an open book on the floor by the chaise, but I couldn't see what he'd been reading. The office faced onto Spadina Avenue and I seized the chance to have a quick look out. Raindrops were rolling down the window pane. In the street, only a few pedestrians were braving the elements and they seemed be moving as fast as they could to get back indoors.

The two men had followed behind me and they shuffled uncomfortably for a moment as they worked out who should sit behind the desk. Rosenthal offered it to the detective and he, himself, drew up two chairs; one was for him and faced the desk. With a smile, he indicated the other was for me. He placed it slightly behind him but, also with a smile, I moved it to be next to Arcady, from where I could see whomever was being interviewed. They both watched while I removed my notebook from my handbag, got my pencil at the ready, and waited to be further informed. I was the epitome of efficiency.

* * *

MR. ROSENTHAL WASN'T a big man, but he conveyed a natural authority that comes with having status from the moment of his birth.

As it turned out, I was wrong about that.

He was well-groomed; his suit was a fine, charcoal grey, worsted wool and his shoes looked to be hand-made. If it weren't for his pock-marked skin, he would have been considered a handsome man. I wondered if he cared about his bad complexion.

At this point, Mr. Rosenthal had asked politely if I minded if he were to smoke. "Of course, I didn't mind," I answered with equal politeness. I regretted saying that almost immediately as he took a cigar from the silver humidor on the desk and lit it. The smell took over the room. Arcady had declined the offer of a similar stinker, but he lit a cigarette from his own pack. I tried not to breathe too deeply. The two men exchanged puffs.

Arcady spoke first, "Why don't you tell me what you know about Mr. Klein. How long has he been in your employ?"

"Four years."

"What sort of man was he?"

Rosenthal blew out a ring of smoke and watched it dissolve before he answered. "I don't know how to answer that. He was reliable. Never missed a day of work and made sure we were hitting our targets."

"Was he a tippler? Of a temperant disposition?

"I don't know. Our relationship was based on business alone. I did not see him after hours. I do not socialize with my employees."

"Wouldn't expect you to, sir," said Arcady. "But I assume you do take down some personal particulars when you hire somebody."

"My son, Joel, does that job." Another smoke ring died on the air. "It's a good way for him to learn the business. I started that way myself," he added, in case we might think the son-and-heir was performing a lesser role. Rosenthal gave a rather rueful smile. "My son takes more after his mother than he does me. People like him. They open up."

"I'd like to take a look at Klein's file."

"Of course."

He balanced the cigar on the ash tray stand and stood up, again showing stiffness in the hips. He limped over to the filing cabinet, fished inside for a moment or two and, rather like Jack Horner, pulled out a folder. He handed it to Arcady who in turn handed it to me.

"Read it out loud, will you Miss Frayne."

I didn't know if he'd forgotten his glasses, or if he wanted to make sure the file had been filled out properly and Mr. Rosenthal was aware of it.

The dossier on Klein was a single page.

"Name: Klein. Christian name: Oscar. Middle name: Nathaniel. Marital status: Bachelor. The line for next of kin was blank. Address: twenty-two Sullivan Street. Boarding. Religion: Methodist. Notes: Klein was a veteran of the Twelfth Battalion. He was discharged with wounds on his left hand."

Arcady spoke up. "I'm surprised that you didn't know he was a veteran. Usually, the only thing some of those men want to talk about is life in the trenches. It's eighteen years since the Armistice was signed. They still can't move on."

He tapped the file. "It says he was discharged with wounds. Do you know what they were?"

"He had a nasty scar on his hand. I presumed he sustained that during the war. He never said."

Rosenthal flicked the ash from his cigar into the tray on his desk.

Arcady did likewise with his cigarette.

"The big question is motive. Any idea why Klein would have been killed?"

"None at all."

"What sort of relationship did he have with the employees?"

"I don't think he was that well-liked. He had a job to do and he played it by the rules. Late-comers lost pay. Shoddy work could get them suspended or even fired if there was no improvement. We've just introduced piece work, but there's been much opposition."

He waved his cigar in my direction. "That's why I hired Miss Frayne. I think there are some Reds here who want to instigate a strike. They want to organize a union. They don't see it from my point of view. If my company falls behind, they will suffer as well. You won't get wages if there's no work. But they don't see that. I'm the big bad wolf." Again, he waved the cigar. "My father arrived in this country as an immigrant from Poland. He had fifty cents in his pocket, but he went on to build up a business. Then he had a heart attack and collapsed. He was not even forty. My mother determined she wouldn't go under and she took over the business. I was working in the storeroom when I was ten. I did every job I was capable of.

I had three younger sisters and I worked for them so they could eat. Those Reds can't talk to me about privilege. I'll match them blister for bloody blister. Scar for scar."

His was clearly impassioned when he spoke and I felt this was not a speech of self-justification. He believed what he said. Arcady was staring at the tip of his cigarette as if it held the answers to all the questions he had yet to ask. But he was inscrutable. I couldn't tell what he was thinking. Few police officers had positive views of the wealthy. Perhaps because they weren't paid very well themselves.

Arcady flicked the ash off his cigarette. "As well as motivation, the most significant question is how the killer got into the building. The sole entrance is from the street and that door was locked. Which employees have keys? Do any others have keys? What is the standard procedure for opening in the morning and closing in the evening?"

"Klein was the only employee with a key. He opened and closed the building. As supervisor, his job was to check the employees off his list as they arrived in the morning. Punctuality is important in our business. I, myself, have a key and today was the only time I have had to use it. No one else has a key."

Arcady nodded. "There are only two keys to the building and both unlock the single entrance. Is that correct?"

Mr. Rosenthal nodded.

I piped up. "A question, Mr. Rosenthal. Isn't it danger-ous to have only one entrance which is also the exit? What would happen if there was an emergency and the workers needed to get out in a hurry?"

"I presume you're referring to a fire?"

"That for example."

"We're very careful about safety. There are buckets of sand on every floor. We have a telephone. The fire department would be here in seconds. The lock is a dead bolt. It locks automatically when the door closes, but doesn't need a key from the inside to open. That ensures safety."

He answered calmly, but the expression that flitted across his face was one he kept away from public view. His answer wasn't good enough and he knew it.

"Was it common practice for Mr. Klein to remain on the premises after hours?" Arcady asked.

"I believe so. He prepared daily tallies, which he placed on my desk for the following morning. Mondays he made up the wage packets."

"Isn't it more common to do that on Fridays so the employees can have money for the weekend?"

Mr. Rosenthal didn't like that question either.

"I thought it was in the better interests of my employees to have their wages on Monday. Less temptation to squander their money."

To my mind, he was being completely illogical. For all his avowal about climbing up the ladder from the bottom, he didn't seem to have an empathy for the less fortunate.

Arcady looked at his watch and started to stub out his cigarette.

"We'd better begin the other interviews." He stood up and offered his hand to Rosenthal. "Thank you for your cooperation, sir. I'm sure we'll get to the bottom of this soon."

"I hope so. I can't afford for our work to be stopped for too much longer."

They shook hands. Rosenthal ignored me. I'd obviously landed on his bad side. The sympathy I'd felt earlier evaporated.

"Would you tell the constable to bring up the first person," said Arcady.

"Be glad to." Mr. Rosenthal was back to being all charm. He left.

Arcady turned around to look at me. "Miss Frayne that was not what I'd consider a necessary question. It was not relevant to this investigation."

"I disagree, sir. If this was the work of a disgruntled employee, having a workshop that was unsafe might be a significant factor."

"Hmm."

I didn't want to point the finger without due cause, but Miriam Cohen was certainly in that category.

There was a tap on the door and Constable Liotta ushered in the woman herself.

At first, i couldn't quite identify a subtle difference in her. When I saw her in the sewing room, she was wearing the ubiquitous white overall top. Then I twigged. She had put aside the tough, hard-nosed, woman-of-action persona and donned the one for alluring femme fatale.

She was wearing a stylish blue polka dot dress that just skimmed her shapely calves. Her hair was perfectly waved. Her use of what looked like freshly applied cherry red lipstick indicated a woman who knew the value of sex appeal. Arcady stood up. Quickly.

"Miss?"

"Cohen. Miriam Cohen."

"Please have a seat. I was expecting Mr. Lishman."

"He wanted to finish his sandwich first so I took his place. As Mr. Rosenthal has given us the rest of the day off, I thought I'd might as well take advantage."

She sat down and tugged her skirt over her knees in a way that drew attention to what she was doing. Arcady certainly noticed. Her eyes met mine, but they were hard to read. I had deceived her, and I could only assume she was angry about that, but so far she had given no particular sign. She might never have seen me before. Perhaps that was the punishment.

Arcady resumed his place behind the desk.

"Just a few questions, Miss Cohen. We won't keep you."

His gallantry made me want to choke.

He asked the routine questions first. She had only been with the company for three weeks. Previously she'd worked at Tip Top Tailors. She'd moved on because she preferred a smaller environment.

"How did you feel about Mr. Klein?" Arcady asked, his voice still gentle and polite. Miriam Cohen had hardly been in the room for ten minutes and she had him eating out of her hand. Clearly, I was missing something in the seduction game.

She answered the question as if thoughtfully and objectively. "He could be strict at times. Perhaps too strict for some people. He was a man who played by the rules."

The coolness of her reply didn't fit at all with the heated conflict I'd witnessed between her and Klein yesterday.

"Miss Cohen, a difficult question, but I must ask it," said Arcady.

"Of course. It's your job to ask difficult questions."

"Is there anybody that you know of, anybody at all, who might have killed Mr. Klein?"

She considered for a moment. "Everyone of us must experience moments of anger when we say impulsively. 'Oh, I could kill that man,' but they are words only. We don't act on them. So, to answer your question, I'd say no."

Arcady went through the ritual of asking about the locked door situation, but again she was not forthcoming. She had no idea how anybody could have entered the building. She did acknowledge her awareness of the routine. Who could not be aware? Mr. Klein was a stickler for punctuality, and they all knew he unlocked the entrance door on the dot of eight. If you had to knock to be admitted, you were considered late and you were fined. He always remained in the building until the last worker had left.

"Thank you, Miss Cohen. You have been very helpful. Miss Frayne will type up what you have said and give you a copy. Before you leave the building, perhaps you would be so good as to sign it and hand it to the constable."

"May I go home after that? This has been such a difficult morning." She drooped. Poor fragile woman.

"Of course, I can see no reason to detain you. But if there is anything you think about later, please don't hesitate to bring it to our attention."

Arcady stood up again and walked over to the door. She looked over at me and gave me a little smile of triumph as if to say, "See it's easy when you know how."

She left and Arcady went back to the desk. I got to the typewriter and started to type up the interview. While I did, the detective fidgeted with a pencil and contemplated his life choices. As soon as I'd finished my task, he went out to the hall to inform the waiting constable he was ready for the next person.

This was Fred Lishman.

He was a husky man with broad features, big hands. He must have been approaching fifty, but his hair was thick and abundant with only a touch of grey at the sides.

He entered the room as if he were a rich client looking to buy real estate.

"So this is where the other half lives. Not as posh as I expected." He sniffed. "Likes cigars, doesn't he."

Usually I don't like bully boys, but I have to admit to a sneaking attraction for the man. Underneath the rough façade, the I'm-a-working-bloke attitude, he seemed intelligent and honest. I couldn't see him stabbing Klein. A fist fight, maybe, but not that kind of violence where the other man had no chance to defend himself.

Unlike Miriam, who had acted as if I didn't exist, he nodded acknowledgement at my presence.

"Have a seat," said Arcady, with a decidedly different tone of voice. We began the routine questions. Lishman had worked for Superior Ladies' Clothes for almost a year. To the question "What was your relationship with Mr. Klein?" he responded, "He was the supervisor, I was the worker. End of story. He was a self-righteous pr—" He checked himself.

"Let's put it this way. There's no way Klein could have been in my good books. He created misery and hardship by dismissing workers for trivial reasons or just to save the boss some money. He acted as if he was better than us. Stuck in my craw." He flashed a grin at Arcady. "Did that make me kill him? No, even though the thought may have flashed through my mind on several occasions."

I felt this was the time to make my presence noticed.

"Mr. Lishman, Mr. Rosenthal is concerned that there is an employee who wants to stir up trouble. He believes that person may be a member of the Communist Party. Are you a communist sympathiser?"

He frowned at me. "Depends what you mean. Philosophically there are many ideas that came from Karl Marx that I agree with. Equal pay for equal work for instance. But I am not a registered member of the CP if that's what you mean."

"Are there Reds working here?" Arcady asked.

"You'll have to ask them."

"But surely you discuss politics, unions and so on."

Lishman shrugged. "We don't have time for a lot of hot air blowing. We just get on with work."

"I can't believe you don't share some views. After all, organizing a union in this shop could be a significant event."

Lishman was not to be baited. "Like I said, we don't have time to blather. You didn't want to get on Klein's bad side. If he took against you, you knew you'd be getting docked in your wages, at worse you could get the boot. Didn't matter if you were long-standing or not. His favourite line was, 'There's plenty more who'd take the job.' So, you just shut up and tried to work faster."

"What was Mr. Rosenthal's position in regard to the supervisor?" Arcady asked.

"Rosie didn't care what went on as long as he got his profit every month. Typical of all Shylocks."

The rest of the interview made me think I was watching two wrestlers circling each other. One trying to find a place to go in for the kill, the other making sure he exposed no vulnerable parts.

Eventually, Arcady let him go with the same instructions as before.

When I went to type up the interview, he stopped me.

"Might as well wait until we've heard all of them. Easier for you."

This also meant Lishman, unlike Miriam Cohen, would have to remain until we'd finished.

A knock on the door and Constable Liotta came in.

"The next two women have asked to be interviewed together sir. They are sisters and their English isn't very good. They thought it would be easier for them to understand if they were together."

Arcady shrugged. "Fine. Bring them in."

The two women entered. I'd have to say they shuffled in. They were the ones I'd called the bobbers. They didn't approach the desk, but from the doorway actually gave their little bob in unison. They looked to be in their forties, although they may have been younger. A hard life had taken its toll on both of them. I called out a greeting.

"Come in please. Have a chair."

I don't know how Arcady felt about my jumping in, but it was painful to see women who were so cowed.

"Yes, er ladies, there's only one chair so one of you will have to stand."

They moved closer and one pushed the other to sit in the chair.

"I understand you don't speak English very well. What is your language?"

"Polish, sir," said the seated one. "We are from Gdansk."

In fact, she seemed to speak quite well.

"And you are sisters?"

"That is right, sir. I am Freda Atanasoff and this is my sister Sandra."

"We have to ask some questions and Miss Frayne here will write down your answers. It shouldn't take too long. All right?"

To my relief, for some reason, Arcady was being quite soft. He started with the routine questions, then moved on to asking what they thought of Mr. Klein.

Their answers were cautious. "He was strict," said Freda, but they just did their jobs and there had been no trouble for them.

"Did he have trouble with anybody else in the shop?" asked Arcady.

Not that they knew of. They weren't interested in quarrels. They just did their work.

He asked about the key, but they had no opinions. The door was always locked when they arrived and Mr. Klein opened it at ten to eight. Mr. Klein saw them out at the end of the day and the door was locked behind them.

Arcady dismissed them and they bobbed their way out.

He leaned back in his chair. "Well that was as helpful as a dish of cold semolina pudding." His simile was confusing, but I got the point. Whatever their life experience, the sisters had learned in Poland the best way to deal with authority was to keep their heads down and not, under any circumstances, to draw attention to themselves. If what Mr. Rosenthal suspected was true, I couldn't see these women joining any mutiny.

The person who came in next, on the other hand, gave the impression she was not only looking for a mutiny, she'd start it herself. This was Bertha Koenig. Her first words were, "How long is this going to take? I've got a lot to do."

She was Arcady's kind of fighter and he gave it right back.

"It will take as long as it takes. If you are co-operative, it won't take long. If you're not, it could take all day. Your choice."

She stomped over to the desk, managing to throw a glare in my direction as she did so.

Arcady gave her the preamble.

"You'll get the statement when we've finished."

"I hope she knows what she's doing," she said rather ambiguously.

She dropped into the chair. No coy arranging of the skirts for her. She was actually wearing a long dark skirt and what looked like a man's plaid lumber shirt. It was hard to tell her age. Probably not more than thirty but, like the two sisters before her, she gave the impression of being older. Life, and no doubt alcohol, had washed away any youthful prettiness she might have once possessed.

"How would you describe your relationship with Mr. Klein?" Arcady asked.

"Relationship? Ha! It wasn't what you'd call a relationship. He was the boss man and I was the hired help. End of story."

"How was he to work for?"

She screwed up her face. "What do you mean?'

"I'd say that's a clear enough question, Miss Koenig.

We've heard he was strict. Not particularly popular. Is that true?"

"I suppose so."

"Most people can accept strict if it's combined with fairness. Was Mr. Klein fair?"

She growled. "What's fair about being docked fifty cents for being two minutes late because you was ill and couldn't get out of bed?"

"That's what he'd do then? No excuses?"

"You betcha."

"How long have you worked in this shop, Miss Koenig?

"Eight months."

"It is my understanding that there is a movement among the employees to form a union, which would go a long way to improve conditions, would it not? Are you going to join?"

"Maybe. You have to fork out dues first off. Money I don't have. And I doubt old Rosie would be happy about strikers. You'd get the shoot in a tick. Then what?"

I intervened. "I'd like to ask a question. If you don't mind, Detective."

"Go ahead." He stifled a yawn.

"Miss Koenig, we're having trouble understanding how somebody got into the building when it was locked. One key was on Mr. Klein's desk and, according to Mr. Rosenthal, he has the only other key. Can you help us here? Who might have a key other than those two?"

She stared at me for a moment, sussing out what might

incriminate her or what could put her in the authority's good books. I could almost read her decision. Her response knocked my socks off.

"You didn't always need a key to get in."

There was a little curl at the side of Bertha's mouth. She seemed to be enjoying this line of questioning.

Arcady leaned forward. "What do you mean by that, Miss Koenig?

Bertha knew exactly where she was in this power struggle.

"I don't suppose you could give me a cig, could you? Calm my nerves."

Arcady silently took out his case and offered her one. He shoved the box of matches across the desk. We waited while she lit up. She blew out the smoke luxuriously.

"Hm. That's better. Now, where was we?"

I answered for Arcady who was beginning to look as if he were approaching the end of his tether.

"You were about to explain why you said you didn't always need a key to get in."

"What I mean is, he left the door open for some people."

Arcady glared her. "Stop talking in riddles woman. If you don't speak in a straightforward manner, I'll charge you with obstructing justice."

Unperturbed, Bertha took another drag of the cigarette. "Let's put it this way. When a new worker is hired, everybody's on probation for a week. Mr. Klein had the power to give them the job or not. The women that is. He'd make a deal. I'll take you on in exchange for a few favours."

She paused, savouring the moment. I could see Arcady was about to explode.

I stepped in. "You mean these were sexual favours?"

"That's one way to put it. He'd take them on, and in return they'd make a visit to him after hours."

Arcady was still glaring. "How do you know this? Did you make a visit after hours?"

"Not me. I'm past the age he liked. He liked them younger. And I know because they told me. Most of us in the sewing room knew what he was up to."

"But nobody spoke up?"

She shrugged. "Why would we? If silly bints wanted to auction themselves off and get a bit more butter on their bread, why not? They chose. Nobody forced them."

"Name names," said Arcady.

"What's the use? They've all left now. None of them stayed long. Frankly, I think he paid them to move on. He knew they wouldn't make trouble and he could keep his little secret going."

"Not so secret if you know. Do other women in the sewing room know?"

She started to stub out her cigarette. "Who'd believe us? Or care? Men will be men after all. Nobody got hurt. No bruises. And as I say they had a choice."

Not much of a choice between dismissal and compliance.

"How many women were involved?"

"Since I've been here, which is going on for two years, I'd say at least four."

"When did these trysts take place?"

"After hours. He always stayed on to do the day's tally. He'd give the girl a little nod and a wink and she'd know to pop in that evening between seven and eight. She'd find the door open."

"And when would you say was the last woman who had such a tryst?"

"Nobody recently so far as I know." She looked at Arcady. "Do you think one of the cast-offs got revenge?"

"We're exploring every possibility. And it would help us considerably, if we knew the name of the women in question."

They stared at each other for what seemed like a long time, Bertha dragging on the cigarette. She won.

Arcady leaned back. "Let's put it this way, Miss Koenig. The police department has a contingency fund which we can dip into for witnesses who are aiding our investigation. I could pursue that."

"All right. Seeing as I'm out of pocket by all of this. Klein kept a record. He has to do that with all employees. Who comes, who goes. It's probably in there. You can just follow up on the most recent."

"Where would that record be?"

"Ask Mr. Rosenthal. He'd know. Or his son. Haven't you heard? He's learning the business."

She didn't say that Joel Rosenthal was involved in the procuring of young women, but the insinuation hung in the air like the smell of stale cigar smoke. That didn't fit the sense I'd had of him yesterday, when he seemed to care genuinely for the injured boy. I hoped what Bertha was insinuating wasn't true.

Arcady pushed back his chair. "Thank you, Miss Koenig. Please wait downstairs until your statement is ready. And if anything jogs your memory, let us know."

She stood up. "And you'll let me know about that fund?"

"I'll pursue it."

She left and it was Arcady's turn to light up another cigarette. I almost felt like joining him.

"What do you think, Miss Frayne? Is she telling the truth?"

I thought back to the uncomfortable moment when Klein had asked me to twirl around.

"Probably."

"And this certainly gives us a possible motive. If Klein did have company and wasn't, shall we say, satisfied with the service … who knows what sort of an argument might have ensued."

"Or somebody was trying to defend herself."

"That too." Arcady wiped at his mouth. "On the other hand, I'm putting my money on Lishman. I wouldn't trust him as far as I could throw him. He was lying. He's a Red, mark my words."

I refrained from pointing out that wasn't an automatic sign of a murderer, but I was well aware of the general paranoia of the police department, Chief Constable Draper leading the charge.

There was another tap on the door and Mr. Rosenthal entered, followed by his son. Joel was carrying a tray from which came the wonderful aroma of freshly perked coffee.

"I thought you two might have need of a little refreshment," said Rosenthal.

Joel put the tray on the desk. "The cheese rolls are a speciality of the bakery," said Rosenthal. "They're still warm from the oven."

He whisked off the white napkin as if he'd suddenly taken up the job of maître d'.

"Help yourself. There's butter and jam if you want."

He waited while Arcady and I did indeed help ourselves. He was right about the rolls and the coffee was fabulous.

"How's the interrogation coming?" Rosenthal asked.

"We're finding out things," answered Arcady. He stuffed a final piece of roll into his mouth. "Matter of fact, we wondered if we could have a look at the employment records."

"Of course." Rosenthal didn't exactly snap his fingers at his son, but he might as well have. "Joel. Get the book, will you?"

Promptly, Joel walked over to the elegant filing cabinet, pulled open a drawer, and took out a ledger. It was the same one I'd seen Klein writing in yesterday.

"Was there anything in particular you wanted to see?" asked Mr. Rosenthal.

"We're thinking we can't rule out the possibility that the killer was a former employee," said Arcady. "Perhaps somebody with a grudge." He rather noisily slurped on his cup of coffee.

I couldn't blame him. The slurp I mean. I hadn't tasted a brew so good. And I don't recall even in Gran's days, drinking out of a china cup of such delicacy that I was afraid I'd crack it if I looked harshly at it.

"Shall we stay or leave you to it?" asked Mr. Rosenthal.

Arcady sipped some more, looking hungrily at the empty silver basket where the cheese rolls had been. He even fished up some crumbs with his forefinger and popped them into his mouth.

"Why don't you stay? We might have some questions."

He flipped open the ledger. "Mr. Klein has conveniently entered all the dismissals in red ink. We can take a closer look at the entire employee list later if we have to, but for now let's just concentrate on the names of the ones who've left." He turned to me. "Right, Miss Frayne?"

I couldn't fault his logic at this point. "Agreed."

"Before we launch into that, though, I'd like to recall Miss Cohen. I have further questions."

Joel spoke up. "I believe she's left, sir. She said you had given her permission to go when she signed her statement."

He was blushing.

Arcady frowned. "I suppose I did. All right, let's get on with it. I do have a question, Mr. Rosenthal. Did you ever meet the new employees? When they were hired, I mean. Or was that all in Mr. Klein's jurisdiction?"

"Usually I left him to do that. I make regular inspections

of the floors and if there was somebody new, I would, of course, introduce myself and learn their names."

He sounded defensive to me. He was very keen to project an image of the good employer.

"Was there a lot of turnover?" I asked him.

"A lot? I wouldn't say that, but people don't always work out. We give them a try, but I can't afford to pay workers who can't keep up."

I looked over at Arcady, who was ready to take his lead on the information Bertha had given us. His eyes met mine and for once we seemed to be on the same wavelength.

He handed the ledger to me. "Just read out the names of those who've left, please. Mr. Rosenthal. If anything strikes you as out of the ordinary or pertinent, please feel free to interrupt. You too, Mr. Joel."

I thought he was being shrewd. He would be able to observe the Rosenthals' reactions to the names as I read them out.

The ledger was heavy, the corners edged with gilt. The writing was neat, the names entered in ink, with old-fashioned precise penmanship.

Other than myself, the most recent hiring was on October twenty-sixth. I read the entry. "Janet Crowdy. Sixty-four Nelson Street. Hired as bin mover. Wages. Twenty cents an hour. Dismissed October thirtieth." That was written in red ink.

"Fairly recently. For what reason?"

Mr. Rosenthal interrupted him. "I remember that young

woman. Unfortunately, she turned out to have consumption. We couldn't keep her. It would have put the health of all the other workers at risk."

"What happened to her?"

"Happened?"

"Where did she go?"

He bit at his lip. "I don't know. I presume to her family. We gave her a subsidy to tide her over."

It wasn't the right place or time to engage him an argument on health insurance. I knew what he'd done was common practice.

Arcady nodded at me to continue.

"September twenty-third. Sylvia Levin. Forty-nine Peter Street. Sewer. Wages twenty-two cents an hour. She was dismissed on October seventh."

"Reason?"

Again, Rosenthal responded. "I'm afraid she was a most unsatisfactory worker. She claimed to be an experienced sewer, but that wasn't the case at all. She did very shoddy work." He grimaced and looked up at his son. "You remember, don't you Joel? She complained constantly. Little skinny woman with dark brown hair? She wore spectacles."

"I, er ..."

Rosenthal waved his hand. "Oh, never mind. Let's go on."

"Next entry is on October eighth. Miriam Cohen. Address sixty-four D'Arcy Street. She's still in your employ."

"So she is. Next?"

"September sixteenth. Alicia Tudsbury. Thirty-one Bulwer Street. Sewer. She was dismissed on October sixteenth."

"She wasn't dismissed," interrupted Mr. Rosenthal. "She left of her own volition. She was getting married. We were sorry to lose her. She was a pleasant young woman with excellent work habits."

For a man who had conveyed a certain distance from his employees, he seemed very familiar with them. Joel shifted and stared out the window.

"Did you, yourself, know these women, Mr. Rosenthal?" I asked him.

"Just in passing," he answered. "To say good morning to, nothing more."

His father glanced up at him. Poor Joel's face and throat had turned red and his nose appeared to be growing long. Miss Alicia of the pleasant personality had left the company about the same time that Miriam had been hired. I wondered if his big pash on Miriam was on the rebound.

"All young women, are they?" Arcady asked.

Rosenthal frowned at him. "How should I know? I don't ask them to show their birth certificate."

Arcady wagged his hand back and forth. "Roughly?"

"As I recall the first two, Miss Crowdy and Miss Levin are mature women, but Miss Tudsbury is younger. She did after all leave to get married."

"The reason I am asking, sir, is that one of the employees has accused Mr. Klein of demanding favours of an intimate nature as a condition of working here. I wonder if you know anything about that?"

"What!" Rosenthal senior's shock seemed genuine. "It's the first I've heard." He looked up at his son. "Joel. Did you know this?"

"No, father. No, I did not."

Like his father's, his reaction seemed genuine.

"Is it true?" Senior asked. "The woman couldn't just be making it up could she? To cause trouble?"

"We intend to investigate further. If Klein was arranging a tryst, it might explain how a person could come and go after hours. We were told he would leave the door unlocked for his prospective paramour."

"And the women went along with this?"

"Jobs are hard to come by these days, Mr. Rosenthal. Perhaps they felt it was the only way to ensure they could pay their rent and put food on the table."

Arcady let the father and son digest the information for a few moments.

"Continue if you please, Miss Frayne."

I turned the page. "On October seventh, a man named Terrence Porter was hired to work in the storeroom. He was dismissed on October fifteenth. He didn't seem to last long. Do you remember this man, Mr. Rosenthal?"

"Indeed, I do. Young chap, but already too big for his britches."

"How so?"

"After our usual two weeks' probation, he demanded a raise. Wanted another five cents an hour. Ridiculous, given he was unproven and he was doing completely unskilled work. So, I said no, take it or leave it."

"He left it, I presume?"

"Quite so. We had quite a confrontation. When I said, 'You can take it or leave it', he used language that I cannot repeat in front of a lady. Atrocious behaviour."

Saul was still burning at the memory.

I went back to the ledger. The next name gave me a bit of a jolt.

"There's one other man listed. On October ninth Thomas Masefield was hired to work in the storeroom. His employment was terminated on October sixteenth."

"Masefield? Different kettle of fish entirely. He was a veteran. Pathetic fellow, frankly. I felt sorry for him and it was my suggestion to take him on."

He paused, chewing on his inner lip.

"Why was he fired?"

"He wasn't exactly fired. He was incapable of doing the required physical work. By the end of the day, he could hardly lift a feather pillow never mind a heavy bolt of cloth. And he had no other skills. I had to let him go."

This had to be the same person who had shown up at the Paradise Café and who was apparently a comrade of Gerald Jessop. The man who had to ask for credit to pay for an extra cup of coffee.

In spite of myself something must have shown itself on my face.

"I do my best, Miss Frayne. But we are not a charity. I cannot hire all the unfortunates in the world. I'd go bankrupt in no time."

Arcady intervened. "Any more, Miss Frayne?"

"No, sir. No more dismissals this year."

"All right then. Copy down the addresses of the most recent. We'll have to have a talk with them."

Joel turned from studying the rain. He spoke fast.

"If Mr. Klein was killed by one of our employees, it could have been someone who has been gone a long time. People can mull over perceived injustices for years."

"That's true, sir. But we've got to start somewhere. If these recent employees are a dead end, then we'll return to the ledger to look further back."

"Does the crime have to be laid at our door?" asked Mr. Rosenthal. "It could have been committed by some vagrant passing by. He may have seen the light on and come in to steal."

"And by sheer coincidence he came on an evening when the door was unlocked?"

Rosenthal's jaw clenched. "Coincidences do occur, Detective."

He was right about that, but according to Bertha Koenig an unlocked door meant an assignation. An assignation that was not as secret as Klein would have liked.

Arcady leaned back. "Thank you for the refreshments, Mr. Rosenthal. They are much appreciated. But now we'd better get back to work. We still have a number of your employees to talk to."

"You will keep me abreast of things, won't you?"

"Of course, sir."

Arcady got up to escort the father and son to the door. As usual, Rosenthal senior led the way, with Joel, the obedient son, following.

I called out. "Mr. Rosenthal, I wonder if I might use your telephone."

"You can, but keep it short. I pay by the minute."

Arcady closed the door behind them.

"Why don't you make your call now, I've got to visit the privy before we continue."

He, too, left.

The telephone was a fancy one, a deep gleaming black with brass bands around the mouthpiece. I'll say this for Mr. Rosenthal, he had good taste. He also favoured the discreet display of his wealth.

I dialled the number of the Paradise. By now it was just past eleven, lunch time, and a rather harried sounding Calvin answered the phone.

"Cal, it's me, Charlotte. Just checking to see if my grand-father is all right and also if you've heard from Hilliard."

Calvin chuckled. "Gramps is having the time of his life. The customers love him. As for Hilliard, he rang about an hour ago. Says his son is not doing too well and he won't be back for at least another week."

In the background, I could hear Pearl calling to him.

"Sorry, Charlotte. I've got to go."

"Go. By the way, did Hilliard leave a message for me?"

"He did. He asked me to be sure and tell you he'd phone in again later tonight. Will you be coming by?"

"I'm hoping to. If by chance I miss him will you ask if there is any way I can call him back?"

"Apparently that is part of the problem. There is only one telephone in town, and he has to go to the general store to use it."

"Okay. Thanks, Cal."

We hung up. I must admit I wasn't happy about the news. It was worrying to say the least and not being able to communicate with Hilliard was frustrating.

Arcady hadn't come back, so I started to write down the addresses of the people we were going to talk to. They all lived fairly close to the factory.

* * *

OUR NEXT INTERVIEWEE was Arthur MacNeil, one of the cutters. He was a taciturn Scot who would probably be good at poker, if he were so inclined. His craggy face gave nothing away. He declared emphatically he had no idea who could have killed Klein. "To say you didn't like the man didn't mean he was an enemy exactly and it certainly didn't follow like the night the day that you would kill said man."

This time, Arcady introduced the accusation that Bertha Koenig had levelled against Klein. McNeil looked sober. "Sorry for the lassies who had to put up with that."

We continued on with the interviews, but got nothing new. Nobody had been fond of Klein, but they had no idea who would have killed him. Shocking that was. As for Mr. Klein forcing trysts on the young women, there was only the one specific assertion. The women workers seemed to shrug it off. The general attitude was, as one of them said, "That's life, isn't it?" You put up with disagreeable things like rainy days and chilblains.

Most of them expressed some liking for Mr. Rosenthal and his son. "He has to make a living," said one woman. "If he didn't, we wouldn't have jobs, would we?" If there were somebody trying to start a union, I didn't think they stood much chance of success. The employees at Superior Ladies' Clothes seemed to be non-combative.

We'd finished the final interviews by half past two. This was Ruby Robertson, a young woman whose job was to dress the mannequins and display them in the front window. She was also responsible for keeping everything neat and tidy in the whole building. For this she got fifteen cents an hour. Like Ben, she looked to be hardly legal working age. She had come to the city a month earlier from a small town near Ottawa. She had a difficult time finding work at first, but had been hired two weeks earlier. She was still on probation. She said that Mr. Klein had been planning to give her a review this week, which would determine if she got permanent work. When she said this, both Arcady and I exchanged glances. She was a pretty girl with blue eyes and fair hair that was braided and pinned around her head, Slavic style. She'd changed into the company uniform of white overall top, as if she'd expected to work today. I thought that life had crushed some of her spirit, even though she was very young. She was nervous to the point of trembling.

Arcady, who seemed to get getting more human by the minute, left me to do the talking.

"You said Mr. Klein was planning to give you a review of you work. Did you make an appointment with him?"

She was trembling more than ever, so I came around the desk and poured her a glass of water. Mr. Rosenthal had sent in a carafe and some glasses earlier. There were some cookies left and I offered her one, which she devoured hungrily.

"You have nothing to fear Ruby. Just tell us what happened."

"He said to come at seven when everybody had left. He said he'd leave the entrance door unlocked and all I had to do was come up to the second floor."

I waited until she'd had a drink of water then I returned to my seat.

"Did you meet him?"

"No. I didn't. I am staying at Georgina House. It's a hostel and it was my turn to help with the evening meal. I took longer than I expected, and it was almost eight o'clock when I got to the shop. The door was locked. I didn't want to knock because he said it was better if we kept our meeting private. He said I was an excellent worker who showed lots of promise and he didn't want the others to say he was playing favourites." Her words were tumbling out now. "I thought he must have changed his mind or even forgotten, so I left.

"How long did you wait?"

"Not long. It was so wet and cold. I was late. I didn't stay more than five minutes."

Arcady leaned forward now. "Did you tell anybody about this proposed meeting?"

"No, sir."

"None of the girls at the hostel?"

"None of them."

"What about people at home? Your mom or your dad?"

"No, sir. I have no family here. My mother has passed away and my father has not been with us for some time."

"Did you tell any of the other workers in the shop?"

"No, sir. Mr. Klein was very adamant about that. Like I said. He didn't want anybody getting jealous."

She was clutching the glass.

"Ruby, did it cross your mind that Mr. Klein's reasons for having a meeting with you after hours might have been …" I couldn't find the right word.

"Dishonourable?" interjected Arcady. "We've learned that he possibly took advantage of his position here to prey on young women."

She flushed. When she spoke, her voice was barely above a whisper.

"He said I showed much promise in the area of fashion. That's all it was. He didn't touch me or anything like that."

We let her go with the usual request to wait downstairs until she received her typed statement. After Arcady had walked her to the door, he sat down and rubbed his forehead as if he had a headache.

"I have a daughter, Miss Frayne. She's fourteen. If I found out some man was preying on her, I don't know what I'd do to him."

I didn't quite know how to respond to this frankness, except to nod.

Arcady left me to type up the interviews while he went to see how the examination of the workshop was proceeding. I was just finishing my transcripts when he returned. He flopped onto the chaise.

"They're going to be here all night. Trying to get usable fingerprints in a place like a workroom is virtually impossible. The scissors are used constantly. Before we send everybody home, they'll have to get their prints. I don't hold out much hope of catching our killer by those means." He yawned. "I feel as if I'm coming down with something. My head aches, my joints ache, even my teeth ache."

"That doesn't sound too good."

He shrugged. "When we're done today, I'm going straight home to bed." He waggled his fingers at me. "Let's start with the employees who've left. Can you write down the addresses?"

"Will do."

He grunted. "To tell the truth, I'd appreciate it if you can come along. You've got a way with people. Jack Murdoch told me you had, and I have to admit he was right." He actually smiled at me. "You've been swell. Big help."

Even though he seemed to speak as if the words had a slightly nasty taste in his mouth, I was chuffed.

"I'd be more than happy to accompany you, Detective. I won't be long with these statements."

Arcady closed his eyes. "This chaise is mighty comfortable. Funny. The sound of you typing is quite pleasant. Makes me almost sleepy."

He fell asleep and I typed. We continued like that for the next half hour. He might have gone on sleeping, but there was a knock at the door. I went to answer and ushered in Saul Rosenthal. Needless to say, he was startled to see the detective sprawled on his chaise.

CHAPTER TWENTY-FOUR

W E HANDED OUT the statements to the waiting employees and when they were signed, Arcady dismissed them. They were anxious to know when work would resume. Mr. Rosenthal declared that they could all have the next day off. They would be paid as usual, but could make up the lost hours over the next few days. Come in a half an hour earlier and work a little later. He said he was considering paying a bonus to those who came in. "For the inconvenience," he said. I gulped at his choice of words, but mostly his employees were happy with his suggested arrangement. Not even Fred Lishman complained, although he continued to look sour. Mr. Rosenthal's popularity had risen by leaps and bounds.

Arcady left a constable at the premises and commandeered young Detective Parrish to be the chauffeur of the police car.

"Klein's landlady is expecting us," he said. "We'll go there first."

This was the first opportunity I'd had all day to go outside and so had not checked on the weather. No change to speak of, except that it was now quite dark. The streetlights reflected on the wet pavements and the few people who were out clutched at umbrellas as if rain had never fallen into their lives before.

"Miserable day," said Arcady. I assumed he was referring to the weather, but he may have been looking back on what had happened at the Superior shop.

"Miss Frayne, why don't you take the front seat? I'll ride in the back."

We did as directed, and Parrish after a couple of tries got the car started. Even to my ears, the engine sounded rough. A reliable working police car obviously wasn't a priority in the department. Arcady muttered some comment that I didn't catch, but the meaning was clear, especially as he said, "We might have to get out and push at this rate. That or hire a horse."

"Sorry, sir."

With a jerk, the car moved off. Parrish was looking worried. He was at the beginning of his career and I could tell how nervous Arcady made him.

Sullivan Street wasn't too far away. We actually drove past Phoebe Street where Mr. Gilmore lived and I had a twinge of guilt. I hadn't had a chance yet to do as he asked and find some accommodations for him. I hoped I could get to it tomorrow at the latest.

As we pulled up, Arcady tapped Parrish on the shoulder.

"What was the landlady like? Is she going to be hysterical?"

"I don't think so, sir. She seemed more distressed at losing her boarder's money than grief for the man. Her first question was, 'Who's going to pay for the funeral?'"

"What did you tell her?"

"I said you would have all that information."

"Don't know if I do. There's usually somebody in the family to take care of such matters. It's not a concern of our department."

Obviously, it wasn't the fault of the young detective that Klein had died without a next of kin, but Arcady had that strange knack of conveying a misdemeanour even if there wasn't one.

"I'll pursue the matter, sir."

He parked the car and we all got out. I was actually glad that he'd told us the landlady didn't seem to care. Possibly having to probe into the dead man's proclivities might add to the pain of grief.

"What's her name?" Arcady asked.

"Mrs. Mary Liddell, sir. She's a widow."

The sad widow opened the door promptly.

"I thought you'd never get here. I've been waiting."

Good manners were obviously not her strong suit.

Parrish, who did possess such, tipped his hat.

"Sorry ma'am. We came as soon as we could." He indicated Arcady and me. "This is Detective Arcady and Miss Frayne, who's assisting us.

"We'd like to take a look at Mr. Klein's room," interjected

Arcady, who had no fear of ignoring niceties.

Mrs. Liddell stepped back a little and we crammed into the narrow, dark hall.

"His room is on the third floor. On the left. The other one's empty."

Arcady started to head up the stairs, but she caught him by the sleeve.

"Who's going to take care of his estate, I'd like to know? Will the city bury him given what's happened? I'm a widow. I can't afford to do it. He was just a boarder here. No relation."

"Did he have any relatives we can contact?" asked Arcady.

"None that came here. He lived a quiet life. Went to work, came home, went to work. That's it."

"No church?"

"Nope. Me, I go regular, but not him."

She conveyed such disapproval I wondered how she could tolerate renting the room at all.

"Let's do this job first, but I'll make sure somebody gets in touch with you about his effects." Arcady began to move away. "We'll need to have a talk later. Where will you be?"

"Where I've been all day. Waiting in my parlour."

Arcady paused. "Are there any other people residing here, Mrs. Liable."

I almost burst out laughing at his mistake, although with him it was hard to tell if it was deliberate or not.

"At the moment, no. I'm careful about who I rent to. You have to be when you're a widow. There's been just Mr. Klein and me for the past two weeks." She softened her voice. "If you do happen to know of somebody needing a nice clean and bright room, meals and laundry extra, you can send them along. Reasonable rates."

"Nobody comes to mind …," he tailed off.

Parrish and I followed him up the stairs. They were carpeted with sisal that was threadbare at the treads. The wallpaper should have been stripped off a long time ago and seemed to have already started the process.

"I'm a widow. I can't afford a funeral, you know," Mrs. Liddell called after us.

Arcady ignored her and continued up to the second floor. There were two rooms here, each with their doors closed. The wattage in the single light bulb was so low it was barely functional. The air could have done with a good blast of oxygen.

We went up an even narrower flight to the third floor, where there was a small landing and two more doors, one open, one closed. Same dim light and same stale air.

Through the door that was open, I glimpsed a bare wooden floor with enough dust to make a beach. Arcady tried the other door which wasn't locked. We went inside.

The room was in complete darkness.

Arcady swore at it. "Where's the bloody light switch?"

He began to pat at the wall, but Parrish beat him to it and flipped on the light. What was revealed by the magic of electricity wasn't edifying. I'd say it was an ugly room that spoke of neglect of place, person, life itself. The iron bed was unmade, the sheets tumbling to the floor. They looked as if they had last encountered a laundry in pre-electricity times. A pair of pyjamas, also in need, were piled on a chair. There was a tiny fireplace, no visible fuel; a wardrobe with a torn curtain. In one corner there was a bamboo screen. Arcady walked over and moved it aside.

"Phew."

I understood the reaction. Behind the screen was a minuscule sink and a commode. The kind that needed regular emptying, which it hadn't. For several days.

Arcady replaced the screen.

"What are we looking for, sir?" Parrish asked.

"You'll know when you see it," answered Arcady. "You take the wardrobe and I'll look in the desk. Miss Frayne, you …"

I interrupted him. "I hope you aren't about to ask me to search the bed. I don't have rubber gloves with me."

He grimaced. "No, I'll do it. Stay where you are. There's no room to swing a rat in this mousehole anyway."

I could understand his sudden fixation with vermin to describe anything to do with Klein's rented room.

There wasn't much for me to do except watch Arcady and Parrish do their jobs.

Parrish pulled aside the wardrobe curtain, which did not reveal many clothes. A pair of trousers and a couple of jackets, all dark colours. He started to go through the pockets of a jacket. Arcady walked over to a rolltop desk by the window; it was certainly the best, perhaps the only piece of decent furniture in the room. He rolled up the top.

Surprisingly, the inside of the desk was empty, except for a blotting paper pad and an inkwell.

Arcady bent down. "Now if I know anything about these old things, they usually have a secret drawer somewhere where you can hide the key to the tea tin or some such thing."

The historical reference surprised me. I had been underestimating the man.

"Ah, ah." He removed a small drawer that was at the back of the desk and started to fish around in the opening. "Thought so," he said, a note of triumph in his voice. He took out a brown envelope and opened it. He removed what seemed to be a bundle of postcards. Whatever he saw caused his head to jerk up as if he were holding something hot.

"Whoa. Lookie, lookie."

Thinking he was asking me to do just that, I moved to approach the desk, but he thrust out his arm to stop me. "No, not you, Miss Frayne. You don't want to see these." He beckoned to Parrish. "Come take a look."

The detective went over and Arcady handed him the postcards. He looked at them and also registered shock.

I have to admit that in the two years since I had been a private investigator, I cannot say I had been forced to deal with the less salubrious side of human nature. Cheating wives and husbands, along with ungrateful pets who had gone on adventures, was about the extent of it. (Not counting this summer's murders and their fallout.)

"Do you mind telling me what they are?" I asked, although from the look on the faces of both men I could guess.

Parrish shoved the cards back into the envelope. "Let's say our Mr. Klein got his thrill from viewing naughty postcards."

"Very naughty," added Arcady.

He replaced the envelope in the desk and pulled down the top.

"Parrish, d'you get anything from the wardrobe?"

"Just this. It was in his suit pocket."

He held out a small paper package. There was a picture on the front of a semi naked woman and the word, *Phantasma*. What he was holding was a popular prophylactic.

"What the crap? Sorry, Miss Frayne."

"Don't apologize, sir. I'm familiar with the word."

"Put it in the desk for now, Parrish. We'll have to collect all these things later."

He walked over to the bed. "What other delights was he hiding?"

He jerked everything off, sheets, blankets, and mattress but there was nothing untoward unless you counted the mousetrap that was underneath the frame. Empty, I might add.

I looked around the room. "Klein was an ex-soldier, but he didn't bring that into his own room. There's nothing that I can see. No service medals, no demob certificate, not a photograph in sight. Except for what we've found so far, it's utterly impersonal."

Arcady scrunched up his face in distaste. "I've had to examine the rooms and belongings of dead people before now, but I'd say this has to be one of the most pathetic. Is there no one to bury him because of the kind of man he was or was he that kind of man because there is no one to bury him?"

"Well, he was a pervert, for one thing. He preyed on young women and tyrannized his subordinates. Those aren't exactly attractive qualities."

Arcady actually laughed. "You're right about that, Miss Frayne. And I think you make a good point about him supposedly being a veteran. I'd like to have a look at his war record. We'll get on to it tomorrow."

He yawned, a wide unprotected yawn. "I'm bagged. I'll have to get a constable to come over and keep guard until we can search everything more thoroughly in daylight. Tell Mrs. What's-her-name that we need to lock up this room. While you're talking to her, ask if she remembers Klein getting any visitors recently."

Arcady leaned against the wall, removed his hat, and rubbed at his forehead with his handkerchief. "I think I'm coming down with something. Don't come too close, Miss Frayne."

No danger there. I was certainly feeling more friendly toward him, but we hadn't got as far as a hug and a kiss.

He wiped his face again. He was definitely looking pale and sweaty.

Parrish gazed at him with concern. "Maybe you should go home, sir. Miss Frayne and I can call on the others on the list. There are only four. I'll report back to you."

Arcady chewed on his lip. "Maybe you're right. Skip the woman with TB. If she's got consumption, she probably wouldn't have the strength to stick scissors in Klein's chest. Who's nearest to here?"

I checked. "Miriam Cohen lives at number sixty-four D'Arcy."

"Did I interview her?"

"You did. An attractive young woman. Nicely dressed. She's the one you allowed to leave early."

I swear my voice was as neutral as cold rice pudding, but Arcady scowled in response.

"I have learned to trust my gut in these matters, Miss Frayne. I don't think she's our guilty party."

"Is your gut pointing at anyone in particular?"

"I told you, my money is on the commie. Lishman. Why were we planning to visit the Cohen woman? She's still employed, isn't she?"

"She is. Because she left early and we hadn't heard from Miss Koenig yet, I wondered if we needed to speak to her further."

He grunted.

"Ruby's statement could be very helpful don't you think?" interjected Parrish. "If Klein was expecting to meet her at seven, he would have unlocked the door then. She says when she arrived at eight, the door was already locked. That's a narrow window of time and we can pinpoint alibis more definitely."

Arcady took his cigarette case from his pocket and started the ritual of lighting up. He didn't offer one to Parrish.

"Assuming she's not lying."

"Why would she lie?" I asked.

"They do, Miss Frayne. People lie all the time."

"What would you like us to do, sir?" Parrish got back into the conversation. "I can drive you home and Miss Frayne and I can continue."

Arcady waved his hand. "You don't need to take me home. A walk will clear my head. Like she says, D'Arcy Street is closest. Go see if you can get any further with Miss Cohen."

It was a relief to leave this pathetic room and go back downstairs.

Mrs. Liddell was waiting for us in the hall. "Well?"

Arcady answered. "A police constable will be arriving shortly to seal the room. Tomorrow there will be other members of the investigative team. In the meantime, you must not enter that room or touch anything that is in there. Or allow any other person to enter or handle anything. Is that clear, ma'am?"

He was addressing her in a very stern voice. It actually seemed to work. At least it appeared that way at first; but, after a brief moment, she said, "This coming and going is very bad for my business. I hope I will be compensated.

I am a widow after all."

For once Arcady answered diplomatically. "We'll talk about all that sort of thing at a later date, ma'am." He tipped his hat. "Thank you for your co-operation."

We left.

Arcady stuck to his decision to walk and Parrish and I climbed into the car.

"Hope the old man doesn't keel over before he gets home," said Parrish as we drove off. He sounded genuinely concerned.

CHAPTER TWENTY-FIVE

D'ARCY STREET WAS only a block away and within five minutes we pulled up at number sixty-four. There was a light shining in the front room. When we walked up the path and knocked on the front door, it was opened immediately.

A woman greeted us. She was in a functional, flowered house dress and white pinafore. The resemblance between her and Miriam was unmistakable. Same dark eyes and brown, wavy hair. Nice complexion.

"Mrs. Cohen? I'm Detective Parrish from the Toronto constabulary and this is Miss Charlotte Frayne. We would like to have a word with your daughter, Miriam, if she's at home."

Alarm raced across the woman's face. "No, Miriam is not at home. Can I help you with anything? She's told me about what happened at her work. Has there been an arrest?"

"Not yet. We're still pursuing lines of enquiry."

Parrish had a polite way of speaking. I thought he'd go far in the police department. Maybe, like Jack Murdoch, he was an example of the new order. Respectful, diligent, not provocative.

"I don't know where Miriam is, Officer. She said she was going out for the evening and she wouldn't be late. She likes to go to the pictures some nights. That's where she might be. Are you sure there's nothing I can help with? She was upset by what happened and I'd rather not have to bother her if it's not necessary."

"Of course, I quite understand."

"Was she at home last night?" I asked.

"Oh, yes. One of the kiddies is sick and she sat with him while I had a rest."

"What time was that, ma'am?"

"All evening. She got home at half past six, had her supper, and went and sat with Rolf until we all went to bed at ten."

Her recital had a rehearsed quality to it, and I thought Mrs. Cohen was the kind of woman who would die in the flames before she would betray a loved one. Her face had become flushed and she was twiddling with the ties of her house dress. "Perhaps you could pass along that Mr. Rosenthal is giving everybody tomorrow off," said Parrish.

Again, the expression on Mrs. Cohen's face was one of alarm. Parrish picked it up. "Mr. Rosenthal has said he will compensate all of the employees for loss of their wages."

Her relief was palpable. "I'll tell her."

We left her. She stayed in the doorway, watching us until I could no longer see her.

If she was lying on her daughter's behalf, I had to wonder why. And what truth she might be hiding.

CHAPTER TWENTY-SIX

"WHO'S NEXT?" PARRISH asked.

"Terry Porter is listed as living on Beverley Street and that should be just on the corner. We can go from his abode over to Masefield, who is on McCaul Street."

"Can we walk? I hate trying to park that bloody car. It would be easier to dock a battleship."

I was getting fed up with splashing around in inhospitable weather, but I didn't protest. The police car was not exactly a smooth ride. To compare it to the trot of a lame mule was to do that animal a disservice.

We walked briskly and number eighty-four Beverley was indeed just south of the corner. The house could have been mistaken for a shed it was so small, wedged between a set of apartments on one side and a dilapidated house on the other. There was a tiny porch in front that looked as torn up as a battlefield. Parrish went up first, I followed carefully behind. He knocked hard on the door.

There was no response. He was about to pound again when the door opened.

"Got here as fast as I could, mate. Did you think I was sitting behind the door waiting in anticipation?"

The speaker was a young man, dark-haired and lightly bearded.

Parrish went for a polite mode. "Beg pardon, sir. I'm Detective Parrish and this is Miss Frayne. I wonder if we could ask you a few questions concerning an investigation we're conducting."

"Did Mrs. Chandler lose her dog again?"

"No. More serious than that. This is an investigation into a homicide."

The rain had increased its tempo. "Do you mind if we come and chat?" Parrish asked.

"As a matter of fact, I do mind. My mother is ill and she's sleeping. Just a minute."

He stepped back into the house and reached for a waterproof. Pulling it over his shoulders, he came onto the porch.

"Who's dead and why do you want to talk to me?"

"I understand you were employed at Superior Ladies' Clothes shop recently."

"That's right." He gave an exaggerated guffaw and slapped himself on the knee. "Don't tell me old Rosie finally got what's been coming to him? Somebody got fed up with being exploited and mistreated? Knocked him on the noggin, did they?"

Parrish glanced over at me. "Would you answer that, Miss Frayne."

I didn't know if he'd tossed the ball to me because he

was losing his patience or if he wanted to play the old police game of good cop, bad cop. I presumed I was stepping in as bad cop.

"It's not Mr. Rosenthal who has been murdered, it's Oscar Klein, the supervisor."

Porter stared at me. "Too bad."

"Too bad it's not Mr. Rosenthal?"

"You got it right, ma'am."

"We understand Mr. Klein was not well liked by the employees. How did you feel about him?"

For answer, Porter kicked the lintel. "Might as well ask me what I feel about this piece of wood. Nothing. I don't care one way or the other. I wasn't there long enough to have an opinion."

He made motions to return into the house. "If that's all you want, I'm going back inside."

"One question, Mr. Porter. Would you mind telling us where you were last evening between seven and eight o'clock?"

He made an exaggerated gesture. This time as if he were pondering the question. "I don't have a lot of appointments these days. I believe I was here in the house with my mother. I think we were listening to the wireless together."

"And she will verify that?"

"Of course. But you're not going to ask her tonight. She's just fallen asleep." He might have been talking about a baby.

Parrish took over. Good cop now.

"We wouldn't dream of doing that, sir. All I ask is that sometime tomorrow at your own convenience, you come to the police station so we can get your fingerprints. I'm sure you understand we have to rule out the prints of any employees."

"Killed in the shop, was he?"

I'd been wondering when he'd ask that question. It was a natural one to ask.

"Yes, he was."

Porter didn't follow up with what I considered to be another natural question. How did he die? Perhaps he guessed we couldn't answer that.

Parrish tipped his hat. "Thank you for your co-operation, sir. If anything occurs to you that might help us with our investigation, please let us know."

"Your name is again?"

"Parrish. You can reach me at headquarters. We're over on College Street."

Porter nodded and stepped back into the house, treating me as if I had suddenly become invisible.

As he closed the door, I called out, "Goodnight."

He did not respond.

Parrish and I proceeded down the front steps to the street; I almost tripped over a raised board and he caught my arm to steady me.

"What do you think?" he asked.

"As my boss, Mr. Gilmore, has said to me many times,

'Just because somebody is a nasty chap doesn't mean he's a criminal. There are some nice fellows behind bars.'"

Parrish laughed. "Got under your skin, did he?"

"Sorry. I'm afraid he did."

"It happens. You have to guard against it. It's what his type wants. Anyway, I didn't have any particular feeling myself. He was wary. He's familiar with police protocol. He didn't seem that shocked to hear about Klein's death, but that could mean anything. Like he said, sheer indifference."

"I wonder if he'd have performed a little dance of joy if it had been Mr. Rosenthal?"

"Probably."

I realized that was the reason Porter had got to me. I liked Saul Rosenthal. I accepted he was many-faceted. Lesson learned.

"Okay. Who's next?"

"Thomas Masefield lives on McCaul Street. It should be just around the corner."

"Another corner?"

"Hey, I didn't put them there."

CHAPTER TWENTY-SEVEN

THE HOUSE WAS indeed just around the corner. Initially, I thought it was completely dark, but as we walked up to the door I glimpsed a light shining through the curtains of the front window.

There was a wreath of artificial poppies pinned to the door, somewhat woebegone as a result of the constant drizzle. Parrish tugged on the bell. I could hear it clanging into the depths of the house.

Nothing happened. He tugged again. We heard somebody shout from inside. A male voice.

"Coming! Hold your horses. I'm coming."

The door opened. A man stood on the threshold. The light was behind him and at first it was hard to make him out, except that he seemed abnormally short. He took an awkward step forward and I realized that he had no legs from the knees down and he was standing on artificial feet.

"Yes?"

The voice was surly.

"We'd like to speak to Mr. Masefield. Is he at home?"

"Who are you?"

"I'm Detective Parrish from the Toronto constabulary. This is Miss Frayne, who is assisting me."

"What do you want with Masefield?"

"Do you mind if we step inside? We're getting soaked out here."

I was so glad he'd asked, but whether or not the man would let us in hung in the balance.

I made an attempt to be conciliatory. "I see you're a veteran, sir."

I could see his face more clearly now. Perhaps once, like Gerald Jessop, he had been a handsome fellow, but in his case it wasn't scars that had spoiled his looks. It was years of bitterness and disappointment that had drawn deep lines on his face. And heavy drinking.

"How'd you figure that out?"

My little attempt at being nice had fallen flat. Worse, it had made him even angrier.

"I'm sorry. I didn't mean to be intrusive."

"Ha. It's always a toss-up between those dolts who pretend there is nothing wrong with me and those parasites who want all the gory details." He adopted a contemptuous tone of voice. "'You poor, poor man. What ever happened to your poor, poor legs?' So which is it? Which kind of idiot are you?"

I did feel badly for the man's disabilities, but frankly I don't like to be made a scapegoat for somebody's rage, justified or not. This was getting off to an even worse start than the interview with Porter.

"I hope neither."

Parrish stepped in. "Now, sir. We're just doing our job. No reason to be insulting. At this moment I'm not asking for your life history. We are here to talk to Thomas Masefield."

"Why?"

"As part of a police investigation."

"What sort of investigation? Is Draper hunting down the Reds again?"

I decided to take over. Good cop. "We are here on official business, sir. We would like to speak to Mr. Masefield because the superintendent at the place where he worked has died under suspicious circumstances and we are conducting an investigation."

"You're saying he was murdered?"

"It looks like that."

The man was jolted.

"Surely you don't think it was Tom?"

"Not at all. We are talking to all of the employees of the company past and present."

"I see. Well he's not home right now." He stared at me. "Come inside if you're coming. It's perishing out there."

He moved back into the hall. An awkward penguin-like movement that looked as if it took a lot of effort.

We stepped in. He hopped onto a stool beside the coat stand.

"May we get your name?" Parrish asked.

"My name's Donald Dunham. Dunham with an 'h.'"

"You live here, I presume."

"You presume correctly, I live here with all the other discards." He scowled. "This is a boarding house for war veterans. The city hands out a pittance so we won't clamour at the doors of the city hall and ask for fair pensions." He raised his shoulders. "It's better than standing on the street corners holding your tin cup with a card around your neck saying 'Ex-soldier.'" He focussed on me. "And in case you were wondering, but were afraid to ask, I lost both my legs at the battle of Vimy Ridge. We were saving the Empire from the wicked Huns. Nobody cares about that now, do they? Germany's getting itself ready for another war. And this one, they'll win."

"Mr. Dunham, I thank you for your sacrifice. I hope what you are saying won't happen."

I meant what I said and rather to my surprise, his expression softened.

"You look like drowned rats. I was just mashing some tea. Come on to my room and I'll give you a cuppa."

Parrish shook his head. "Thank you, but we'll only be a few minutes. I have to get back to the station."

My point of view was considerably different; I thought a more intimate chat might render some information about the mysterious Mr. Masefield that would benefit both the investigation into the murder of Klein and my investigation on behalf of Mrs. Jessop.

I spoke to Parrish. "Look, Detective. It's been a long day. You go on ahead, I'll stay and have a cup of tea with

Mr. Dunham."

Parrish hesitated, but I was in a rather ambiguous position in terms of officialdom. If I wanted to stay with Mr. Dunham, there was no reason I couldn't.

"I'll say good evening then. Miss Frayne."

"I'll see you tomorrow."

Rather reluctantly, he left.

Dunham hopped off his stool.

"Come on. I'm down the hall."

I followed him. My impression of this house was a far better one than the one I had formed of Mrs. Liddell's. The hall was fresh-smelling and well-lit by two overhead electric lights. The walls were painted a biscuit colour that was a good background to the numerous framed photographs that were hung. As far as I could tell, they were all of groups of men in army uniform. Dunham ushered me into his room.

"Welcome to my abode. Humble, but mine own. Please to have a seat."

His demeanour was much different now and he seemed to be genuinely pleased that I had taken him up on the offer of a cup of tea.

His room was somewhat larger than Klein's and infinitely more appealing. It was sparsely furnished, but a cheery fire flickered in the grate and two oil lamps gave off good light. Against one wall was a single day bed. Dunham appeared to have retained his army discipline and the edges of the cover were tightly tucked, but colourful cushions softened the lines. One low brown couch and two matching armchairs knew their place in the universe. A new-looking battery radio was playing softly.

I was about to sit down, but I noticed a set of deep shelves that lined the near wall on which were a half dozen doll's houses in various stages of development. There was a narrow table in front which was scattered with bits and pieces of wood and coloured paper.

"You've got quite a village there, Mr. Dunham. Is this your hobby?"

Dunham had shuffled over to a hot plate standing by the window to tend to the steaming kettle. He glanced over his shoulder and took note of where I was looking.

He grimaced. "I wouldn't call it a hobby. It's my work. I couldn't live on the pension I get, so I make these doll's houses and furniture. I sell them in the Kensington market once a month. Buys some groceries."

I took a closer look. The houses had been fashioned from cardboard boxes and they were each different, some fully furnished with tiny exquisite furniture, some not yet complete.

"It must take you a long time to create all of these."

"It does. This bunch I'll have to have done by the end of the month."

He manoeuvred himself over to me and pointed to an empty white box that might once have held shoes.

"I'm just starting on this one and I was considering making it into a hospital ward. I can put in about half a dozen patients, each with a different problem. The kiddies could nurse them. Cut off a leg or two or an arm? Then glue it back. They could have a blind patient or a deaf one. What do you think? Would it sell?"

For a moment I thought I might be dealing with a man who had truly lost his mind.

"It's hard to say. It is certainly a novel concept."

Then I realized he was grinning at me slyly. "Might teach children to have empathy, don't you think?"

I smiled back with relief as much as anything. "It might."

"Tea should be ready. Do you want milk and sugar?"

"Thanks, a little of both."

He lurched back to a tea wagon that was lined up near the hot plate while I took my place by the fire. One of the chairs was a rocker and I guessed that was Dunham's. I took the other one and, as unobtrusively as possible, I stretched out my legs closer to the fire. My shoes and stockings were damp; the heat was soothing.

Dunham wheeled the wagon over to me. Gran would have been impressed. The tea pot wore a red woollen cozy, the cups and saucers echoed Mr. Doulton's best blue and white. My host had even added a plate of biscuits. He poured the tea and handed me one of the cups. I took a sip. And almost spit it out. The tea was so strong and bitter and so laced with sugar that, as Gran would have said, you could have stood a spoon in it.

"Strong enough?"

"Er, yes, thank you."

He took a gulp from his own tea. "Old army habit. The Tommies I was with liked their tea very strong. First I thought it tasted like squirrel soup, but after a while I got used to drinking it like that." He indicated the biscuits. "Help yourself. I'd like to say I baked them myself but I didn't. No kitchen in the house. I get them from a bakery."

"How do you manage if you don't have a kitchen?"

"We go out. There's a blind soldiers' club just up the street. You don't have to be blind to go there. Just a former soldier. Get some grub if you need it."

I had another taste of the tea. In the interim it had evolved from squirrel soup to racoon stew. I chomped on a biscuit as fast as I could.

"How many men live in this house?"

"Six. Among the lot of us we've got two arms gone, four legs, one eye. Never mind the nerves, the feet, the lungs. But we manage."

I didn't know what to say; he wasn't asking for pity, just stating the facts.

"Do you think I'll be able to talk to Mr. Masefield tonight?"

"'Fraid not. He's on a leave of absence." His shoulders slumped. "Every so often, Tom falls into arrears with his rent. I function as the superintendent here. If that happens, I'm under instructions to lock him out. I'll make sure he's never thrown out completely, but we operate on a week-to-week basis and if he can't come up with the rent he can't stay here."

"What does he do, then?"

"Goes over to Pearson Hall. The blind soldiers' club. If they've got a space, they'll give him a bed for the night."

"And if they haven't?"

"He has to go over to the House of Providence or the city relief house. He's not got work to fall back on like me. Has to depend only on his pension. He gets the occasional job, but he's not strong so it usually don't last."

"I gather he was injured in the war as well?"

"Gassed. They said he'd recovered, but you never really do. His lungs are barely functioning." He pointed at my tea cup. "D'you want another?"

"No, no thanks. That was plenty."

"Put hair on your chest that will."

Out of politeness, I didn't say I didn't particularly want hair on my chest. I finished my biscuit.

"Mr. Dunham, you have been so kind. I should get going, but I wonder if I could just ask you a question before I do."

"Sure. I'm enjoying your company. Don't get to see much of the soft side of the world."

"The detective told you he was investigating the death of a man at a workplace on Spadina. It happened most likely between seven and eight o'clock last evening. Was Mr. Masefield at home then?"

He regarded me doubtfully. "I don't like answering questions about my friends."

"I understand. We have to ask everybody who was connected with Superior Ladies' Clothes. But if he was home, it gives him a solid alibi."

"Okay. Like I said, Tom has been staying off and on at Pearson Hall. But tell the truth, I was out myself yesterday. I went over to the Labour Lyceum on Spadina. We had a nice concert going on. I didn't get back until about ten o'clock. If he did come back in for a better kip, I wouldn't have known."

"And how long has he been away from home?"

"What's today, Tuesday? Been almost a week now. Had to close him out last Thursday."

"One more thing. Does the name Gerald Jessop mean anything to you?"

"No. Should it?"

"He, too, was a war vet. Got badly disfigured at Valenciennes. I believe he knew Mr. Masefield. and that they met recently."

Dunham drank more tea. "Tom has never mentioned him. Don't tell me this is another 'suspicious death,' as your detective put it?"

"Jessop has been declared a suicide."

"There's a lot of us end up like that," Dunham said with a sigh. "Put them in the trenches and shell them day in and day out and you won't find a tougher group of men, but bring them back to civilian life and they've got no purpose. People are kind enough, but them that wasn't there, can't understand. Some of our lads just can't deal with it. You'd think after all this time it would get easier, but it don't necessarily."

He put one of his artificial feet against the wooden fender so that the flames were only an inch away. The prosthetics were fixed into regular shoes I suppose for cosmetic reasons. I started to smell burning leather.

"Mr. Dunham, I think your shoes are singeing."

He laughed, enjoying his little drama. "Don't hurt."

"But you're going to ruin them."

That really made him laugh. "They're my second pair. The ministry says I won't get any more."

"All the more reason to take good care of them."

He withdrew his foot which I could see was blackened along the sole. It looked like this was something he did regularly.

"My feet always feel cold." He shrugged. "It's true. The medics call it phantom pain. Happens to a lot of fellows who've lost their parts."

Perhaps it was the schoolboy trick, but Dunham's face had relaxed. He could only have been in his late thirties, not much older than I. And I could see for the first time that he was quite good looking. His hair was cut short at the sides, military style, and the top was wavy.

"I hate to say it, Miss Frayne, but I do believe there's going to be another war before too long. And more good blokes will be destroyed. And more women will weep. We haven't learned anything."

He stamped his smoky feet on the floor as if to extinguish the flames.

CHAPTER TWENTY-EIGHT

I EXTRICATED MYSELF from Mr. Dunham as quickly after I finished the tea as I could. I would have liked to sit and talk more with him, but I was getting quite peckish. Cheese rolls and biscuits can only sustain life for so long. And, truth be told, I dreaded having to down another cup of his tea. Promising I would return, I left and I headed down Spadina intending to stop in at the Paradise.

Given I had my head tucked into my collar, I might have completely missed the man who was saying good-bye to a young woman at the door of one of the houses near the corner of Spadina and Bulwer. He was wheeling a bike onto the street and started to mount it. She called out to him.

"Good night, dear. See you tomorrow."

As he pedalled off, he passed under the light of the street lamp and I saw him clearly. Lo and behold, it was Sam Weaver.

As the woman closed the front door, I saw the house number. Thirty-one. This was on my list of addresses of employees who had left Superior Ladies' Clothes. This was where Alicia Tudsworth had lived. She, whose very name had brought a blush to young Joel's cheeks; she who had supposedly left to get married.

From the sense of intimacy I'd just witnessed between the two people, the man she had married, if indeed she had, was Sam Weaver.

Over at the Jessop household, there had been no mention of his nuptials, legitimate or otherwise. I guessed Mrs. Jessop didn't know he was maintaining a separate residence. Not only a residence, from the look of Alicia, it seemed that a family was on the way

I was tempted briefly to go and talk to her, but I didn't. If Sam wasn't acknowledging her to his employer, it wasn't likely she would betray his secret.

A gust of rain-soaked wind decided for me. I wanted to get indoors as fast as I could.

CHAPTER TWENTY-NINE

SHORTLY BEFORE I reached the café, I saw a crowd gathered outside. This wasn't the quiet exodus of customers departing. There was a police car parked at the curb and an officer was leaving the café carrying a large box. I should say more accurately, he was trying to leave because his path was blocked by two people who were gesticulating angrily. I recognized both of them. One was Miriam Cohen and the other was Wilf Morrow. Miriam was dressed for the outdoors, Wilf was not. The other person I recognized was Detective Jack Murdoch who was attempting some kind of amelioration of the situation. Gathered around, but at a safe distance, were several people, men and women, most of whom seemed to be on the side of Miriam and Wilf.

"Detective Murdoch, what's going on?"

He didn't have a chance to answer because Wilf yelled. "They're trying to prevent the lawful presentation of our play. They have no legal right to do that."

Jack, speaking calmly and reasonably, was the one who answered.

"We are not at this moment preventing you from presenting a play, Wilf, as you well know. The commissioner of police has received instructions that given the incendiary nature of this particular play that you are informing the public honestly and properly as to its exact nature." He looked over at me. "We are confiscating the pamphlets until such time as they are appraised for seditious content. When that process is concluded all the material will be returned."

Wilf's face was flushed with anger. "Or not. And I'll bet you will make sure nothing is decided until it is too late. We need to inform the public that the play is opening."

A sort of rumble went through the crowd. It wasn't an ugly group, but it certainly seemed to have the potential to get that way.

"I give you my word I will expedite this as fast as possible."

Miriam frowned at him. "You might be a decent enough cop, but that's not a guarantee you can do what you promise. We all know Draper has bloodshot eyes. He sees Red everywhere."

She was playing to the galleries and they laughed.

"What if you can't do what you say you'll do?"

Jack looked at her. "I can't answer to 'what ifs.' I've said all I'm going to say, especially as we're all getting wet and cold. If you and Wilf will stand aside and let my officer through, I'll come indoors and we can talk about this some more."

It was interesting watching Jack deal with the situation. He wasn't placating them or pleading, "I'm just a bloke doing my job," which I thought would have stirred up contempt in some of the onlookers. He was making his position clear and behind him was a lot of authority.

Miriam and Wilf hesitated briefly, then they moved out of the way of the constable who immediately hurried over to the police car.

"Thank you," said Jack. "Let's go in, shall we?"

I could see Gramps hovering on the other side of the door, but Pearl and Calvin seemed to have disappeared.

Jack turned to the crowd. "Excitement's over folks. I suggest you get on home where it's surely warmer than out here."

They began to disburse and straggle off, except for one man I'd noticed on the fringes. He called over to Miriam.

"Want me to join you, Miss Cohen? I'm always up for a good chin wag."

He was rather shabby and could do with a shave and hair cut, but his voice was not the least shabby. In fact, as Gramps might have put it, he spoke with a posh accent. This was the same man I'd seen last night talking to Miriam and Wallace Workman.

Jack regarded him doubtfully and I thought he was about to refuse, but the man said, "This isn't in any way a legally defined meeting is it, Detective? As long as nobody has any objection, I believe I have the right to be present."

Miriam had been about to enter the café, but she stopped and walked back to us quickly.

"It's all right, Detective Murdoch. This man is a good friend of mine. I have no objection to his being present. If Miss Frayne is going to join us there is no reason why Mr. Masefield cannot." Her emphasis on my name made it obvious what she thought. Not much I could do about that. I hoped I'd have a chance to tell her why I had been at the shop yesterday.

The man put out his hand in a friendly fashion.

"Tom Masefield."

"Murdoch," said Jack and they shook hands.

"All right, let's go," said Jack and we all headed into the café.

Once inside, Wilf stepped up as host. "Let's sit over here," he said. "Mr. Frayne, you have this chair. Miriam, sit here. Detective, why don't you sit at the head? Charlotte, take this one. Mr. Masefield, I'll get you a chair."

To my astonishment, I saw my grandfather slip a rolling pin onto the counter. He'd been holding it at the ready behind his back. I wasn't sure who he was prepared to bonk on the head.

We hung up our coats and got ourselves settled into our chairs. Wilf spoke up, addressing Jack.

"You said we've got your word you'll get his matter settled as soon as possible." He reached behind him to a side table where there was a pamphlet that had been left behind. He slapped it down in front of Jack. "Now tell me what's seditious about this."

The pamphlet depicted a row of chained men being shoved toward a jail by a sadistic-looking guard who was holding a gun.

Jack picked up the pamphlet. "It says here, '*Eight Men Speak* remounted for the first time in Toronto since it was brutally suppressed three years ago by the chief constable who was afraid of the truth. Injustice must never go unchallenged. Join us to watch the play and express your solidarity in our fight against tyranny.'"

"That doesn't sound too seditious to me," said Miriam.

Masefield moved in. "As the detective is no doubt well aware, this place is not a public theatre. It will be strictly a private performance, put on for invited guests. No licence is required, nobody is breaking the law." He smiled. "All of the players will be fully clothed. Not a frilly pair of knickers in sight."

Jack sighed. "The pamphlet will have to be examined by police lawyers."

Gramps was looking most upset at this point. "What if they decide the pamphlets are seditious? That's a serious crime. What would happen?"

"Let's cross that bridge when we come to it," said Jack.

Masefield spoke up. "It would be too costly and protracted for the police department to bring a charge against the café on such flimsy evidence. 'Express your solidarity' can mean nothing more inflammatory than waving your arms in the air and shouting, 'Yes!'"

Gramps looked over at him. "You're a fellow who seems to know what you're talking about. Lawyer, are you?"

Masefield smiled again. He actually had a pleasant smile and the deep lines that scoured his face temporarily vanished. "No, not a lawyer. Just somebody with experience in the ways of the law."

I must admit I was transfixed for the moment. I could only guess at what that experience had been. Donald Dunham said Masefield had been gassed in the war, which was why he wasn't strong enough to work at Superior Ladies' Clothes. I thought it was most unlikely he knew about Gerald's death as nothing had been made public. Pearl said they had greeted each other like long-lost pals. Were they?

I was brought back from my reverie by Jack rising from his chair.

"As I said, I will get back to you as soon as I can, Wilf."

"Shall I go ahead with the play or not?"

"I don't see why not. Maybe hold off on handing out the pamphlets for now. Just tell people to tell their friends. You'll get a good crowd."

"We can only hold forty people, max. The first production had fifteen hundred. We're not going to start a revolution with forty people."

Gramps shook his head. "Jesus had only twelve followers and he started a revolution."

"And look what happened to him. He was crucified," said Masefield.

We all grinned a little nervously. Was this a joke?

Jack got his coat and headed for the door. "Good night everybody." He turned around. "You might not all believe me, but I'm a big supporter of justice."

CHAPTER THIRTY

THERE WAS SILENCE for a few moments. Masefield spoke first.

"The good detective may see himself as a supporter of justice, but his concept of what that means and ours might not be the same."

Wilf rubbed at his hair which was already springing up from his head. He looked as if he had encountered an electric live wire.

"At least he said we could go ahead with the play. So we will."

"What does Hilliard have to say about this?" I asked.

"Not much. He's too caught up with his family problems."

"But he thought it would be better to open the Cave with some musical entertainment."

I knew all too well Wilf had seized on Hilliard's absence to put on this play. They'd been bickering about it for weeks.

"We can do that later, when he gets back. By the way, Hill asked me to tell you that he'd be away for at least another week. He'll call or write as soon as he can."

I wished he'd picked a different time to tell me this. I nodded, aware that Miriam had taken in the conversation.

She, too, was preparing to leave, smoothing at her hair that didn't need smoothing. She addressed me.

"I presume you are not in fact in need of a job at Superior Ladies' Clothes, Miss Frayne? You are employed by the police department?"

"Actually, I'm a private investigator."

"So, you were there to investigate?"

"Yes. I'm sorry I had to be there under false pretenses, but there was no alternative."

"Really?" Her tone was acid with sarcasm. "Did this have anything to do with what transpired?"

"I don't know yet."

She walked over to get her coat from the rack by the door. Wilf jumped up to help her. I noticed Miriam Cohen seemed to have that effect on men. She brought out a powerful impulse toward gallantry. This seemed never to happen to me.

Coat suitably on, she called out goodbyes and left. Wilf came back to the table.

"Splendid woman. She'd face down a marauding tiger without blinking."

"She's faced worse than tigers," said Masefield. "At least they tend to be afraid of us humans."

Perhaps unreasonably so, all these metaphors were irritating me. I decided to face my own challenges.

"Wilf, I know it's getting late, but I wondered if you'd mind if I had a few words with Mr. Masefield in private."

"Sure. I've got to clean up the kitchen. I think Calvin is still in there."

"I'll help," jumped in Gramps. "Come and get me when you're done, Lottie."

Masefield had slipped back into his guarded expression.

"I hope you don't mind, Mr. Masefield? Believe it or not I was trying to find you earlier tonight."

"Me? Why?"

I waited until Wilf and Gramps had retreated into the kitchen before answering.

"The supervisor at Superiors, Oscar Klein, was killed sometime last night. I have been helping the police to investigate."

I gave him a moment to react, but he didn't.

He replied calmly, "I've actually had this news from Miriam. Suspicion has inevitably fallen upon the employees has it?"

"Not exactly. There is an issue about the murderer having access to the building, so the police are questioning everybody who was working there. You were an employee until fairly recently, were you not?"

"I was indeed, Miss Frayne. Now let me guess. You would like to know what my relationship was like with Klein. How did we get along and so forth? Just in case I resented being dismissed at such short notice and felt moved to exact revenge and kill him? Is that not so?"

"That's right. Were you? Full of resentment?"

"Let's put it this way, Miss Frayne. Loading heavy bolts of cloth from one place to another isn't exactly my idea of an exciting job. I didn't grieve for it."

"But you were let go with no notice to speak of. That must have been hard without an income to fall back on."

I admit I was being a bit devious. I'd got this from his housemate, Donald Dunham. Masefield regarded me for rather a long time. I tried not to quail.

"Klein was only the mouthpiece of Saul Rosenthal," Masefield continued. "You could say I despised him, but thatis too strong a word. You don't despise a dog that barks at you because it has been ordered to do so. You don't have contempt for the ventriloquist's dummy. Oscar Klein was a stupid man who used his little bit of power to get what he wanted. He thought he was much more important than he was. Rosenthal craves to be seen as a good and fair man. He is not. There is one motivation for everything he does. That is to make as much money as he possibly can off the sweat and toil of his employees. He sees his company the way other people see their car. Is it working efficiently? Good, we'll keep it. If not, then we must simply discard the parts that are malfunctioning and replace them with parts that do work."

Talking about facing down tigers, there was something about Tom Masefield that was definitely scary. Physically, he didn't look very strong, he was too thin and pale-faced, but there was an expression behind his eyes that made me nervous. It wasn't coldness exactly, although that was there, it was more the sense that nothing would move him from his convictions. He had the eyes of a fanatic.

"It does seem that Mr. Klein was killed sometime between seven and eight o'clock last evening. Do you mind telling me where you were during that time?"

He actually laughed. "Of course, I mind. You have no authority at all to ask me this."

He was right of course. "In other words, you won't tell me."

"Correct. If the detective wants to question me, he should do it himself."

It was his turn to rise from his chair. "It's time I went home. I'm tired."

"One more thing, Mr. Masefield. I have also been hired to investigate a case unrelated to this one. You don't have to answer my questions on this matter either, but I would appreciate it if you would."

He raised his eyebrow.

"I understand you are acquainted with a man named Gerald Jessop?"

Again, I got the wary look.

"Might be. What of it?"

"Did you know he has died?"

That did elicit a response.

"What! No, I did not know. When?"

"Last Thursday."

"What happened?"

"His death has been determined to be a suicide."

"I see."

He turned his head and for a brief moment I thought tears had come to his eyes, but I might have been mistaken about that.

"What were the circumstances?"

"He ingested morphia and alcohol."

"They're sure that's what happened?"

"That's the coroner's verdict, but his mother and wife won't accept it. Mrs. Jessop senior has hired me to confirm or refute that verdict."

I waited, letting him absorb all of this.

Finally, he took out a handkerchief and blew his nose. The male equivalent of wiping away embarrassing tears.

"Did he leave a note?"

"Yes. His intention seemed clear. His life had become intolerable."

There was a momentarily distracting burst of laughter from the kitchen. Masefield coughed harshly, almost losing his breath completely. He put away the handkerchief, his own softness rebuked and stowed.

"You knew him during the war, did you?"

"Let's say we were in the same battalion at the same time."

"I understand you encountered each other here in the café. After the war, you'd lost touch I presume."

"I hadn't seen him since demobilization. I haven't been living on this side of the country for a long time."

"Was it a chance encounter? Here in the Paradise?"

Masefield was staring at me. "What do you want from me, Miss Frayne?"

"The night you met him here was the night he killed himself. When you saw him, did you suspect he was in a distressed state of mind?"

Masefield's eyes darkened. "Who isn't distressed these days, Miss Frayne? If you're not, you're stupid."

"Pearl says you left together."

"We did. We walked and talked, and I deposited him at his house. I can see you are going to ask me what time that was?"

"I ..."

He didn't let me finish. "It was almost nine o'clock. I just had time to get over to Pearson Hall before they closed the doors. I was planning to spend the night there. They take pity on former soldiers."

"And you weren't worried about Mr. Jessop?"

"If you mean did I suspect he was suicidal, no I did not. I was sorry to see the war had so injured him, as it did to thousands of others. All now trapped in the No Man's Land of public indifference." He stood up. "If you will excuse me, I will say goodnight."

He started to head for the door.

I called after him. "Mr. Masefield, would you like to be notified about the funeral arrangements?"

He turned around. "I think not. I have no desire to grieve a coward."

How's that for an exit line?

At that moment Gramps popped his head around the kitchen door.

"All done?"

"Yes. I'm all done."

"Did you find out what you needed to?"

"I suppose I did, Gramps."

"That chap didn't look too happy."

"He wasn't."

If I'd had a small fortune, I'd have gladly handed it over to Tom Masefield. But I didn't have one and I also knew money wouldn't alleviate the despair he carried within him.

CHAPTER THIRTY-ONE

B Y SHEER LUCK Gramps and I managed to hail a taxi just returning from a fare. The driver grumbled about having to turn around as he was heading for home, but I charmed him with a smile and the promise of a dollar tip. Gramps and I piled into the car and out of the rain. We had to wait until we got home and went inside before I could fill him in on what had happened this long day.

"My, oh, my," said Gramps. "And I thought my day was filled with drama."

"Why? Did you spill the soup? Did somebody else spill the soup and demand their money back?"

"You may jest. What happened was sort of like that. Somebody did complain about the soup. He demanded to see the cook. Calvin came out and the man insulted him. Called him a stupid black you-know-what. Said he'd never be able to eat here again as long as they had a negro cook. Although that wasn't the word he actually used."

"Good grief, Gramps. What came of it?"

"I said that seeing as how he didn't like his soup, we

might as well get rid of it and I poured it over his trousers."

"You didn't."

"I did. It wasn't terribly hot, so it didn't scald his private parts, more's the pity. But he was not happy. He left in a huff."

I had to laugh.

"I know it's nowhere in the same league as a murdered man, but at the time it was quite dramatic."

"I'll bet it was. How did Calvin take it?"

"He didn't say much, but I know he was humiliated. When I went to speak to him after, he said it happens sometimes. He's learned to keep out of sight."

I felt badly about this incident. I liked Calvin a lot. He didn't deserve that kind of treatment.

"Are you going back to the café tomorrow, Gramps?"

"I am. I told Wilf I'd fill in until Hilliard came back."

"What's your feeling about this play that's causing all the trouble?"

"Me, I'd rather watch some lively singing and dancing, but if Wilf wants to do the play, it's up to him. I'm looking forward to playing my part. I've never been on stage before."

He yawned. "I'm up the wooden hill, Lottie. Good luck with your investigation. Promise me you'll be careful."

"Of course, Gramps. In terms of the Oscar Klein case I'm not really involved. Just the note taker."

Who was I trying to kid?

CHAPTER THIRTY-TWO

I WAS WOKEN up by the sound of a loud shout from downstairs. After a few moments, the shout was repeated. I grabbed my robe and hurried down to the kitchen. Gramps was standing by the stove, pointing at the wall.

"Guilty!"

"Gramps. What on earth are you doing?"

"I'm practising for the play."

"It's only a quarter past seven."

"Oops. Sorry, pet. Didn't mean to wake you up."

He was wearing his ratty, old robe and his hair was sticking out in tufts from his head. I was irritated at being robbed of an hour's sleep, especially after yesterday, but I hadn't seen him that happy since before Gran died.

"That's okay. I'll live."

He put down the paper he was holding. "Shall I make you a pot of coffee?"

"Make that a bucket."

I sat down at the table while he busied himself at the stove and glanced at the script. He had the part of one of the proletariats who had to point at the slimy character named "Capitalism" and cry "Guilty." He'd already marked his line with red pencil.

"Do you want me to give you your cue?"

"Don't be sarcastic, Lottie. It's not that hard. I know when to say my bit."

"I wasn't being sarcastic, Gramps. That one word is a lot to practice."

I grinned at him as I said this and he responded by bursting out laughing.

"All right. So I'm overdoing it. But I've never been in a play before. I want to get the right tone."

"True. Have you read through the entire script yet?"

"Not yet. I was going to do that this morning."

"You know it was banned for, quote, 'fomenting sedition,' a couple of years ago. It's considered Communist propaganda. Are you all right with that, Gramps?"

Arnie Frayne's politics leaned to the right. He was keen on personal responsibility and hated anything he construed as mollycoddling by the government. We'd had many lively discussions on the subject. But he was full of contradictions, my grandfather. Gran had said he had a heart of mush and it was true. Out-and-out begging wasn't allowed in the city, but Gramps never failed to slip some money to a derelict on the street if he felt he needed it.

"Of course, I'm all right with it. Hopefully it will get people thinking."

"Especially if they hear you shout 'guilty' like that."

"Doing a good job, am I?"

"James Cagney himself couldn't do better."

"Cagney? I was thinking more of Gary Cooper myself. The strong, honest type. Not to mention he's better looking."

He swivelled around, pointed at the stove and shouted, "Guilty!"

* * *

MY EARS BUZZING from Gramps's potent cups of coffee, I practically ran up Yonge Street to the Arcade. I needed to get the blood moving in my veins against the chill. The dull, overcast sky indicated more rain was on the way.

I made myself run up to our floor. Darn, another light was out near the door to the office. The caretakers were not what I'd call attentive and unless I changed the bulb myself, the light would probably be out for several days.

I wished we could move to a better place, but Mr. Gilmore was reluctant. "People know where to find me." That was true, but I thought there were also benefits to taking an office that projected a more affluent image.

Thinking of Mr. Gilmore reminded me that, so far, I hadn't put any energy into finding accommodations for the mysterious relatives he was bringing from Munich. I'd better get on to that today.

Just as I was turning the key in the lock, the telephone rang. I scrambled to answer. I lifted the receiver while at the same time taking a deep breath so I could convey calm and serenity.

"Gilmore and Associates, Charlotte Frayne speaking."

"Miss Frayne. I apologize for ringing you so early, but something has come up and I need to speak to you." It was Mrs. Jessop.

"Of course."

"I wondered if I could prevail on you to come to the house right away. I'd would prefer to deal with this in person."

"Of course."

"I can send the car for you. Will that be all right?"

When would a luxury Packard not be all right?

"Thank you, that would be excellent."

"Would nine o'clock be suitable?"

"Quite suitable."

She paused and I could almost see her struggling to keep her feelings under control.

"Mrs. Jessop, can you give me some indication of what has transpired?"

"Early this morning, Ellen discovered that Gerald wrote a holograph will the night he died. According to our lawyer whom we consulted this morning, such a thing is quite legal. It is definitely Gerald's handwriting."

"I see." Actually, I didn't; but I thought she was not to be rushed. "I gather this is a departure from his original will."

"Precisely. It seems that Gerald has bequeathed his entire estate to someone he refers to as an old friend. A man we have never heard of, nor seen. A man called Thomas Masefield."

CHAPTER THIRTY-THREE

T HE NOW-FAMILIAR smell of the interior of the Packard greeted me as Wilson opened the door for me to climb in. I thought there was a fresh overlay of tobacco and I assumed the chauffeur was the smoker. He hadn't fixed the windshield wipers as yet; they still squeaked. The morning hadn't given up the intention of being the most miserable day of November, but at least it hadn't started to rain.

I wasn't sure how much Wilson knew about this new occurrence and I was contemplating how to be discreet when he saved me the trouble.

"I thought we had laid everything to rest, but not so. The house is in an uproar."

"I can understand why. Another shock."

He turned a corner but, so distracted, he didn't notice the huge puddle near the curb and ran right through it, splashing a well-dressed couple standing on the sidewalk. On his behalf, I said, "So sorry." Wilson glanced in his side mirror, saw what had happened and shrugged.

"They should know to stand back."

I let him proceed a little further. "Mrs. Jessop has told me about this new will. Where was it found?"

"Inside the piano. Miss Ellen decided she'd practice. She likes to play when she can. Mr. Gerald's piano has a good sound. At least that's what she says. Me, I think it makes her feel in touch with him even now."

Given his callousness about soaking the pedestrians we'd just passed, this was quite a sensitive remark.

"What do you mean the will was inside the piano?"

"Exactly that. It was placed behind the keys. She started to play and realized some of the keys were jammed. She checked inside the lid and found the envelope."

"Has Mrs. Jessop told you what the will said?"

"Oh, yes. She got us all together and read it out loud. Shocker that was. Not that it affects me as such. I work for Mrs. J. She's already settled a pension on Greta and me."

"Did it affect anybody in the household?"

"If you consider his wife to be a member of the household, yes, it did. She was cut out completely. I'm sure she'll be all right. Mrs. J. will look after her, but considering she'd have got a lot of money from the original will, this was a shocker. A slap in the face really. I know I'd be pretty upset if Greta died and cut me out of her will. I'd wonder what I'd done to offend her. If you see what I mean, Miss Frayne. Sort of like Shakespeare leaving his wife the second-best bed."

The man was full of surprises.

"Was anybody else affected would you say?"

"Sam Weaver of course. He's been Mr. Gerald's valet for years. Since the army days. Mr. Gerald was very dependent on him. He wouldn't have heard of him leaving even if he'd wanted to."

"And did he?"

"I beg your pardon, I'm not sure what you mean?"

"Did Mr. Weaver ever express the desire to branch out? Get married for instance?"

"Never. He always said Mr. Gerald needed him too much.'

"There are other valets in the city surely?"

Wilson shook his head. "It wasn't what you'd call an ordinary situation. Sam Weaver was Mr. Gerald's bat-man during the war. He looked after him when he was injured like a mother would look after her child. Mind you, Mrs. Jessop made sure he was paid handsomely. As I say, it's not the money so much as the implications."

He had a point. I was just trying to sort all this out. Never mind all the stuff about Sam being too devoted to leave the Jessops. He'd got himself a wife on the side.

"One more question, Mr. Wilson. Have you heard about this old friend, Masefield?"

"Not a word. Mr. Gerald never had visitors. Any friends had dropped off long ago. He made it clear he didn't want company."

He fell silent and we were soon at the house. He got out to open the door. I walked up to the entrance. Strange how familiar it was beginning to look to me.

CHAPTER THIRTY-FOUR

THE MAID, DOLLY, took my hat and coat. "I'm glad you've come. The mistress is very upset. I am not sure of how much her constitution can withstand."

She led the way to the drawing room. Even through the closed door I could hear Mrs. Jessop's raised voice.

"This is intolerable. I cannot accept it."

Dolly tapped on the door and ushered me in. Ellen was sitting in the armchair, Mrs. Jessop standing near the fireplace. Sam Weaver was also standing. The little dog raced over to greet me, yapping wildly.

"Duffy. Stop that," called Sam. The dog barely hesitated, then continued to inform me as to just who was boss. Sam came over and, with another command, also ignored, he swept the dog up and returned to his place by the fireplace with Duffy tucked safely under his arm. After a couple of muffled reprimands in my direction, the dog subsided.

Mrs. Jessop greeted me. "Miss Frayne. Thank goodness you are here. We are in utter disarray. Please have a seat. Would you like some refreshment?"

I would have liked something, but declined. This was going to be an intense session and I didn't want to have to worry about balancing tea and cookies on my lap. I sat in the wing-back. Ellen nodded at me, but she looked if possible even worse than when I'd seen her last.

Mrs. Jessop picked up a piece of paper from the table and handed it to me.

"Ellen discovered this inside the piano. It is a holograph will. We intend to have it properly examined, but so far, it appears to be genuine. According to the date, Gerald wrote it the night he died."

I unfolded the paper.

October 29, 1936

I, Gerald Somerset Jessop, being of sound mind and body, do declare this to be my last will and testament to replace any previous will and testament that is now in existence. I hereby leave all of my goods and chattels to my friend, Thomas Masefield. He can be reached at number 25 McCaul Street in the city of Toronto, Canada. I trust that my executors will respect and honour my wishes.

Signed this twenty-ninth day of October,
the year of our Lord, 1936.

It certainly seemed genuine.

Mrs. Jessop picked up another sheet of paper and showed it to me.

"This was with it. Tell her, Ellen."

Ellen's voice was hardly more than a whisper. Fortunately she was seated close beside me. She looked as if a breath of wind would blow her quite away.

"Gerald loved music and even with his disability, he sometimes played for us."

"Difficult as you can imagine with three fingers missing," interrupted Mrs. Jessop. "Sorry. Please continue, Ellen."

"I haven't been sleeping very well since he died and I thought I might find some peace of mind if I sat for a time in his room. We've had to keep it locked for the police while they finish their investigation, so this was my first opportunity to be in Gerald's room alone." Tears began to roll down her cheeks. "I went to his piano. He seemed close when I sat on the bench. I started to play one of his favourite pieces. He wrote the words and music himself." She paused to wipe her eyes. She must have been referring to the music I'd seen. *Dreams Gone*.

She took a deep breath and went on. "I realized the notes didn't sound right. Some of them were jamming. I opened the lid to the piano and I could see there was something inside. It was an envelope, which I removed. It contained this will and a letter."

Mrs. Jessop thrust a piece of paper into my hands.

"This is what she's referring to."

I should add that Sam Weaver had not made a peep during this entire recitation. He was scratching the dog's head in an absent-minded way.

The letter was also dated October twenty-ninth. The handwriting started out neatly enough, but rapidly worsened until near the end it was almost undecipherable. Similarly, the content began in a fairly matter of fact way and descended into a wail from hell.

It seems only fair that I explain why I am changing my will. In my previous will I divided up my estate, leaving almost everything to my wife, Ellen. I no longer wish to do that. She will be more than adequately taken care of by the insurance policy that I have taken out. She is the beneficiary, together with Sam Weaver, my personal valet. I cannot imagine how I would have survived without his loving care.

I have left the policy in the hands of our lawyer Deacon. As for the bequests to the other servants which I listed in my previous will, I expect my mother to honour them. I am sure they will be well taken care of.

So why have I chosen to write this final testament? You will not know the man to whom I am leaving this money. Thomas Masefield was under my command during the battle of Valenciennes. This was where I received my own injury. But not before I had led four men to their deaths, something for which I cannot forgive myself. How vainglorious are the young. Private Masefield saw that I was struck and at risk to his own life he carried me to safety. He then returned to action and was subsequently gassed on the field. I was in no condition to take care of my duties for many months and was eventually told he had been discharged and returned to the place of his birth, Shropshire, England. I attempted to contact him, but with no success. I did not see him again. Until tonight. We met by chance, by sheer chance if there is such a thing, in a café where I go sometimes. I was sorry to see he had fallen on hard times. The gas had compromised his health to the point there is not much employment he can maintain. I want to ensure he has no such further worries. I knew he was an intelligent man, thoughtful beyond his station. I was right about that. He has great plans to change the world. As we all did back then. He wants to fight for equality for the poor and the working people who, together with our discarded soldiers, sacrifice so much they are barely surviving. I am confident he will be a force in the world with this inheritance behind him. I have faith that you will understand, dear Mother. I ask you not to impede the facilitation of this will in any way. It is my deepest desire.

His signature, sprawling but legible, was underneath.

"What is your opinion of this letter, Miss Frayne?" Mrs. Jessop asked.

What could I say? "It seems genuine, Mrs. Jessop."

"I don't doubt Gerald wrote it, but why? Was he coerced? Who is this man, Masefield?"

She turned her head away abruptly. "It makes no sense to me at all. That he would betray his family in such a way. For what? It sounds as if this man is a Red."

I had little doubt that was the case. To my surprise, Weaver spoke up.

"Don't worry, madam. We are all taken care of financially. At least Mr. Gerald made sure of that."

"There is too much about this situation that is strange. Why, for instance, did he put the document inside the piano? What if Ellen had not discovered it? What then? Gerald wrote this was his dearest wish. But we might not have found the will and the letter. How could we have carried out his wishes with these documents and the wishes he expresses in them hidden away in his piano?"

I'd been wondering just the same thing. The previous will would have stood was the simple answer, but I held my tongue.

"Perhaps he changed his mind," said Ellen. "He may have written all that then decided to wait for further reflections. He was so unstable at the end, who can guess what he was truly thinking."

I decided to enter the discussion. "This may be an obvious question, but I would like to ask it, if you don't mind, Miss Ellen. When you found your husband, did you notice any papers on the table?"

"Papers?"

"An envelope?"

"No. I ran to fetch Sam. It was the police who found Gerald had left a final note."

"And you, Mr. Weaver? When you came into the room, did you see anything?"

Sam grimaced. "My only concern was to check on Mr. Gerald's condition. As Miss Ellen said, it was the police who found the note."

"And you heard nothing untoward after you said goodnight at — what time was it? Ten o'clock?"

"That is correct. He was in his room getting ready for bed. He said he had everything he needed, so I left him and I went to my own room."

I went for blunt. "Did he seem to you to have been drinking?"

Sam answered promptly. "No. He seemed tired and a little morose, but he did get that way sometimes."

"And he didn't say anything about meeting up with this old friend?"

"No. To tell the truth, our exchange was fairly brief."

"When you said he was getting ready for bed, was he in his pyjamas already?"

"Yes. That is to say, he had his trousers on. I usually helped him with the buttons on the jacket of pyjamas."

"And if he had been drinking, you would have been able to smell that?"

Sam stiffened. "Yes."

Mrs. Jessop and Ellen listened to this exchange with great attention.

I continued to question Sam. "And that was the last time you saw him alive?"

"That is correct."

Mrs. Jessop addressed him. "I have a question, Sam. Is

it possible that Gerald invited this man Masefield back to the house? He may have listened to some sob story. What if this person returned later that night? After we had all retired. Gerald could have let him in himself. Perhaps this person tempted him? He may have plied him with alcohol in order to get him into an irrational state. It is not entirely impossible, is it?"

"No, I suppose not." He looked over at Ellen. "But you would have been aware would you not, Miss Ellen?'

She shook her head. "I had a severe headache on that night and I took a sleeping draught. Unless Gerald were carousing, I would not have awakened."

I wondered why Mrs. Jessop was so determined to pursue this tack. But then I realized that if she could find a villain, she would shift any responsibility for his own actions away from her son. Actions that she saw as the worst of betrayals. As for me, I found it hard to imagine a strange man coming and going in the household in the middle of the night, or that if he did, he and Gerald would have been so quiet they didn't wake anybody up. Drunken comrades didn't usually act that way.

Mrs. Jessop began to fold up the piece of paper. "I have asked Deacon to come here and examine these documents. I have already asked Detective Murdoch to look them over." She addressed me. "Given this very odd turn of events, Miss Frayne, I would like you to continue with your investigation. I rather doubt Detective Murdoch, pleasant man that he is, will see the necessity for reopening this case. But to my mind, it is not yet closed. Maybe you can find this Masefield person and see what he has to say."

"What shall I tell him about the will?"

"Nothing until that is verified. It may well be that he will get nothing. But do what you can to persuade him to come here. I am most curious to meet with him."

"I'll pursue that immediately, Mrs. Jessop."

"I'll have Wilson take you back to your office."

"Thank you."

She nodded at Weaver. "Will you see Miss Frayne to the door? Wilson will bring the car to the front."

Sam placed Duffy on the floor. The dog's tail started to wag.

"Please contact me as soon as you can," said Mrs. Jessop.

Sam led the way out, closing the door in the dog's face.

"You stay here."

He led the way into the hall where he proceeded to collect my coat and hat. He wasn't saying much.

I jumped in. "I think it's such a pity nobody heard Gerald that night. You might have been able to prevent him doing what he did."

I knew I was being cruel, but I was frustrated with the many unanswered questions in this case. Sam winced as if the arrow I had shot were a physical one.

"I have been wishing that every minute, Miss Frayne. It does not leave my mind for one single minute."

He turned away from me and was looking through the glass panel of the door. I gave him another chance at honesty.

"Why do you think you didn't hear him, Mr. Weaver?"

"I sleep soundly, I suppose."

His answer was unconvincing. Chance forfeited.

Suddenly there was the sound of the car horn from outside. The car was waiting. I pulled on my hat.

CHAPTER THIRTY-FIVE

I DECIDED TO check out Pearson Hall first to see if I could get any solid information as to Masefield's whereabouts. I gave Wilson the address on Beverley Street and, with its customary purr, the Packard started up through the wet streets as fastidiously as a cat walking through grass. We slipped into a parking space a few houses down.

"Do you want me to wait, Miss Frayne?"

The weather was less inhospitable, and a feeble sun was struggling through the clouds. I could easily walk to the office. On the other hand, I didn't know when I might get another chance to have a chauffeur drive me around in a leather-upholstered, mahogany-trimmed luxury car.

"Thank you. I'll say yes to that. I don't think I'll be long here. If you don't mind waiting, I'd like a lift to the office when I'm done."

Pearson Hall was a grand, red brick house, once a home to George Brown, one of Canada's Fathers of Confederation. Typical of such homes built in the 1870s, it conveyed affluence, albeit modestly. There was a beautiful wrought iron fence around a small lawn and a broad flight of steps swept up to the impressive entrance of tall wooden doors and an arched doorway. Not that the original residents would have been able to see this splendour. And probably not most of the current users.

Just as I reached the steps, the door opened, and a man came out. He had a white cane in one hand and the other on the shoulder of the young boy who was leading him.

"There's seven steps, sir," the boy called out and they walked down together. There was a slight stumble near the bottom as in fact the boy had miscounted. "Sorry sir. One more."

No harm done and they turned a sharp left and walked off down the street.

A plaque beside the door instructed me to press the bell and walk in. It was reproduced in Braille.

I obeyed instructions and pushed open the door.

I stepped into an airy, pleasant foyer with high ceilings and as much light as the day was going to allow. A woman was seated at a large desk, situated to one side of the door. Everything about her was neat. Her fair hair was coiffed into an old-fashioned coil at the nape of her neck, and her sombre attire consisted of an unadorned navy blue dress.

She appeared to be typing, although the typewriter was unlike any machine I had seen before. As I entered, she turned her head in my direction, and the way her gaze sort of missed me gave me to understand she was partially or completely blind.

There was a brass plaque on the desk that identified her

as Miss L. Smiley. Whatever her affliction, she lived up to her name. Her voice was cheery.

"Good morning. May I help you?"

"Good morning. I'm trying to get in touch with a Mr. Thomas Masefield. I understand he may have been a temporary resident here."

Her head adjusted slightly to the sound of my voice.

"May I ask why you are enquiring?"

"My name is Charlotte Frayne. I am private investigator and I am working for a family who recently lost their son. Mr. Masefield was an acquaintance of the dead man and they would like to meet him. I am hoping to trace him on their behalf."

She nodded. "How sad for them. Well, at least that doesn't sound like you're bringing completely bad news."

"I don't believe so."

"Sometimes people come here trying to recoup debts. There is rarely a happy outcome." She sighed. "Life can be a struggle for some of our veterans, especially if they were badly treated by the war." She pulled open the drawer, counted the folders and removed one.

"Let me see what I can do for you." She began to run her fingers lightly over the pages. She was reading Braille.

"Masefield? He's not a permanent resident, but he did have a temporary stay on October tenth and again on the fourteenth. I have no record of him being here since last week. He did apply for a night's residence on Thursday last, but he arrived too late to get a place. We have to close our doors at nine, you see. The note here says he showed up at half past nine which is too late. We do try to help our men, but we are not a hotel. Our resources are limited."

"Of course. Just to confirm, Mr. Masefield came here on Thursday, October twenty-ninth, but did not stay overnight?"

She touched the paper again. "That is correct."

Where had Masefield gone if he had not ended up in the soldiers' residence?

"Did he come here this past Monday?"

She checked her paper again. "No. Not at all. He did not even apply. We have to note down everyone who asks for relief."

So no alibi for Masefield on the night Klein was stabbed.

Miss Smiley beamed pleasantly into the space in front of her. I wondered how she had lost her sight.

"Is that all?"

"Yes, thank you. If Mr. Masefield does show up, will you ask him to get in touch with me. I can be reached at T. Gilmore and Associates."

She turned back to the machine, which I realized was a Braille typewriter.

"I'll just enter the information in here. Do you have a telephone?"

I gave her the number and repeated my name.

"Please assure him it is good news."

At least I hoped so. Receiving a sudden windfall was surely good news. Unless the circumstances were equivocal. And I didn't yet know if this was the case.

CHAPTER THIRTY-SIX

WILSON DROPPED ME off at the Arcade and, as I got out, I gave the back seat a regretful pat. It wasn't likely I'd be driven around in it in the near future.

The telephone was ringing as I let myself in to the office.

Gramps's voice came over the wire. He sounded very agitated.

"Lottie, can you get over here soon as possible. There's a big ruckus going on."

"What happened?"

"I can't go into details now, but Hilliard phoned and he says Wilf can't put on the play. Wilf says he will. They've had a big row. Apparently, Wilf has threatened to break up their partnership. Wilf says he'll shut down the café. Would you come and talk to him?"

I didn't know what good I could do, but I heard how upset my grandfather was.

"I'll come as soon as I can."

"Thanks, pet. I know you'll be able to sort it out if anybody can."

We hung up. He had much more confidence in my ability to create a truce between two equally pig-headed men with entrenched ideas of where their mutual venture might go.

There was no beautiful Packard to whisk me away. I had to walk. Talk about dreary. Grey skies, grey pavement, grey people.

* * *

I GOT TO the Paradise as fast as I could. As I approached, I saw Pearl was ushering out the last few lunch customers. One of them was still munching on a cookie and the way they were all moving, so reluctantly, said to me they weren't too happy about having to leave. Hilliard always gave each shift a grace period of ten minutes to exit and to allow the next group in. This was the second lunch shift and clearly they felt short-changed.

"Café's closed. Hurry along now," called Pearl.

She was about to close the door when she saw me.

"Thank goodness. I hope you're able to sort things out. It's a free-for-all in there."

I slipped through.

"They're in the kitchen."

As I approached the kitchen, I heard Wilf shouting. As I couldn't hear anyone answering I guessed he was on the phone. I walked into kitchen just as he slammed down the receiver.

"Hilliard still thinks he's the captain and everybody has to do what he says."

He glared at me as if I was complicit in this brazen misuse of authority.

Gramps was at the table with Calvin and he gave me a nervous smile. He wasn't comfortable with conflict. He was pressing a cloth to his boil. The onion compress, I gathered. Calvin gave me a little wave.

"What's going on?" I asked Wilf.

He didn't answer directly, but stood at the table. If steam could have come out of his head, it would have powered a freight train.

"Wilf?"

"Hilliard says I can't open the Cave with the play. Either I have to wait until he gets back, or put on something less controversial."

"He'd probably like to be here, no matter what. You two have planned this for a while."

I was being diplomatic, mostly for Gramps's sake, but that's not how I felt. I thought that Wilf was behaving like a spoiled and inconsiderate brat. The competitive feelings he displayed toward Hill were rarely far from the surface.

He returned to ranting.

"Who knows when Hilliard will get back? Could be weeks. Why should I have to wait that long?"

"Is that what he said? It might be weeks?"

Wilf blinked at me. "What? No, he didn't say that exactly. He doesn't know when he'll be back."

"Then it seems only fair that you wait."

"We're all ready to go. I was going to start rehearsing tonight. We've been spreading the word like mad. We'll get a full house. If we postpone, people will lose interest."

Pearl came in and joined the others at the table.

"I'm going ahead. Screw Hilliard," said Wilf.

I lost my patience. "You might be surprised to know, Wilf, that there are people out there who, unlike you, do in fact have more of an attention span than a gnat. If you have to postpone for a short period of time, they will still come."

I could feel my face had gone red. I had been shrill, but I was truly fed up.

He didn't relent, but scowled even harder. "I might have expected you to take Hill's side. He snaps his fingers and you jump."

"What?! That isn't true."

Who knows where this would have all gone, but at that moment the door swung open and in walked Detective Murdoch.

"Sorry to interrupt folks, but I'm returning your flyers." He took in the situation. "I obviously came at a bad time."

"Not at all. I'd say you came at exactly the right moment to stop Wilf and me from killing each other."

"I see. I can come back, if you want to go ahead."

He said this in a dry tone of voice and I burst out

laughing. Even Wilf grinned. Calvin seized his opportunity and jumped up.

"You know what. I think we all need to taste some of my latest chocolate cookies. And tea and coffee are at the ready."

"I'll help you," said Gramps and he dropped the compress on the table.

Pearl didn't move.

"What's the verdict on these pamphlets?" Wilf asked Jack.

"The commissioner couldn't find clear evidence that they were seditious. Said he might come himself."

Wilf gaped at him. "You're kidding?"

Jack laughed. "Sort of. The commissioner's idea of entertainment is a lively prayer meeting with lots of singing."

"But no dancing, I'll bet," said Gramps, who was returning to the table with a plate of cookies. Calvin was right behind him, carrying a tray with a tea pot and accoutrements.

"Do you mind if I join you?" asked Jack.

"Have you had lunch?" Cal asked.

"Not had the chance yet."

"Take your coat off, sit down, and I'll bring you some soup. It went over well today didn't it, Arnie?"

Gramps shuffled a little. I could tell he was searching for the narrow winding path between the truth and tact.

"There's nothing like a bowl of hot soup with toast, served by a lovely young lady such as Pearl."

That's my granddad!

She beamed at him.

"Done," said Jack.

Wilf was sitting at the table by now, looking at the flyers.

"Thanks, Jack. We can start handing them out at tonight's sittings."

He looked over at me. "Sorry for the shouting, Lottie. It'll be all right. We'll do a good job. I'll make Hill proud. Just wish he could be here to see it."

"I'm sorry for what I said too, Wilf."

Jack raised his eyebrows. "What did you say?"

"Never mind. Not worth repeating." Wilf pushed the plate of cookies in Jack's direction. "Here. Have one."

Jack took a bite of one of the cookies. "Wow, Cal. You've outdone yourself."

"Not too sweet?"

"Nope. Perfect. You're a master."

I noticed he hadn't tried the soup yet.

Calvin had brought me a cup of coffee the way he knew I liked it. Very hot and strong. Peace was restored. The cookie was indeed delicious.

"How are your hands, Calvin?" I asked.

"Much better. My fingers might all fall off, but you can't have everything can you?"

"As long as nothing else of importance falls off, you'll be all right," said Pearl.

All five of us gaped at her. "What do you mean?" Wilf asked.

"You know, his nose. You can't be a cook without a nose, can you?"

She looked rather pleased with her joke. I could see Jack was trying hard to stop from laughing. He drew the bowl of soup toward him.

"Wilf said I can take a rest here, Lottie," said Gramps. "Rather than tromping all the way home and back. Calvin and I are going to have a game of cards and then we'll start preps for the evening."

He pressed the cloth compress against his neck again.

"Is that helping?" I asked.

"It will soon."

"We should clean up the dining room" said Wilf. "We'll put the flyers on the tables."

"I'll help," said Gramps.

"I'll meet you upstairs then," said Calvin. In spite of what he'd said, he still looked as if he were hurting.

"How's the soup?" he asked Jack.

Jack waved his spoon. "Nothing like hot soup on a cold day."

"Good. You can leave the bowl in the sink when you've finished."

The three of them left. Pearl got up.

"I'm going home to see my mum," she declared. I saw that Jack was struggling with the soup which was a rather unappetizing beige colour. Another taste of mutton scrag.

"Cheery bye," said Pearl and off she went.

Jack put down his spoon and pushed away the bowl.

"Charlotte, I was hoping to find you here. Arcady has come down with the flu, so I'll be taking over the Klein case. There's been a new development."

"Quick question before we get into that. What's your take on the Jessop case? The new will and all that?"

Jack fished out a cigarette case from his jacket. "Do you mind if I have a smoke?"

I waved permission at him and he performed the usual ritual of lighting up. He had a dainty silver match case.

"Mrs. Jessop called me and informed me of what they'd found. Frankly, I don't see any reason to reopen the case or treat it like a suspicious death. As I understand it, the will is quite legitimate."

"There are a couple of things that are a bit odd."

Jack blew out some smoke. "Such as?"

"The man he names as his beneficiary, Thomas Masefield, was somebody he'd been in the war with, but he hadn't seen him since 1918."

"I don't find that so odd. One of the chaps in the division got a nice sum of money from an aunt he didn't even know existed. Supposedly she said he was a sweet little boy and very deserving. People do that with their wills sometimes." He grinned. "That's why lawyers love sorting out complicated estates. They earn a lot of money."

"It's not only that. The papers were hidden in the piano. They were found by chance."

Jack puffed out more smoke. "Was it chance?"

That question had squeaked in my mind like a little mouse.

"Ellen certainly didn't gain by the new will. Just the opposite. She was shut out entirely."

"Who would have preferred to keep that new will undiscovered?"

I have to admit I was rather enjoying this back and forth.

"Anybody other than Ellen? I'd say all of the servants who were the original beneficiaries, especially Sam Weaver, the valet. He did get some of the insurance money regardless, but he was also set to have a nice bequest from Gerald's first will." I hesitated for a moment. "I did wonder briefly if he could have helped Gerald on his way, as it were. But the fact is: he wasn't home when Gerald killed himself."

Jack frowned. "I didn't know that. Where was he?"

"He's married and has been going back and forth to his wife on a regular basis. He was with her. However, he may well have been the one to put the will in the piano. Frankly I don't know who else would have the opportunity to do so."

"Give me the name of the former soldier again. It sounds familiar."

"I was going to get to that. Masefield worked at Superior Ladies' Clothes for a short time. He left a couple of weeks ago. Apparently wasn't strong enough to handle the work."

"Right. His name was on the list Arcady gave me."

"So far, I haven't been able to pin down an alibi for him for Monday night."

"Surely these two cases aren't connected?"

"I don't know, but there is an odd crossover. Sam Weaver's wife, Alicia, and Masefield were both employed at Superior Ladies' Clothes. Oscar Klein, Sam Weaver, Gerald Jessop, and Masefield were all in the same battalion during the war."

"Okay. Where is Masefield now?"

"I don't know that either. Occasionally he stays overnight at Pearson Hall for former soldiers, but he hasn't stayed there since the fourteenth. I was going back to his lodgings on McCaul Street to see if I could speak with him."

Jack stubbed out his cigarette. "I'll come with you."

"By the way, you said there had been a development in the Klein murder."

He started to gather up his things. "A woman called the station today and said she had seen somebody leaving Superior Ladies' Clothes on Monday night."

"Good heavens. Did she give a description?"

"That's all I know so far. She wouldn't talk on the phone. Says she doesn't trust them. Phones, I mean. She wants to talk in person. I was going over there now."

"Can I come with you?'

He grinned at me. "I hoped you'd say that."

I grabbed my coat and we headed for the dining room. Just as I opened the door I heard somebody shout, "Guilty!" Another voice joined in, "Guilty!" Jack and I stepped through into the room. Gramps and Wilf were dancing around each other, pointing accusing fingers. "Guilty!" yelled Gramps.

I started to clap. "Bravo! Bravo!"

Gramps laughed. "I'm getting better at this by the minute."

Jack clapped too. "This show is going to be a smash hit."

Wilf and Gramps swirled around and in unison pointed their fingers. "Guilty!"

CHAPTER THIRTY-SEVEN

Jack INDICATED A black sedan parked on Queen Street. "It was the only one available. Get in at your peril."

"This one belongs in a museum, if you ask me."

"We've offered and been turned down."

He opened the door and I climbed into the passenger seat. The upholstery was split and stained, the crumbs on the floor would have sustained an aviary.

"I've got to crank it up," said Jack.

"You're joking."

He wasn't.

When he finally got the engine going and got into the car I had stopped laughing. With a jerk, we set off.

"The witness lives on Spadina right across from Superior Ladies' Clothes. Apparently, she has a heavy accent so the clerk didn't quite get her name. Something like 'Borkman.' The house number is one-sixty-six."

"And she says she saw somebody leaving the shop?"

"Supposedly."

He pulled over to the curb and the car shuddered to a stop. "Here we are."

Superior Ladies' Clothes was dark. Nobody working. Number one-sixty-six was indeed almost directly opposite. It was a nondescript house that fronted directly onto the street. Before Jack had time to ring the bell, the door opened. Given the information about this woman not trusting telephones and heavy accents, I had expected someone older. But, in fact, this woman didn't look much older than me.

But to my eyes she looked very odd indeed.

She was wearing a crisp, white blouse under a bright red, laced bodice. Her skirt, which fell to her ankles, was red and black striped and was covered by a black apron. Her fair hair was tucked into a plain white cap.

It took me a moment or two to realize she was wearing a traditional national costume. I didn't immediately know which one.

Jack raised his hat. "Mrs. Borkman?"

"It is pronounced Bjorkaman."

"Sorry, ma'am."

She nodded. "You must be police. *Hyvaa iltapaivaa.* Good afternoon. *Tule sisaan.* Come in."

She stepped back, inviting us to enter.

It was as if we had been transported into another and a far distant country.

We were standing in a single open room, wood panelled except for the far wall which was papered in a pattern of large blue flowers cascading from ceiling to floor. The wooden floor was half-covered by a deep blue woollen rug and in the centre of the room was a white painted table with four coloured chairs. Where were we?

The woman walked over to the table and pulled back two chairs.

"*Istukaa alas*. Please sit down. You may take off your outer clothes if you wish." I did wish and slipped off my raincoat and hat, draping them on the back of my chair. Jack removed his hat and undid his coat.

Mrs. Bjorkaman waved her hand toward the kitchen area. "Some refreshment? I have a drink that is very popular in my country."

Jack shook his head. "No, thanks."

I was game to give it a try. I hadn't travelled much so far in my life. Truth is I hadn't ever been out of Canada, so I was curious even though I still didn't know what country we were in.

I nodded heartily. "Yes. Thank you. Yes."

The woman went over to a cupboard, also blue and white, and took out a jug and two glasses. She returned to the table, poured a small amount of reddish-coloured liquid from the jug and handed me the glass.

"We call this, *lakka*. It is made from cloudberries."

She did indeed have an accent, but it was actually slight and her English was totally comprehensible, if not decidedly idiosyncratic. She also had a way of saying something in another language first, followed I think by its translation into English. I wondered if that was what had befuddled the police clerk.

"Where is your country?" I asked, sincerely curious.

"I come from originally Finland. However, together with my recent husband who is Swedish, Canada is now my country."

"I see you have brought a lot of your homeland with you."

"*Joo.*" She shrugged. "We never really leave our first countries behind do we? I enjoy these reminders."

She sat down at the end of the table and poured herself a glass of the *lakka*. I sipped on the drink. It was cold and sweet and tasted somewhat like raspberries.

She was watching me and there was a little smile lurking at the corner of her mouth that was disconcerting.

"I should perhaps warn you, madam. The drink is made with alcohol. It might be a little strong for you."

The warning came a little late as the *lakka* burned a path down my throat before setting my stomach on fire. I was seized by a fit of coughing.

Mrs. Bjorkaman got up and went back to the kitchen. She returned with another glass. This time it looked like she was offering me milk.

"Drink some of this."

Gratefully, I gulped down some of the milk, but almost spat it out. It tasted sour.

"Take a couple of more swallows."

I did and my burning throat started to ease.

Jack was watching me. I couldn't tell if he was amused
or dismayed.

"I beg your pardon, madam, we haven't yet introduced ourselves. I'm Detective Jack Murdoch. This is Miss
Charlotte Frayne. She is assisting me."

I intended to say hello, but my voice had vanished. All
I could do was waggle my fingers.

"I understand you telephoned the police station this
morning," continued Jack. "You said you had information
concerning an investigation we are conducting?"

"*Joo.* I have to understand that a sudden death has occurred at Superb Clothes. On the Monday night."

"That is correct."

She took another swallow of the *lakka*, but seemed
unaffected. Familiarity breeds familiarity I suppose.

She was sitting at the table, back straight, head up, in
her crisp white cap and red bodice. I felt positively dowdy
in my brown dress, even with the lace trim which was old
enough to be a holdover from Toronto's first settlers.

Jack took out his notebook. I should have taken out mine,
but I couldn't recall where I'd left it.

"Mrs. Bjorkaman," Jack pronounced it correctly. "I believe
you claim to have seen somebody leaving the Superior
Ladies' Clothes building on Monday night."

"*Joo.*"

"What time was it when you saw this person."

"Exactly two minutes past eight o'clock. My wireless

progamme had just finished so I walked over to the window wherein I looked out onto the street."

"Can you give me a description of the person you saw?"

She frowned. "*Ei*. That's not quite accurate, detective."

"How so, madam?"

"It wasn't just one person. It was two. A man and a woman."

CHAPTER THIRTY-EIGHT

T HAT STATEMENT WAS certainly enough to blast away the clouds that the cloudberry drink had created in my brain. I remembered that my notebook was in my purse and I took it out at once. Later on, I typed up her statement.

REPORT ON THE INTERVIEW WITH Helmi Bjorkaman, 166 Spadina Ave. November 4, 1936.
PRESENT: Detective Jack Murdoch. Recorded by Charlotte Frayne.

(I omitted the Finnish words with which she seasoned her statement because I was not sure of the spelling and asking her to spell them for me slowed up the narrative considerably.)

"I had just finished listening to a lovely rendition of the Nabucco chorus on my wireless. I went over to the window to see what the climate was like and to close tight my curtains. It was raining. There is a street lantern close to the Superb Clothes doorway.

I could see a woman was standing there. She was holding an umbrella and was wearing dark rain gear. I might not have paid attention except that it was a misery night and I wondered why she was not indoors. She began to walk away. She had just gone past the light when the door of Superb Clothes opened and a man emerged. He, too, was within rain clothes. He appeared to see the young woman and he moved fast to catch up with her. It is possible he called out as she turned, but I did not hear from my advantage point. They stood for a moment, conversing, then walked off together. He took her arm."

That was it. Jack pressed her, but she said she would not be able to recognize each person again. She could not see their faces clearly. The woman was of ordinary build and the man was rather shorter and seemed slighter. She believed the woman was younger, as she had more of a spring to her step.

"Are you absolutely certain the man came out of the building?" Jack asked her.

"I speak with complete certitude. The woman tried the door, but it was not possible for her to enter. She walked away. Then the man emerged. I thought perhaps she had come to meet him."

"Was there anybody else at home who might have also seen them?" Jack asked.

"*Ei.* No. I only lives at this moment. My husband is working in a mine shaft in the north country. He will be home to make the Holy Birth."

It turned out she was referring to Christmas.

Mrs. Bjorkaman escorted us to the door. She said she had a meeting to attend later in the evening of the Finnish National Society. That was why she was dressed the way she was in the traditional costume of Finland. Usually she wore ordinary clothes. I thought she had indulged in a smile at this point. My expression when first seeing her must have been a dead giveaway.

"*Hyvaa iltapaivaa,*" she said as she closed the door behind us.

CHAPTER THIRTY-NINE

"LET'S SIT IN the car for a minute and sort out what we've got," said Jack.

The car had the look of a vehicle that had no intention of ever starting again, but Jack gave it some hearty cranks and it roared into life. He joined me.

"What are your thoughts, Charlotte? What, or more exactly, who, did Mrs. Bjorkaman see?"

"Her account of a woman trying to get into the building fits with what Ruby told us. She says she went for her rendezvous with Klein about eight o'clock. But who is the man who came out? Ruby said nothing about seeing anybody."

Jack sighed. "The description could fit anybody. 'Average height, overcoat, cap.' But what it does confirm is that a man was inside the building before eight o'clock."

"Dr. Lewis determined that Klein died between six and eight and unless there was a veritable trolley load of people coming and going between those hours, I'd say Mr. Man-with-a-cap is most likely our prime suspect."

"And he and the unknown woman knew each other."

"Quite well from the sound of it. They linked arms. And the only concrete thing Mrs. B. said was that the man seemed older."

Jack shifted the gears. "Let's go and have a word with Ruby." With a frightening squeal the car moved forward.

Georgina House was on Beverley Street, not too far south of Pearson Hall. It was roughly the same vintage, but whereas the Hall had been converted from a private residence, Georgina House had been built specifically as a hostel for young women who were from out of town and needed a protective and decent place to live. It was a gracious two-storey building with a side porch and a front sun parlour. The second floor had several windows that faced the street. A large front garden which, even in November, managed to appear well tended. It seemed a residence I could have imagined staying in.

Jack parked the car and together we walked up to the entrance.

There was an up-to-date electric bell to one side of the door and above it a neat sign asked us to please ring and wait. We did. From somewhere inside, I could hear the sound of singing. Female voices, singing a hymn.

Fairly soon, a woman appeared. She was older, wearing a plain black dress, grey hair pinned back. Her demeanour was definitely not that of a maid.

She opened the door and smiled at us pleasantly.

"May I help you?"

Jack removed his hat. "Good afternoon, madam. I'm Detective Murdoch and this is Miss Frayne. We were hoping to speak to Miss Ruby Robertson. I understand she is a resident here."

The woman frowned. "Is there something wrong?"

"We were hoping she can help us with our enquiries. Is she at home?"

"No, I'm afraid not."

"When do you expect her back?"

The woman's reserve began to crack. "Actually, she left this morning. She has returned to her home." She stepped back. "Perhaps you should come inside. I'm the matron here, Mrs. Hartley. It's all been so upsetting." She waved her hand. "We can meet in here."

She led the way into a small foyer and opened a door to the lounge. With perfect timing, a blast of music assailed us. "Amen. Amen." About half a dozen young women were clustered around a piano. The amens were the robust conclusion to the hymn they had been singing.

They turned to regard us curiously.

Mrs. Hartley clapped her hands to get attention.

"Ladies, I wonder if you wouldn't mind adjourning to the library for the time being. I must speak to this gentleman and this lady for a moment."

Good naturedly, they gathered up their song sheets and hymn books and trooped out.

When the door closed behind them, Mrs. Hartley indicated the armchairs that were near the fireplace. A cheery fire was in the grate. We sat down and the matron took one of the other chairs. She regarded us anxiously.

"Can you tell me what is going on, Detective? Miss Robertson came to me early this morning and said she had to return home immediately. She said she had received word that somebody in the family was ill. She was so upset and had obviously been crying for some time. She said she didn't know if she would be returning to Toronto." Mrs. Hartley clasped her hands tightly together, prayer like.

"You said you were conducting an investigation. Your presence here says to me it is of some seriousness. Is that true?"

Jack paused for a moment. "Yes, madam, that is true."

"And it concerns one of our residents, Miss Robertson?"

"I believe so."

"Dear me, dear me. I must say, Detective, I believe her to be a young woman of excellent character. She has been with us for four weeks and got employment at a women's clothes shop two weeks ago. She has not had an easy life for such a young woman, but I thought that things were looking much better once she acquired steady work."

"Mrs. Hartley, was Miss Robertson in the residence on Monday evening?"

"As far as I know she was. She was certainly present at supper. I saw her then."

"What time was that?"

"We eat at a half past six. Some of our young women

aren't finished work until six o'clock, so we try to accommodate them. We always have a prayer service right afterward. I myself was feeling a little out of sorts, so I retired to my room."

"You don't know if Miss Robertson remained in the residence for the evening?"

"She didn't ask for a pass." She lowered her head. "We take our responsibility seriously, Detective Murdoch. We ask that our residents report to us if they are intending to be out for the evening."

"And where they are going?" I asked.

"Yes, that as well." She frowned. "That is not as restrictive as it might sound. Of necessity, we have a curfew and the front door is locked at ten o'clock. We have to keep track of who is in and who is out. We are *in loco parentis* after all."

I had ruffled her feathers somewhat, which was not my intention. Jack stepped in to appease her.

"Of course, Mrs. Hartley. Frankly I'm not looking forward to the time when my children start demanding more freedom. I'm going to trust my wife to be wiser about these matters than I think I am."

I was almost envious that he had shared that particular confidence with the matron. She, of course, became putty in his hands.

"As I said, I went to my room quite early. When I am not personally available, I make sure one of our monitors is in

charge. The women who have shown maturity and responsibility become monitors if they wish."

"Who was on board on Monday evening?"

"That would have been Miss Sharon McKinley. She is
in today. I can fetch her if you wish."

"Thank you, Mrs. Hartley. I would like to have a word
with her if possible."

"I'll be right back."

"One question, you said that Miss Robertson told you
she had received word that a family member was ill."

"That is correct."

"How would she have got that word? A letter? A telegram? A telephone call?"

"Ah, I see what you are getting at, Detective. I don't
believe she did get a letter. Certainly not recently. Definitely
not a telegram and not a telephone call. We only permit our
residents to receive calls in the evenings after prayers. For
cost purposes I always check the log book in the mornings.
There was no such call recorded for Miss Robertson."

The matron's cheeks became a little pink. "Is it possible
she was not telling the truth, Detective?"

"I'm afraid that is a possibility."

She stood up.

"Can I have some tea or coffee sent in?" Jack was the one
she addressed.

"Not for me, thank you."

I was still feeling the effects of Nordic hospitality and I
beamed at her. "Coffee would be most appreciated."

Mrs. Hartley didn't look in my direction with the same chipper aspect, but she responded politely. "Very well."

The door closed behind her.

"Are you really afraid of your children growing up?" I asked Jack.

"Are you kidding? I'm terrified. I know nothing. I've always considered child rearing the mother's job. I'm just to come in and lay down the law. Administer punishment and so forth."

"What! Is that how it was when you were a child?"

He grinned at me. "Not really. My mother died when I was young, so parenting fell to my father."

"And?"

"He sort of disappeared for a long time. Emotionally, not physically. Now I can see that he was devastated himself, but I didn't understand it at the time. It was only when I came back from the war, a complete disaster, that we started to get close. He's been wonderful since."

In spite of his cheerful words, a shadow came over Jack's face. Since I'd known him there had been moments when the past had opened up. They were few and far between. All I could tell was that his war experiences had been horrific. I got the feeling that the emotional weight and pain of them never quite went away.

He nodded at me. "Now that we're swapping personal histories, what about you?"

"My father died before I was born and my mother decided eventually that motherhood was not for her. She left me with my grandparents, on the paternal side. They raised me from the age of two. I couldn't have asked for better. Gran died two years ago, so it's just Gramps and me now. You met him at the Paradise Café. He's great. Don't tell him, but our roles have changed. Now, I'm the one to do the looking after."

Mrs. Hartley returned with a young woman following. I recognized her as the piano player who had been infusing such vigour into the old hymn.

"This is Miss McKinley, one of my most trusted monitors."

Jack and I introduced ourselves.

"I'll go and get the coffee," said Mrs. Hartley.

Miss McKinley sat down and Jack resumed his chair.

There was something very likeable about this young woman. She was rather fashionably dressed considering this was a residence run by the Anglican Church. Her navy skirt hovered more closely to her knees than her ankles and her blue blouse was decorated with two polka dotted flounces. She had an abundance of dark wavy hair which was subdued under a flowered bandeau. She didn't seem rebellious so much as independent.

Jack repeated his statement about conducting an investigation.

"I understand from the matron that Miss Robertson left the residence this morning. Did you speak to her?"

"Only briefly. She was up and on her way out before I'd even left the bathroom." She shook her head. "She certainly seemed most upset about something, but wasn't inclined to share what it was. She had a suitcase with her. When I asked about it, she explained there was a family crisis and she had to get home right away." Sharon chewed on her lip. "I asked her to wait a minute so at least I could walk with her to the station, but she said somebody was meeting her outside. A cousin, she said. Then off she ran."

"Was it a man or a woman who met her?"

"A woman." She scrutinized both of us. "Can you tell me what's up? I got fond of young Ruby. Is there anything I can do for her?"

"We were wondering if Miss Robertson was at home on Monday evening? Mrs. Hartley said she left the monitor in charge. That was you, was it not?"

"Monday? Yes, that's right. And no, Ruby wasn't at home. She said she was going to meet somebody, but she'd be back by curfew."

"How did she seem?" I asked.

"Seem? I didn't pay much attention. A bit jumpy, but she's a little mouse most of the time so that wasn't so unusual. She said she was late and had to hurry."

"What time was this?"

"About a quarter to eight."

"And she was back by curfew?"

Sharon grimaced. "She barely made it. Good thing it was me on the door and not Mrs. Hartley. Ruby probably would have got a demerit point. If you get five in one week you have to do extra chores." She gave us a rueful smile. "It's considered good for our characters. Who knows, they may be right about that."

"When Ruby did come home, was she by herself?"

Sharon sat back in her chair. "I'd rather you didn't pass this along to matron unless you have to …"

"Understood."

"In fact, she was with a gentleman. It was a miserable night and she wanted to bring him in. I had to say no. We don't allow gentlemen to enter the premises after curfew. Not even family members. By now it was ten minutes past ten. Curfew's at ten sharp. Ruby started to plead with me, another unusual thing for her. She's such a regular mouse most of the time. Won't say boo to a goose. The man stopped her. Said she shouldn't worry. He would come back tomorrow and continue their chat. That's how he put it, 'chat.' I don't know what the heck was going on with them. It all seemed very tense. But he didn't seem like a boyfriend or such. Too old for her for one thing."

"Can you describe this man?" I asked.

She paused. "He wasn't particularly outstanding. I'd say, medium height. On the thin side. Black mackintosh. A brown cap. Honestly, I didn't get a good look at him. The porch isn't too well lit at the best of times and he was sort of hanging back." She stopped. "Hold on. I just remembered. He wore spectacles. You know those funny round ones." She actually made the same gesture that Pearl had made when she was describing Masefield.

"One question, Miss McKinley. Please take your time to

answer. What you say is important ..."

"Go on."

"How would you describe the way they parted company? Was there any sign of affection between them for instance? Did they kiss? Hug? Shake hands?"

Sharon gave it some thought. I liked that about her.

"He gave Ruby a kiss on the cheek. Brief, to be sure, but affectionate."

"Did she respond?"

Again, Sharon considered the question. "She didn't kiss him back or anything like that, but she did stand and watch him as he left. I say, he hasn't got her in trouble has he?"

"I don't believe so. Not in the way that you mean."

Sharon looked relieved. Unplanned pregnancies were a serious issue for most young women.

"Tuesday, she went into work did she not?" I continued.

"Yes. I saw her at breakfast. She looked awful. As if she hadn't slept much."

"Did you see her after that?"

"I did. I was here when she came home. She skipped supper and went straight to her room. Mrs. Hartley had to have cook send up her meal."

"Did the man come yesterday as he said he would?"

"No, he didn't. I was on monitor duty all that evening. I would have seen him. Ruby did have a visitor though. A woman. She said she was Ruby's cousin. I don't think Ruby was expecting her. She brought her into the lounge and they were in quite a hugger mugger for a while. She didn't stay that long and I was actually going to speak to Ruby myself because the little mouse looked in such a pother. But she went straight up to her room when the other woman left."

"What time was this?"

"It was getting late. Our house curfew is nine o'clock. All visitors must leave by then."

"Can you describe this person?"

"Young. Younger than me probably." She glanced over at me. "About your height."

Tall.

"Hair colour?"

"Brown. Wavy. She was what would be considered pretty."

"How long did she stay?"

"About an hour."

"You said somebody came to fetch Ruby this morning? Was it the same person?"

"As a matter of fact, it was."

"Had Ruby called for a taxicab?"

"No, I believe they were walking to the train station."

She frowned at me. "I would appreciate it if you can tell me what this is all about. I can guess something very serious has happened."

"I'm very sorry, but we are not at liberty to give you information at this time. I would, however, like to have the address that Miss Robertson gave when she first came here. It must be on file."

"I can get it at once from the office."

She stood up and hurried away. I faced Jack.

"So, let's have a recap. The woman that Mrs. Bjorkaman saw outside Superior Ladies' Clothes I think we can assume was Ruby Robertson. Timing fits and the description. The man who apparently came out of the shop and followed after her is the same man who came with her to the hostel. Her description fits Tom Masefield. We can't assume he is connected to Klein's murder, but it's sure stretching coincidence if he's not."

"I agree with all of that. At the very least, he may help us with our enquiries, as we always put it."

Miss McKinley returned and handed Jack a piece of paper. "I wrote it down. She is from Perth."

Jack in turn gave her his calling card. "If Miss Robertson does happen to return any time soon, please have her telephone me or come to headquarters. Say it's urgent."

We headed for the door. A couple of the young women drifted back to the lounge, eyeing us curiously. One of them went straight to the piano and began to pick out a tune. Another hymn by the sound of it.

"Rock of Ages, cleft for me. Let me hide myself in Thee."

We had just stepped outside onto the porch. Dimly lit as Sharon had said. Suddenly, she came rushing out.

"Sorry, I got all scrambled. I just remembered something. The woman who said she was Ruby's cousin? The first thing I noticed was how cheerful she looked on such a gloomy night. She was wearing a bright red raincoat and a matching beret. Is that helpful?"

I stared at her for a moment.

"Indeed, it is. Thank you."

I swear there was only one cherry red raincoat in the entire city. The mysterious visitor had to be Miriam Cohen. And the mysterious man? Lots of men wore round spectacles, but lots of men didn't necessarily know Ruby and Miriam Cohen both. It had to be Thomas Masefield.

CHAPTER FORTY

ONCE OUTSIDE, JACK paused to light a cigarette. I told him who I thought the so-called cousins were.

"Maybe they are related, maybe not. They both work at Superior. Or I should say, 'have worked.' It's possible Miriam dropped in on Ruby to see how she was doing."

"I don't know. We are fairly sure that Ruby met up with a man who we suspect has something to do with Klein's death. Then Miriam shows up and the next thing we know, Ruby has vanished."

"Not to mention the fact that Miriam Cohen appears to be chummy with a man named Masefield."

Jack grinned. "Sounds like he could help us with our enquiries."

We reached the car. "I'm going to go back to the station and send a wire to the Perth police department. See if they can get hold of our Miss Robertson. We may also have some results from the lab. Perhaps a beautiful, intact fingerprint from the scissors which is the perfect match for another print we have on file that belongs to a known criminal."

"Want the easy life, do you?"

He laughed. "Wouldn't that be nice. Okay. What do you want to do next?"

"I'm going over to the café. See how Gramps is doing. Then I'll go back to Masefield's known place of residence and see if he is there sitting by the fire."

Jack gaped at me. "You will not. He's a prime suspect in a vicious murder. I will do any interviewing that needs to be done."

He was right. But I needed to track down Masefield on another matter. I'd challenged Detective Arcady on listening to his gut instinct. Challenged him scornfully I might add. But here I was, not willing to believe that the man I'd met recently was capable of committing murder. Or even a double murder.

Jack was frowning at me. "Charlotte, promise me you won't be foolhardy! I will take this from here. Hey. Look at me. Give me your word."

"Okay, okay. I promise I won't do anything foolish."

"Hm. Knowing you, that could be quite an elastic word." He opened the car door. "Get in. I'll drop you off at the café."

"Before that, why don't we go back to D'Arcy Street. Maybe Miss Cohen of the cherry red beret is home. Further talks are warranted."

He was looking doubtful.

"Jack. I can't just drop out. I want to get answers as much as you do."

"All right. But we will be careful, won't we? You gave me your word."

"Of course."

CHAPTER FORTY-ONE

H E CRANKED UP the car and we chugged off.

There were a few more people hurrying home. A river of umbrellas flowed down the sidewalk, eddying at the stop lights.

Jack pulled up in front of the house on D'Arcy Street. We both went to the door and I rang the bell. To my surprise, Miriam Cohen herself answered. She didn't look pleased to see me. I smiled at her just the same.

"Miss Cohen, this is Detective Jack Murdoch. We wondered if we could have a word with you."

"Why? I've gone through everything I know with the other fellow."

Jack lifted his hat. "Detective Arcady has come down with the flu and I've taken over the case. There are a couple of loose ends we thought you might be able to help us with. I don't think it will take too long."

She looked a little mollified, but didn't invite us in. "My mother is about to serve our supper. Can it wait?"

"I'm afraid not. It concerns Miss Ruby Robertson. I

believe you are acquainted."

"Slightly. We work at Superior Clothes."

"We were talking to somebody at Georgina House and we were told she has left there and has returned to her home town. You helped her I believe?"

"That's not a crime is it?"

Her tone was belligerent; this was a different Miriam from the one who had presented such an alluring face to Arcady. Was it the difference in the two men or had something occurred in the meantime to make her change her approach?

"Not necessarily, Miss Cohen, unless you are knowingly aiding and abetting a criminal."

"What? Don't be ridiculous. Ruby isn't a criminal."

A woman's voice called from inside the house. "Mimi. Your dinner is getting cold."

She called over her shoulder. "Be right there, Mama."

She stepped forward and pulled the door part way closed behind her.

"I can't speak to you right now. It's out of the question. Can you come back in about an hour? I'll be able to then."

"Of course," said Jack.

Miriam glared at me. "You as well?"

I smiled back at her. "Me too."

She stepped back into the house and Jack and I headed for the car.

"I'll pick you up in an hour at the café? All right?"

"Sounds good."

CHAPTER FORTY-TWO

Jack dropped me off at the perfect time as the final dinner sitting was just dispersing. I did a quick assessment of the departing customers. They moved away slowly, reluctant to leave the warmth and camaraderie of the café. One of them was studying the flyer that announced the play. I thought that was a good sign.

I went in. Pearl was sweeping the floor and Gramps was wiping off the tables. He waved me over.

"Lottie, you just missed Hilliard. He rang up about ten minutes ago."

"Did he settle things with Wilf?"

"I believe so. He thinks he'll be back on Saturday."

I must admit that was a big boost to my spirits. That darn Cupid's arrow had penetrated deep into my heart.

"Do you have time for some dinner?" Gramps asked.

"What's the soup today?"

"Fish mulligatawny."

"I think I'll skip it, Gramps. How was it received?"

He grinned at me. "Let's say the enthusiasm was a

tad underwhelming."

I thought Hilliard or Wilf might have to have a word with Calvin soon. Given the climate in the city at the moment, I didn't think the café was in danger of losing customers. There was always a line to get in. However, we wanted them to be happy with the food. A good lunch or dinner was one of the few bright spots in the lives of many of the people who came to the Paradise.

"I've got to keep at it, Lottie. Cal is waiting to do the treatment on my neck."

"I'll be right there, Gramps."

"That poultice is making a big difference. My boil has gone right down."

I was about to follow him into the kitchen to say hello to Wilf and Cal when Pearl called over to me. "That man you were interested in, the poet? What was his name again?"

"Masefield?"

"Yeah. That's the one. He was in here earlier."

"Really! What time was that?"

"First sitting. Matter of fact he had a girl with him."

"A girl?"

"That's what I said. Are you going deaf, Charlotte? Well, I say a girl. She might have been sixteen. They sat over there in the corner."

She pointed at a table near the chess board.

"What did this girl look like?"

Pearl swept up some crumbs into her pan. "Look like? I

don't know. Like a girl. Fair hair. Nervous type, if you ask me. She couldn't decide what sweet she wanted, but when I asked her to please make up her mind she looked as if she would burst into tears. I mean, it wasn't a big deal. I might have been a teeny bit sharp, but I had other customers waiting didn't I?"

I walked over to her. "Pearl, this is important. How did they seem?"

"What do you mean? Like everybody else, as if I had four pairs of hands."

I took a breath, holding back an impulse to shout at her. "I know some of the customers can get impatient, Pearl. They're usually hungry. What I mean is, did you notice anything in particular with Masefield and this young woman? Did they talk to each other for instance?"

She shrugged. "I didn't notice." She lowered her voice. "To tell the truth I had to deal with a few complaints about the soup. It wasn't a big favourite. Most people thought it was much too curry-flavoured."

"We'd better tell Calvin."

"I will. That's two flops in a row."

Pearl started to put away her broom.

"To back up for a moment, Pearl. About Masefield and his companion. Is there anything at all you can tell me about their behaviour?"

She pursed her lips in that familiar way. "She didn't finish the soup, he did. She had the plum duff. He had a Shrewsbury cake. He had money this time and he paid up and they left." She bobbed her head from side to side. "Neither of them looked exactly chipper, but in this place that's not so unusual. I'm not sure what you're getting at."

I could hardly say what I was fishing for. Did Masefield look as if he had recently stabbed somebody to death? Did the girl, who surely was Ruby Robertson, look as if she knew that?

At that moment, Wilf popped his head through the kitchen door.

"Jack Murdoch is on the phone, Lottie. He wants to talk to you."

"Thanks, Pearl." I followed Wilf into the kitchen. Pearl came behind me.

Gramps was sitting at the table with Calvin, chopping come carrots. There was the all too familiar reek of onions. He had a bandage wrapped around his neck holding the onion poultice in place.

I picked up the receiver. "What's up, Jack?"

"Charlotte, two things. First of all, I'm delayed for at least two or three hours. Sorry, we're short-handed here. Another man has come down with the flu. Secondly, I was able to talk directly to the police department in Perth. He said the address I gave him no longer exists. Several months ago, the houses on that strip caught fire. All of them razed to the ground. No survivors."

"Good grief. None?"

"Apparently not. There was a woman living at that number, but she was one of those that perished. If Ruby

Robertson was indeed going back to Perth, I don't know who she was going to see. He has no record of any people by that name."

"I can tell you that so far she hasn't left the city."

I told him what Pearl had reported.

"The man she was with fits the description of our suspect."

I could hear his intake of breath over the wire.

"I wonder where they've gone. Or are going? Listen, Charlotte. I'll come as soon as I can. Where will you be?"

"I was planning to go back to the office."

"All right, I'll see you there."

We hung up. Wilf had joined in the preparations for dinner, but he came over to me.

"Hill says to tell you he misses you. He hopes to be back on Saturday, as long as his kid continues to improve. He might not be able to stay, but at least he'll be here for opening night."

"He's okay with the play now is he?"

Wilf actually turned red. "I didn't tell him. He thinks we're opening with a vaudeville."

"Wilf!"

"It'll be all right when he gets here. The response to the flyer has been really keen. We'll be sold out. You'll see. We can do the vaudeville next week."

"I think it might be only courteous to let him know, Wilf. I'm sure he'll be okay with it."

"You don't know him like I do, Charlotte. He can dig

in his heels. I'm not going to say anything, and I'll thank you not to leak it either."

"It's your business, Wilf. Yours and Hilliard's. Either way I'm happy to be at the box office."

"What?"

"You need somebody to handle the tickets, don't you?"

"Pearl says she will do that. She's used to handling money."

"Okay."

"No, I was actually going to ask you to be one of the crowd in the last scene."

"What?! I'm no actress."

"You don't have to do anything except come on stage with the others and then you all point and yell, 'Guilty!'"

Gramps had been listening to this exchange and he chuckled. "We can practice together, Lottie. It'll be fun."

I had massive doubts about that, but this wasn't the time to argue.

"I'm going to the office, Gramps. I'll check back later."

He waved a dishrag at me. "When we've finished, Cal is going to rehearse my lines with me."

"I thought all you had to say was, 'guilty.'"

"Wilf liked what I was doing and he's added another line. I now say, 'You are guilty.' Then we all repeat 'guilty.'"

Wilf grinned. "He's got a touch of Fredric March to him. He'll be a big attraction."

I had to laugh. I was glad my Gramps was having such a good time.

CHAPTER FORTY-THREE

To be honest, D'Arcy Street wasn't exactly on the way back to my office, but a vigorous walk is always a good thing. The rain had stopped, leaving a soft washed feeling to the air. I had many things to think about. I decided I'd go back and have a chat with Miriam Cohen. I wasn't sure Jack would be happy about that, but I was keen to do it. I was still in search of Tom Masefield.

I had reached the corner of McCaul and D'Arcy. My brush with the ecclesiastical at Georgina House had suddenly infused me with melancholy. I had chosen to be a private investigator and I was not sorry. However, it did mean that I often had to deal with the darker side of human nature. Oscar Klein might have been a less than exemplary human being, but he had died savagely. I was getting closer to finding out who had committed that act. I wasn't glad about it.

I knocked on the door and this time it was opened by her mother. She regarded me anxiously.

"She hasn't come back yet, Miss."

"She's gone out? I was expecting to see her."

"She went out not too long ago."

"Did she say where she was going?"

"No, I'm afraid not."

"Or when she'd be back?"

"No, I'm afraid not."

A child started to cry from inside the house. Were they ever cheerful these Cohen children?

Mrs. Cohen was already stepping back to the door.

"I'll tell her you called."

The door shut firmly.

Damn.

Now that I was so close, I thought I might as well carry on to the Legion House. Perhaps Masefield had been in contact with Donald Dunham.

I wasn't paying attention and didn't notice a sizeable puddle which was hugging the sidewalk. My shoes got soaked. Perhaps I could prevail upon Mr. Dunham to let me dry off in front of his fire.

In fact, he didn't answer the door. Just as I approached the house, Miriam Cohen was coming out.

"Hello, I just called in at your house," I said.

She didn't look too happy to see me.

"I was going back there. Where's your detective?"

"He had something to take care of at the station. I've returned as promised."

She frowned. "How did you know this is where I was?"

"I didn't. I came here to talk to Mr. Masefield. And lo

and behold here you are. I gather you are a friend of his. Is he at home?"

"No, he's not."

"Any idea where I might find him? It's rather important?"

"No, I don't."

"Can you and I have a chat then? Save me a trip."

She shook her head so vigorously she might have been a dog shedding water. "No, no. We can't. I've got to get back home." She paused for a moment. "What do you want to talk about anyway?" She came down the steps and started to hurry away. "If you want to talk, you'll have to come with me."

She reminded me of a mother bird trying to draw the potential predator away from her chicks. I scurried after her.

"Miriam, wait. This is serious."

She stopped. "What is it?"

"I understand you met up with Ruby Robertson this morning. She's the one I want to speak to. I was wondering if you could tell me where she is."

"What do you think I am, a travel convener? Where's this person? Where's that?"

She was glaring down at me, but I had the feeling much of the expression was sheer bluster. She was very upset about something.

"Why do you want to talk to Ruby so badly?"

"I'm assisting the police in the investigation into Oscar Klein's death."

"She doesn't know anything about that." Miriam's voice was sharp. "Why would she?"

It was my turn to shrug. "I'd prefer to speak to her directly. Do you have any idea where I might find her? When I spoke to the matron at Georgina House, she was under the impression Ruby was going back to Perth. She thought you were taking her to the train station."

"That's right, I did."

Miriam was a woman full of contradictions. On the one hand, she seemed to feel no compunction about not telling the truth, on the other hand, she wasn't very good about being convincing.

We had reached the corner and I didn't want to get out of sight of Masefield's house. I made a big display of checking my wrist-watch. Gramps and Gran had presented me with a special watch for my birthday. It was designed for nurses' use, and it looked highly functional with large numbers and a luminous dial. The kind of watch a nurse might need when taking a pulse at the bedside of a fevered patient in a darkened room.

"I must get back to the office. You get on home and I'll come by later. If by chance you do happen to encounter Ruby, please tell her that the police want to speak to her. Routine questioning."

It was me fudging the truth a little. So far, I thought the young girl was implicated in this case up to her timid neck.

Miriam could hardly reverse her story about having to get home at once. She nodded at me and reluctantly she continued along D'Arcy Street. I made a brief pretext of heading down McCaul, away from the Legion House. She glanced over her shoulder once more, but I was now ostensibly heading south. She seemed satisfied by that. I gave it a few minutes, then retraced my steps.

I needed to see whether or not Masefield was indeed at home.

CHAPTER FORTY-FOUR

DONALD DUNHAM OPENED the door. He broke into a big smile when he saw me.

"Miss Frayne. Just in time for some tea. And I've finished my hospital. I'd love you to see it."

"Mr. Dunham. I'd love to accept your invitation, but I need to speak to Mr. Masefield first. Is he at home?"

His face fell and I felt cruel to disappoint him. "No. He's not. That other girl was looking for him as well, but he went out almost an hour ago."

"Do you know where he went or when he's coming back?"

"Yes and No. He's gone over to the church. He does that sometimes. I don't know how long he'll be."

"You mean St. Patrick's?"

"That's the one. Just down the road."

"Thanks. I'll just go and take a look. But I promise I'll keep you to that tea offer."

His face lit up. "Done. I'll be here. Not going anywhere soon."

* * *

THE CHURCH JUST down the road was St. Patrick's, the beautiful Catholic church run by the Redemptorist fathers. Their monastery, equally grand, was adjoining. They were both constructed in the soft, buff-coloured brick that distinguished the city and, after the recent rain, the buildings seemed to glow.

I trotted up the steps and entered.

The interior was also grand, but not overwhelmingly so. Tall, pale columns directed the worshipping eye to the stained-glass windows behind the altar but there was minimal statuary; the pews were dark wood and simple in design.

Tom Masefield was easy to pick out among the handful of people scattered around the church, some kneeling in fervent prayer. He was seated close to the entrance and near the aisle. I slipped in beside him. He turned quickly, an old reflex, but when he saw me, he smiled.

"Miss Frayne. How nice. How'd you know I was here?"

"I went to your house and Mr. Dunham said you might be here."

He nodded. "I am not in the least religious, but I do admit that I come here more and more. I find it peaceful." He grinned at me mischievously. "If smoking were allowed, it would be perfect. So, Miss Frayne, you come across me in a contemplative mood. Why are you searching for me?"

I'm not sure if it was being in the church that made me feel I was fed up with dancing around the truth, but I was.

"You are not obliged to talk to me, Mr. Masefield. I am a

private investigator not a police officer."

He held up his hand. "You don't have to justify yourself. I have no desire to run away or avoid the truth."

"Okay. I need to ask you one important question."

Despite what he'd said, I could feel that he immediately became wary.

"Go ahead."

"When you encountered Gerald Jessop last Thursday, you said you left him at his house and then you went on to Pearson Hall."

"Correct. That is what I said."

"They have no record of your staying that night."

"Indeed?"

"Indeed."

The sound of organ music suddenly burst forth. There weren't many people in the church so I could only assume the organist was practising. It has never been my favourite musical instrument, and I hoped he would be brief. Masefield sat straighter in the pew.

"I was brought up in a devout Methodist family who considered the Catholic church to be the agent of the devil. I never set foot in a Catholic church until I was an adult. It was fancier than the one we attended, but otherwise they seemed the same. We worshipped the same God and adored the same Jesus."

He nodded his head in the direction of the altar. "One thing the Catholics do have over us Protestants is Confession. You pour out all your sins and a priest, as

God's representative, forgives you. Leaves you feeling all peaceful and clean inside."

I wasn't sure where we were going with this, but I knew I had to wait. The organ music had ended. The smell of incense hung in the air. I saw a man in a black soutane scurry down the aisle, genuflect at the altar, and disappear off to the side.

Masefield continued. "I did go to the Hall that night, but I had left it too late. I could not get in."

"What did you do then?"

"I came here. The Redemptorists give shelter to the homeless. I spent the night as their guest. I did have to share with a dozen others, but it was better accommodation than the pavement."

"Mr. Masefield. I have said I have no legal authority to question you, but for the sake of honesty and perhaps to put a tragedy to rest, will you tell me on your honour, in this sacred place, if you had anything to do with the death of Gerald Jessop?"

Masefield removed his spectacles and rubbed at them. "On my honour, Miss Frayne? You are taking a chance by asking me to swear on that. I believe I lost my honour long ago."

"All right then, here in this sacred place, will you answer my question truthfully?"

Masefield replaced his spectacles. "I will swear I had nothing to do with Captain Jessop's death. We met, we talked, and we parted."

"He drank a lot of rum that night. The household was maintaining strict abstinence. Where would he have got it?"

"Not from me, if that's what you are asking. I don't touch rum anymore. It was the drink of death. 'Here swallow this down and you will feel brave as a lion, tall as a tree, and fierce as a tiger.' So, we did. Unfortunately, bravery and fierceness were an illusion. A dead man is no longer brave or tall or fierce, is he?"

I had no answer to that.

"Are you a Catholic, Miss Frayne?"

"No, I'm not. I was brought up Anglican."

"During the war, I learned that these distinctions didn't matter much. There were men who were brave and decent, who would put themselves in danger, risk their own lives, to save somebody else. And there were the cowards, the cheats who had no compunction about stealing from the dead or the dying. Some of them were on our side, some of them were considered the enemy."

The man who had been wearing a black soutane returned now wearing a white lace surplice. As before, he genuflected in front of the altar and went off to the side. I felt as if I were holding my breath. The more he talked, the more Masefield seemed to retreat into his own dark world.

He was staring down at the ground. The wooden floor was scuffed from many devout feet.

He went on, his voice lower. "I was a soldier, trained to kill an enemy that I was taught to believe wanted to destroy everything I held most dear. That wasn't true of course, but I did what I was told in those days. And I did kill men, other human beings. How many? I don't know exactly. The first time I was with Bill Nelson and we each had a Thompson repeating gun. We went over the top and advanced across Hell toward the Kraut trench. I thought we had reached it at the same time. My buddy, my fellow man-at-arms, Joe didn't. His head was blasted from his shoulders within a few feet of the trench. His body moved on a few more feet before he dropped. Bill and I opened fire on the five Germans in the trench. Did he kill three and me two, or the other way around? Did I kill three? Or even four? At one point, his gun jammed as they often did. I kept firing or he would have been shot himself. He said afterward that I saved his life. Maybe I did. He lived. Five Germans didn't."

There was more activity up at the altar. A boy, also in a surplice, emerged carrying a long taper and started to light the candles in the candelabras. I was reminded of a play getting ready to start.

"You seem to be adept at saving lives. Gerald Jessop said you saved his life."

"Did he? I'm not sure. I didn't know what had happened to him. He was bleeding to death. His jaw had been sliced off. I carried him to the field ambulance. They saved him. Not me. A waste, if you think of it. I am truly sorry he killed himself. I wish it had been different and he had found the courage to keep on through this vale of tears."

Masefield slumped a little lower. He had a story he needed to tell.

"The worst was the Kraut in the shell hole. The firing was so heavy I went to take cover in a shell hole. Unfortunately, it was already occupied by a Kraut. One of the enemy. He hadn't done anything. I think he'd even put down his rifle. He was a boy, really. I didn't think, 'I'm going to get payback.' Nothing as articulate. I saw a man in a grey uniform. He started to come toward me. I thought it was going to be him or me. So it was him. I stabbed him through the eye with my bayonet. I wish I could say he died instantly, but he didn't. It took a while."

Somebody entered the church and a blast of chilly air swept in. Masefield lifted his head, but didn't turn around. I saw that the person who had entered and who was now standing at the end of the pew was Jack Murdoch. Beside him were two uniformed constables.

Masefield continued, calmly, as if we were just finishing up a conversation.

"I regret that I killed those men. The only person I do not regret killing is Oscar Klein."

* * *

MASEFIELD PUT UP no resistance as Jack arrested him. It was all done so quietly and calmly that I doubted if any of the worshippers kneeling in the front of the shrine or in the pews farther back knew what was happening.

CHAPTER FORTY-FIVE

I FOLLOWED JACK to the police station. There, he took a formal statement from Masefield, then took him down to the cells. The regular police clerk still had the flu, which meant I was recommissioned to take down what had transpired. By the time it was all over, I have to admit I felt shredded. The law doesn't always run side-by-side with justice and, having heard what Masefield had to say, I hoped the judge would grant him some clemency.

He was not a big man, and I guessed he was seriously underweight. His hair was sparse, he was short-sighted, and he coughed a lot. In spite of these characteristics, he was one of the most commanding people I'd met. Possibly a fanatic, but a man you might follow anywhere.

This is his statement.

November 5, 1936
Statement of Thomas Masefield.

I want to say first of all that I am taking complete responsibility for my actions. I acted alone. The balance of my mind was not disturbed. In fact, given the same circumstances, I believe I would act in the same manner.

I decided to confront Oscar Klein. I had been employed briefly at Superior Ladies' Clothes. I was dismissed because the job was beyond my capabilities. Fair enough. It was indeed more than I could handle. However, I was owed money, a day's wages to be precise. Two dollars. It was money I needed.

I'd heard that Klein stayed late on Mondays so he could put up the wage packets. It seemed a good time to pay him a visit. I got to the shop about half past seven. The downstairs door was not locked so I went in. He was in his counting house, counting all his money. Although of course, it wasn't his money. I can't say I was surprised. Klein was a malingerer through and through. That scar on his hand was a giveaway. I knew as soon as I saw it, he'd done it himself. Some men did that. Shot themselves through the foot or the leg. The hand was the best. You stood a better chance of not being seriously crippled. You could get sent back to Blighty. Who could prove it wasn't a Kraut sniper that had got you?

When he saw who it was had come into the workroom, he came out to meet me. He wasn't afraid. Why should he be? I was a weakling in his eyes. Couldn't even lift a bolt of cloth. I said I was owed for the last day of work and he laughed. He was deducting the two dollars because of shoddy work. I might have swallowed that and shrugged it off, but he was the one who wouldn't let it go. He started to jeer. Threw out insults about my masculinity. Not that it bothered me. I've become impervious to insults, truth be told. But then he said I had to scram. He said he was waiting for somebody. It was the way he said it that made me realize what he meant. I'd heard rumours about his predilections. He said the one he was expecting was the morsel, as he put it, who had just started to work in the mannequin room. (Here Masefield paused and for the first time, showed some emotion.) I tell you, when he stood there literally licking his lips, I saw red. I shoved him hard and he fell across the table. I wanted to bang his head and I jumped on him but, even prone, he was a lot stronger than I am. He managed to grab me by the throat. (Briefly, he pulled aside the collar of his shirt and revealed livid bruises.) I could feel myself starting to lose consciousness. He would have won, but something got hold of me. I've experienced it before. You're not human anymore. You're an animal trying to survive. I grabbed at a pair of scissors which were on the table, and before I knew it, I had stabbed him in the chest. I think he died instantly. I was obviously stronger than we both thought. Rage will do that for you. I decided to take the money that was owed to me. I went into his office and helped myself. Two dollars. Nothing more, nothing less. That's it. I swear this is the truth.

I put down my pencil. "I will type this up and have you sign the statement; but, before I do, there is something I need to say."

"Yes?" He was wary again.

"I believe that you have been truthful about the killing of Oscar Klein, but you haven't told the entire truth, have you?"

"What do you mean?"

"The 'morsel' Klein referred to was Ruby, wasn't it? That's what sent you off the deep end. He had arranged to meet her and assault her. That's why you killed him. She's your daughter."

There was long silence. Both Jack and I sat quite still.

I spoke first. "Does she know what happened while she was waiting at the door?"

"No," he almost shouted the words. "She is not a strong young woman. I blame myself for that." He rubbed his head as if he could erase the memory. "When she needed me, I was not there. Her mother was troubled and perhaps I had more to do with that than I'd like to believe."

"Didn't Ruby wonder what you were doing at the shop? She's not a fool. The very next morning was when Klein's body was discovered."

"I told her I'd been on my way home when I saw her."

"Why is she running away if she is so oblivious?"

His eyes grew dark, his voice angry. "She isn't running away. I was worried about her well-being. I asked Miriam Cohen to look after her for me. She thought it was a good idea and she has brought her to stay at her own house."

"Does Miriam herself know what happened?"

"No, she does not. I must repeat. I acted alone. Completely alone. No allies."

There was an expression in his eyes that I thought martyrs might have. Men who died horrible deaths rather than betray their comrades.

Jack spoke. "I'm sure you will receive clemency if you tell a court what was underlying your actions."

Masefield's fists were clenched. "Then they will drag her into it. She has suffered enough. I will not do it. It is irrelevant. The events occurred as I have described them. I wanted my wages. That is all. Please type up my statement as is and I will sign it. I will say nothing more."

He sat back and folded his arms. Nothing was going to move him.

I had no choice but to type up the statement as he had given it. He signed it.

Masefield was looking exhausted and once again I wondered about the state of his health. But there was one final important piece I had to deal with. Talk about going with a gut instinct. I had to trust that Mrs. Jessop was fundamentally a woman of honour.

I asked Jack if I could speak to Masefield further, and explained why. He was quite agreeable and we both sat down again opposite him.

"Miss Frayne says she has some important private information she has to give you."

"What now?"

There was an expression on Masefield's face that I'd

heard described by observers of post-battle survivors. Not exactly total indifference, but something akin to that. The expression of a man whose emotional fatigue is so profound he has given up fighting for his own life.

"It's to do with Gerald Jessop."

"I've told you already what happened. I can say no more."

"I accept what you have said, Mr. Masefield. What I have to tell you, however, is that on the night in question, after you left him, Gerald Jessop wrote a new will. It is quite valid. He has left his entire estate to you."

That woke him up.

"To me? What are you talking about?"

"In the will he says that you saved his life when you were in Valenciennes. He was not happy with how the world has treated you ever since the end of the war. He wanted to offer his own compensation."

"Good heavens." Masefield stared at me. "You said his entire estate. How much money are we talking about?"

"Close to twenty thousand."

He whistled between his teeth. "Too bad it's come now. I don't suppose I'm going to get a chance to take a trip to the Riviera, am I?"

As capital punishment was the sentence for murder in this country, I thought there was a chance he could be right about that.

"The money is legally yours."

"What about Jessop's wife? Is she going to be all right?"

"I believe she will get a good portion of the insurance money. She'll be fine."

"Good. I can accept with a clear conscience? I wouldn't want somebody to be cheated out of their rightful dues because of a drink-inspired illusion."

"I don't think that's what it was. The money is legitimately yours."

He smiled and actually clapped his hands.

"I know exactly what I'm going to do with this money."

"Which is?"

"I shall leave one half to the Communist Party, and one half will go to my daughter, Ruby." He raised an eyebrow. "How did you figure out she was my daughter? That was clever."

"She mentioned her father was not with the family anymore, but she didn't say dead. Our witness thought the man and woman walking away from Superior Ladies' Clothes were familiar with each other. Mostly though, my brilliant deduction was based on the fact she's your spitting image. Same colour hair and eyes, same chin."

That made him chuckle outright. "But she's better looking. I hadn't seen her for a long time. I didn't even know where she was living. Then by chance she got a job at Superior Clothes. I had just been hired myself. I persuaded her it was best if we kept our relationship quiet. I certainly didn't want to hurt her chances. And …," he took a deep breath. "I profoundly regret that I left her mother and her. Truth is, I found the pressure of being a father unbearable. I didn't seem able to provide for them. You might not believe me, but I thought they would be better off without me."

"That is rarely true."

Masefield turned his head away.

I stood up. "We need to get you a solicitor."

He caught hold of my arm. "Is it solid? Did Captain Jessop really leave me that much money?"

"It is solid. Quite legal."

"Excellent. The Party has a lot of work to do."

CHAPTER FORTY-SIX

I SAID GOODBYE to Jack and headed back to the office. I had to get to Mrs. Jessop and tell her I had found Tom Masefield. I wasn't sure how she'd react when she discovered he was charged with murder. But there was one more thing I had to tie up before I did that.

It was dark when I reached the Arcade, but the place itself was blazing with light and filled with people in the grip of wishful thinking. "If I buy this, my life will change and I will be happy ever-after." Mostly women shoppers.

I hurried into the office, divested myself of my wet clothes, and got to the telephone.

As I had hoped, it was answered by Sam Weaver.

"Mr. Weaver, this is Charlotte Frayne. I wonder if it would be possible for you and I to have a private talk."

"Could you tell me what it's about?"

"I think you can guess. But I'd rather not talk in the house. Can you come to the offices of T. Gilmore and Associates in the Arcade as soon as possible?"

"We've just finished dinner. I can come now if you like."

"Excellent. I'm on the second floor."

"Be there in half an hour."

And he was. He had obviously run most of the way and was still panting a little from coming up the stairs. The lift was out of commission as usual.

I brought him into the office, and I pulled over the visitor's chair for him. It seemed like eons ago since Mrs. Jessop and her daughter-in-law had been here.

As soon as I took my place behind my desk, he blurted out, "I appreciate you giving me a chance to explain my side of things."

"You realize I can't promise I won't have to pass it on to Mrs. Jessop?"

"Given what's happened ...," his voice tailed off and I wasn't totally sure what he was referring to. "By the way, how did you flush me out?"

I couldn't help myself. "The dog did it."

"What?"

"Duffy is attached to you. She was barking about eleven o'clock and again at six in the morning. I guessed she heard you leaving and returning."

"I see. You're right, she does yap when she hears me."

"I also happened to be going past your house just as you were saying goodbye to a woman I'd heard had recently married. Alicia Tudsworth, as she was then known. It wasn't a big leap to figure out you were the man she had married."

"I see," he sighed.

I leaned forward. "Why the subterfuge? Why not just tell the Jessops you were getting married? Surely, you would still keep your job? You could just come and go."

"You'd think so, but the Jessops aren't like most people. Ever since Mr. Gerald returned from the war the way he did, Mrs. Jessop has done everything she can to protect him. She made it clear to all of us that there were to be no changes to his way of life. He didn't want to go out, therefore he wouldn't. Neither would we."

"Servitude indeed."

"Oh, I got my days off. One day a week until supper time. But Mrs. Jessop wanted absolute loyalty. She would not have tolerated me getting married. And I probably wouldn't have considered it neither if I hadn't met Alicia." He smiled at me, a sweet shy smile. "She's quite a girl, Miss Frayne. She stole my heart away."

"Where did you meet each other?"

"At a church picnic. It was a Sunday afternoon one day in early March. Mr. Gerald had been going through a particularly difficult time and Mrs. Jessop persuaded him to go to yet another clinic for inebriates. Usually I went with him to take care of things, but I had come down with a cold and she excused me." He smiled again, his lopsided, endearing smile. "Never thought I'd be happy to have a cold in the head, but ever since that magical day, I have blessed my fate. You see I went to the picnic and there was my dearest Alicia. What a sight for sore eyes. She was wearing a pink sun bonnet. I had never seen such blue eyes, such a lovely face, not just the perfect features, but what they reflected. Kindness and intelligence."

He paused, which gave me a chance to get my breath. I didn't know if I could handle any more superlatives about a human being. I thought Mr. Weaver might have grown up on a steady diet of romantic novels. But I could also tell the man was utterly sincere.

"There you have it. I couldn't believe my good fortune that she took kindly to me in spite of my ugly mug. I started to see her as often as I could. She knew of my situation, but was willing to tolerate it. We got engaged and then married. I know we couldn't have carried on like this forever. We've got a baby coming. But we thought if we could just get to the end of the year, we'd have enough savings that I could move out on my own."

He lowered his head, his face suddenly contorted by sadness. "I intended to look after Mr. Gerald as long as I could. We could have worked it out."

"I'm so sorry about what happened, Sam. You were with him for a long time."

"I was just seventeen when I joined the army. I had to lie about my age, but they were taking any lad who moved and talked by then. 'You'd make a good batman, sonny,' said one of the brass hats. 'We'll send you to France right off if you agree.' I'd been hoping to see a bit of the fighting, but he said I would be taking care of a front-line officer and that would be as good a contribution to the war effort as any of those infantry fellows. So off I went, and

I was assigned to Mr. Gerald." Sam chuckled. "He wasn't much older than me and green as grass, but we hit it off right away. I'd grown up in what you'd call the school of hard knocks, you see, and I was used to doing things. Not so good at proper schooling, but Mr. Gerald didn't mind that. 'I've got more than enough for both of us, Sam,' was what he said. Then he got himself wounded and things were never the same. He suffered so bad. There was more than once when I thought we'd lose him."

"You mean he tried to commit suicide before?"

Sam's voice was sharp. "No, not that. He took to the bottle. Who can blame him? Kiddies ran away from him. He was in pain most of the time. But he never turned against himself. But he'd get down and fall into moping."

"And you'd pull him out of it? "

"I suppose you could put it that way."

"Just you?"

He shifted in the chair and I could see this was a point of pride to him.

"I was the only one he'd listen to. We'd sit on that darn blue bench for hours on end. He said only somebody who'd been there could understand."

"Been in the war you mean?"

"That's right. A lot of ex-soldiers feel that way. But you just have to go on, don't you? What else is there to do?"

I flashed on the remark Masefield had made when I asked him if he would go to Gerald's funeral. "Why should I pay my respects to a coward."

"One more thing, Sam. I am sincerely sorry I have to bring this up, but I must."

"Okay."

"It's the matter of this new will … It makes no sense that Gerald would go to the trouble of writing a new will then hide it."

"Okay," he said, this time much less agreeably.

"As far as I can see, the only person who would have the opportunity to drop the papers into the piano was you."

He didn't speak, but sat motionless watching me, waiting for what came next.

"I believe that when you sent Miss Ellen to fetch Wilson, you saw the envelope. You had enough time to take a look. You realized what this would mean in terms of the estate and you stuffed it into the piano. I presume you intended to retrieve the papers later and destroy them? Nobody would be harmed."

He was staring at me in horror. I tensed myself, not sure what his response was going to be. When he spoke, his voice hard and bitter.

"He wasn't in his right mind. I suppose if he'd left his money to the local orphanage, I wouldn't have cared. Like he said, I was taken care of. So were the others. What I couldn't stand was that he left everything to a man like Masefield."

I was startled. "You knew him?"

"Not personally. But he worked for a short time at Superior's where Alicia was. She couldn't stand him. Said he was a commie sympathiser. A troublemaker who was trying to stir up the workers. When I saw what Mr. Gerald had written I knew it had to be the same bloke. He said they were both at Valenciennes. 'Great plans to change the world,' my eye. Men like Masefield are only interested in getting power to do what they want. They want to leech off those more fortunate. They might dress it up with fancy words about equality and fairness, but that's like putting a silk dress on a whore. What's underneath is the same poxy body. The rest of us end up getting screwed. For money."

He sank down in the chair.

"Excuse my language, Miss Frayne."

"Did you intend to destroy this will even though Gerald specifically asked that his wishes be honoured?"

Sam rolled his head back. "When he came to his senses, he would have torn it up himself." He was almost shouting.

"We can't know that, can we?"

He groaned. "And we'll never know."

CHAPTER FORTY-SEVEN

S AM SAID HE wanted to see his wife.
I rang the Jessop house to explain that I was coming
over.

Dolly Jones opened the door. She was most unfriendly.
I could have been the baker, whose bread was under par,
making a delivery. I almost expected her to send me around
to the back door.

"I'd like to speak with Mrs. Jessop."

"She and Miss Ellen are having tea in the drawing room."

She did not of course say, "Buzz off," but she might as
well have.

"Good. Will you tell her I'm here?"

"Come in."

I stepped into the foyer and she scuttled off to announce
me. I wondered why Dolly had gone from so friendly to
cold as ice. I did not hold myself responsible for any of the
things that were troubling this household. Perhaps she did.

In the next minute, Duffy came racing down the hall,
barking furiously.

I held out my hand, "Hi Duffy. What a good girl you are." She stopped abruptly and took an extremely cautious sniff. By great good fortune and foresight, I had a half a cookie in my pocket and I handed it to her. She gave me a suspicious look, took another sniff, then condescended to swallow down the treat. I'm not sure what the next move would have been on either side, but at that moment Dolly returned. Still friendly as a glacier.

"Mrs. Jessop said to come in."

I followed her down the hall to the drawing room. Duffy trotted after us. A dog who knew on which side her bread was buttered.

Dolly ushered me in.

As before, I had the feeling I was stepping into an oppressive silence. The two women appeared not to have been talking to each other.

Ellen got up and drew a chair closer to the table.

"Miss Frayne. Please have a seat. May I offer you some tea?"

I declined the tea, but took the chair. If possible, Mrs. Jessop looked more ravaged than the last time I had seen her.

"You wished to see me, Miss Frayne?"

"I think I have completed my job. I must concur with the judgement of the coroner that your son, Gerald, did indeed take his own life."

Her jaw tightened. "What is making you so sure?"

"I have been able to trace Thomas Masefield. He has stated that he met Gerald at the Paradise Café earlier on the evening in question. They indeed had been soldiers-in-arms.

According to Masefield, they talked for a long time and then he accompanied Gerald back here. This would be about nine o'clock. Masefield had planned to spend the night at Pearson Hall and he left. As it turned out, there was no room there so he spent the night at the Redemptorist fathers' refuge."

I paused to let this sink in.

"Is that confirmed?"

"It can be. I believe it is what happened."

"Did he give Gerald the liquor?"

"He says not. He's been trying to stay sober for a time now himself."

"So had Gerald," burst out Ellen.

Mrs. Jessop's back straightened even more. "We must be realistic, Ellen. Gerald had frequent lapses in the past. Please continue, Miss Frayne."

"It wouldn't be too difficult to track down where your son purchased the liquor. It may have been in his room for some time."

For some reason, that particular statement seemed to ring true for her. I guessed Gerald had done a lot of squirreling away.

"According to Masefield, Gerald was upset to see his circumstances. As we know, he considered that Masefield had saved his life. He felt that our soldiers who returned from the war were being treated shabbily."

"And so he decided to right that wrong by changing his will?"

"Yes."

Mrs. Jessop was no fool. "In that case, why did he put it in the piano where it was not necessarily going to be found?"

"Sam Weaver put the will there."

"He has admitted this?"

"He has."

"I see." She took a moment to pour herself more tea. I could see her hands were shaking.

Ellen didn't speak either.

Breaking the suspense their silence was creating, I launched into the explanation. I included the fact that Sam was married.

"Did you know this, Ellen?" she asked her daughter-in-law.

Ellen was almost inaudible. "I didn't know he was married, but I did suspect he had a sweetheart that he visited some nights."

More buying time on the part of Mrs. Jessop, who drank some of her tea.

"I am sorry he did not inform us. We would have given him a nice send-off."

That way of putting it was ambiguous, but I let it ride. Sam might be right about his fate had he told the Jessops of his plan to marry. I took a chance.

"Sam Weaver's actions have in no way been illegal, Mrs. Jessop. At least, that is until he hid the will. Perhaps we might consider that more unethical than illegal."

She nodded. "My son expressed his appreciation of his

valet on more than one occasion. I will accept that Weaver acted on the spur of the moment. And I now know that he was not at home with Gerald on the night he died."

"That is correct. He was with his wife."

She had given no indication that she had even suspected Sam of double dealing. Clearly it had never crossed her mind. I wondered if there was someone else she had worried about. I knew there was someone on my mind. I now faced her.

"Miss Ellen. I am convinced we have a true and accurate picture of what transpired the night of Mr. Gerald's death. However, there is one more thing I would like to verify."

"What is it?" she whispered.

"You said that you told Gerald you were pregnant. He was delighted, you said."

Mrs. Jessop was watching her daughter-in-law with intensity.

"Is that true? Are you really expecting a baby?"

"No."

This time she raised her head and her eyes met mine. "Far from it. I have discovered I am unable to conceive. My time has passed."

"Did you tell Gerald that?" Mrs. Jessop burst out.

"Yes, I did."

"And was he upset? Was that why he did what he did?"

Ellen gave a small whimper. "Frankly he didn't seem to care. He said, 'Just as well, given the state of the world. We don't need more children.'"

Mrs. Jessop reached across the table and touched her daughter-in-law's hand.

"That sounds like a cruel thing to say. I'm sorry, Ellen."

"Thank you, Mother. When I myself heard the doctor's verdict, I believe I was more disappointed than Gerald was. We had dearly hoped for a child. I now regret I did not stay with him, but …," her voice tailed off. "I found his black moods hard to handle. Sometimes my presence just seemed to aggravate him rather than soothe. I thought it was more prudent to leave him alone."

My heart ached for the poor woman. Gerald Jessop must have been hell to live with.

"Why did you not tell me the truth? Why did you let me believe you were with child?" The question was harsh, but actually Mrs. Jessop's voice was kind.

"Because you wanted so badly to believe it."

I turned to Mrs. Jessop. "As far as I am concerned, the investigation is completed. I am satisfied that Gerald died by his own hand. Nobody aided and abetted him. No person was the cause of his death except he himself."

It was my turn to reach out. Mrs. Jessop's hand was icy cold under my touch.

"I am sorry, Mrs. Jessop."

I can't say this was exactly a happy conclusion, but no matter how much we all might wish Gerald had not killed himself, or that Masefield had not brought about the death of another being and ruined his own life, those were the facts and we had to come to terms with them.

CHAPTER FORTY-EIGHT

M RS. JESSOP PAID my bill and added a generous bonus, which reluctantly I accepted. She told me she would consider keeping on Sam Weaver as a member of the household and, although she didn't promise, I thought she probably would. He was an irreplaceable link to her dead son.

The following day, I received a visit from Jack Murdoch. He told me that a doctor had examined Masefield. The gassing he had received during the war, coupled with the hard life he'd led since returning home, had severely damaged his lungs. In the doctor's opinion it was unlikely Thomas would survive any kind of long-term incarceration. He had doubts that he would even make it to a trial. Jack said he would do everything he could to appeal for clemency. He considered Masefield a casualty of war. I hoped this would happen, but I knew there were still too many veterans struggling to survive in an increasingly callous world.

* * *

I FOUND THE accommodations that Mr. Gilmore had requested.

I went back to Mrs. Liddell, whose rooming house on Sullivan Street was not far from Mr. Gilmore's home on Phoebe Street, and made her a very attractive proposition. We would take the three rooms she had available. The family would have use of the kitchen and the minuscule backyard. They would pay two dollars less than asking but, in return, Mr. Gilmore would pay to have the house cleaned up and refurbished. He would also advance Mrs. Liddell some money to purchase new furniture. I was taking a risk because I'd had no chance to consult him, but I was pretty confident he would agree. Why bring people out of a dangerous situation to a new world if you didn't help make it better for them? I wanted to make the refugees welcome.

I was tired of misery and unhappiness. I made no mention of the fact that her new tenants were refugees and Jewish.

My last task was to speak to Mr. Rosenthal. After an initial stiffness, he was surprisingly open. He agreed to convene a meeting of his employees and discuss with them what sort of conditions they would like to see in the shop. "I can't promise, but I will consider," were his words and I had to be content with that. Given Miriam was still employed, I trusted he would be held to that.

* * *

THERE WAS NO word from Hilliard, but I was so preoccupied with closing the case for Mrs. Jessop and finding the accommodations Mr. Gilmore had requested that I didn't pine too much.

* * *

THE CAFÉ CLOSED promptly on Saturday night and most of the customers plus others trooped down to the lower level to watch the opening of *Eight Men Speak*.

Gramps had been so excited he'd dropped two plates and forgotten several orders.

The place was packed. Jack Murdoch grabbed a seat at the back, but he'd brought along his wife, Fiona, to make it clear he was there unofficially. He even helped Wilf and Calvin put out some extra chairs. The only place to put them was on the stage itself so, Elizabethan style, some patrons found themselves almost a part of the drama. One fellow was so caught up with the story he even shouted out comments. Gramps forgot for an instant he was supposed to be acting and answered back. Things might have become very awkward, except that the other more experienced members of the cast sailed right on with the script as written. Finally, Gramps got his moment and he was able to yell at the scum capitalism with the others, "Guilty!"

Clapping wildly, the partisan audience leaped up. Somebody started to sing the "Red Flag." A couple of men were banging on the backs of chairs. The actors on the stage, including my Gramps, stamped their feet.

I had been taking tickets, so I was standing near the

door. I felt somebody tap me on the shoulder and I turned. Hilliard was beaming at me. I couldn't hear a word over the noise, but he leaned forward and spoke directly into my ear.

"Hello, Lottie. I'm back. What have you been up to while I've been gone?"

ACKNOWLEDGEMENTS

A S USUAL MANY people gave me invaluable help during the process of writing this book. I particularly want to thank my friend, Howard Waxberg, who went out of his way to introduce me to David and Daniel Sliwin, who own the Athletic Knit Factory. They kindly gave me a tour so I could see a working factory in action. I'm happy to say, it is quite different from the one I depict in the book.

I would be totally adrift without the help of my wonderful research assistant, Keara Langford.

And then there are the books, too many to list, which are like friends. The memoirs and the diaries of the soldiers; the early socialists and the courageous folks of the living theatre of the time. Against great odds they struggled to enlighten playgoers about the injustices perpetrated against those who "didn't agree."

All the menus referred to in the Paradise Café come from my fabulous old book of Nautical Recipes (1930s).

Finally, great thanks my editor and publisher, Marc Côté and all the wonderful folks at Cormorant, Barry and two Sarahs who, like so many book people, have had to struggle with the restrictions imposed by Covid but still brought this book into the world.

May the words continue.

We acknowledge the sacred land on which Cormorant Books operates. It has been a site of human activity for 15,000 years. This land is the territory of the Huron-Wendat and Petun First Nations, the Seneca, and most recently, the Mississaugas of the Credit River. The territory was the subject of the Dish With One Spoon Wampum Belt Covenant, an agreement between the Iroquois Confederacy and Confederacy of the Ojibway and allied nations to peaceably share and steward the resources around the Great Lakes. Today, the meeting place of Toronto is still home to many Indigenous people from across Turtle Island. We are grateful to have the opportunity to work in the community, on this territory.

We are also mindful of broken covenants and the need to strive to make right with all our relations.